DOORS
OF DEATH
AND
Life

Tor Books by Brenda W. Clough

How Like a God
Doors of Death and Life

DOORS OF DEATH AND *Life*

BRENDA W. CLOUGH

TOR®

A TOM DOHERTY ASSOCIATES BOOK
NEW YORK

DOORS OF DEATH AND LIFE

The epigraph on page 7 is quoted by permission of Daniel Ardrey, from *African Genesis,* by Robert Ardrey, published by Atheneum in 1961.

The lines on page 77 are quoted by permission of Oxford University Press, from *Myths from Mesopotamia,* translated by Stephanie Dalley, published by Oxford University Press in 1989.

This book is printed on acid-free paper.

Edited by Delia Sherman

A Tor Book
Published by Tom Doherty Associates, LLC
175 Fifth Avenue
New York, NY 10010

www.tor.com

Tor® is a registered trademark of Tom Doherty Associates, LLC.

ISBN 0-312-87064-7

First Edition: May 2000

Printed in the United States of America

0 9 8 7 6 5 4 3 2 1

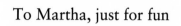

To Martha, just for fun

It is our innate necessity for society as a means of primate survival that has demanded of man those capacities which we regard as ethical. The dual nature of man is the supreme product of the social territory.

—Robert Ardrey, *African Genesis*

For murder, though it have no tongue, will speak
With most miraculous organ.

—*Hamlet,* Act II, Scene 2

✳ CHAPTER
I

The fight was the natural, inevitable conclusion to a horrendous evening. "You promised me," Julianne said. "You *promised*, that if I let you quit the rat race you would at least give me moral support on *my* job."

"That is really unfair, Jul. Home improvement is always seasonal. It's not my fault I had to finish a deck today." Rob tried to keep his voice down, but a passing hotel bellboy smirked at them anyway.

Julianne punched the elevator button, her bosom heaving in the tight blue taffeta cocktail dress. "Handing your business card to that woman, and offering to build her a swing set? What would Portia do with a swing set? She's the biggest slut in Milan! Debra actually asked me if that was the latest in pickup lines!"

Rob's jaw was set so tight his blond beard bristled. "I know she's easy. Everyone in the room knew. Why do you think I told her I was a carpenter? To get her to quit hitting on me, that's why."

"Or maybe it was just to get your pager number into her hot little hands, huh?"

"Jul, you can't possibly believe—"

The elevator doors slid open to reveal the smiling elevator boy. "Lobby, miss?" They stepped in, not touching, and stood in seething silence as the elevator descended.

The Willard Hotel's lobby was historically accurate to a painful degree, restored to look just as it had when Mark Twain strolled through in the 1890s. When they stepped out onto the antique-look mosaic floor, Rob got in the first shot. "And I didn't appreciate being appraised by that old vulture, either."

"Rob, the Signora is famous for her sense of style. She's the greatest fashion designer of her generation. If she ogles you, it's an honor, that's all! I mean, she's eighty-four years old."

"If a sense of style means dragging around the world with a planeload of whores and gigolos, it's an honor I could do without."

"You are just so impossible!" Julianne's hazel eyes flashed magnificently with rage. "Oh, for God's sake, go get the van. I can't walk another step in these heels." She sat down heavily on a red leather chesterfield sofa.

"High fashion makes people do such melonheaded things. I'll bring the truck around front."

"The truck?" Julianne sat up straight again, electrified. "Rob, you didn't drive that hunk of junk to a black-tie reception, did you?"

"It's not junk," Rob snapped.

"Well, it looks like a junker! You are trying to embarrass me, just out of meanness, because you didn't want to get dressed up!"

Rob forgot not to shout. "It was force of habit, okay?"

"I don't want anybody I know to see me riding in that clunker! Pick me up at the bus stop across the street!"

Snarling, Rob strode out through the revolving doors and down the street to the parking garage. His dress shoes pinched, and the warm May evening made him sweat where the old tuxedo jacket was too tight under his muscular arms. Jul hadn't appreciated a bit the aggravations he'd gone through—building decks all day, rushing home to wash up and climb into the monkey suit, and then battling rush-hour traffic all the way from Fairfax downtown for the Association of Garment Design's damnable reception. And it was ten o'clock at night, and they hadn't even served any real food. Why did he let her do these things to him?

He felt better when he got to the garage. Slowly over the last several years, Rob had marshaled his private coping mechanisms into a deliberately mundane armor. His carpentry work was always a calming and centering influence, and by extension his tools and truck had become talismans of normality. Automatically, he checked the light blue Ford over. The white truck cap hid all his tools, and the ladder rack on the roof was empty. He had locked all the doors and paid for garage parking to keep from getting ripped off. Once, he had forcibly trimmed back the crime rate of the entire District of Columbia, just to see if he could do it. But these superficial societal fixes were never permanent. After three years the local economy was still reeling from the '99 Quayle recession to the point where even Lewis Home Improvement's truck could be a target. But the truck was untouched tonight. Satisfied, he climbed into the cab and started the engine.

As he eased out onto the street, Rob's hyperactive sense of justice came to the fore. Julianne did have a point. This was not a vehicle to ride in wearing blue taffeta. The heavy-duty bumpers were spattered with red construction mud, and the vinyl front seat was invisible under a clutter of tools, maps, construction sketches, and notes. Hex nuts and odd carriage bolts rattled back and forth on the dashboard as he turned the corner towards the hotel. Of course he hadn't had time to clean up the cab, but would it do him any harm to tell Jul she was right?

Then Rob remembered that Julianne was waiting across the way at the bus stop. He was on the wrong side of the street, and would have to pass the hotel and pull a U-turn. He peered ahead and to the left to see if Jul was there yet, and gasped.

The bus stop had a shelter, a roof and two Plexiglas walls. Inside it several people were scuffling. Between them he could clearly see the blue sheen of Julianne's party dress.

The crisis mind-set fell over Rob like an icy cloak. He stamped on the gas and set the truck barreling at the bus shelter, screeching to a halt at an angle to the curb. On high beam, the headlights flooded the bus shelter with 110 watts of shadowless light.

Any other rescuer would have dashed to intervene. Rob had the time to cut the engine and turn on the emergency flashers. He got out slowly, sucking the air down deep into his chest because it was important not to get too mad, not to lose control. Still, his step was unsteady as he went across to Julianne and helped her to her feet. "Don't try to talk, dearest," he said, holding her close.

Her dress was torn open at the vee of the neckline, and her ash-blonde hair straggled down from its topknot. She trembled in his arms like a frightened bird. "My purse," she stuttered. "My shoe. And—oh my God, Rob, what are they waiting for?"

The three young muggers stood eerily still, staring into the glare of the headlights like jacklighted deer. Their hands, tattooed with gang emblems, hung limp at their sides. A knife glittered on the pavement beside Julianne's beaded evening bag. "They're waiting for me," Rob said grimly. "Let me cope with it, Jul. Into the truck with you." With tender care he helped her into the cluttered front seat, and fetched the missing shoe and the bag. "You're not hurt, right?"

"Just shook up. Oh Rob, let's go!" Tears ran down her face, smearing the mascara into raccoon rings around her eyes.

"One more minute, dearest." He pushed a hanky into her hand and shut the passenger-side door. Then he went around to the front of the truck and stood between the blazing headlights, leaning back a little against the truck's dusty grille. "You little swine," he said to the muggers. Suddenly his voice didn't sound like his own.

Very rarely now did Rob use his full power. Ordinary daily life didn't call for it, any more than it called for tactical nuclear missiles. But the ability was always there, leashed but vast, and he clenched it now like a fist around the three lowlifes in the bus shelter. He wasn't interested in their miserable past histories, or what drugs they were on now, or what half-assed rationales they could construct for their criminal behavior. Rob was out for blood, and the only question was how.

"A bus or a car accident is too messy," he said softly, remotely. "So is jumping from a roof. The Potomac River, that'll do. Walk yourselves halfway over the bridge down there, and jump in where it's deep."

The power hummed like thunder in his voice. The three young men turned obediently and began to walk, around the corner and then south along 14th Street towards the river. The doorman at the Willard had noticed the commotion at last and ran up. "Is something wrong, sir? You want me to call 911?"

Rob turned his berserker gaze onto him for only a second. As the doorman's mouth dropped open in terror Rob got a grip on himself. This guy was innocent. "They tried to snatch her purse," he said, breathing deeply. "But I sent them off with a tongue-lashing."

"You should press charges!"

"They'll never do it again," Rob said. "Forget it." Again it was a command, not a suggestion. The doorman held the truck door for Rob and waved cordially as they drove off.

Julianne wiped her streaming eyes with the smeary hanky. "Oh, Rob, I was so frightened! I let them have my handbag, but then they pulled the knife, and began to claw at my dress—"

For a second Rob could hardly see, he was so angry. Automatically he eased up on the gas as they rolled down Constitution Avenue. "I should've dropped them onto a railroad track," he muttered.

"What did you say, hon?" Julianne peered through the dark at his face.

"You don't have to worry about them anymore," Rob said hastily. Very few people knew about his weird abilities, and Julianne wasn't one of them. The glare of the headlights would have kept her from seeing anything, and he had stood with his back turned in case his expression revealed too much. But all this caution would be wasted if he didn't act normally now. "As long as you're not hurt, that's the only important thing."

"My dress is shot." Julianne pulled the torn edges together to cover her lacy black bra.

"You'll have to get a new one."

"That's right!"

Rob smiled at her, secretly congratulating himself. She would deny it to her last breath, but sometimes Jul was just like a child, thinking about a new gown. The tigerish fury drained out of his body. It was like recovering from a sharp high fever.

They were over the Memorial Bridge and heading up 66 before the realization hit him. He had just murdered three people! The compartments in his life were so habitual, the clash now between the powerful and the mundane stunned him. His first foolish thought was, Am I too late? Rob cut the truck into the exit lane and zoomed up the Glebe Road ramp.

Julianne turned to look at the exit sign as it flicked past. "What are you doing, Rob? This isn't our exit!"

"Wait, Jul." There were two red lights on Glebe Road before the left turn to the eastbound ramp, and halting at them gave Rob time to reach out mentally. Unseen, unfelt, he could find them. He didn't know their names or ages, but he

could recognize those three punks anywhere in the world. Swiftly he reached back towards the river and across at the 14th Street bridge. No. They were gone. He was too late.

The light turned green and he put the truck in gear. His mouth had gone desert-dry, and he swallowed and swallowed again so he could speak in a natural tone. "Sorry—I must've been more upset than I knew. Thought this was Route 123. Let me get us back on the highway."

Julianne leaned her head on his tuxedoed shoulder. "You are such a sweet man, Rob. I don't appreciate you properly."

Rob flinched. "You aren't a very good judge of character, dear." With an effort he kept the bitterness out of his voice, kept the tone light.

Safely at home, the routine carried him along. He paid off the baby-sitter and stood in the doorway while the teenager crossed the street to her own home. He turned the deadbolt on the front door, looked in on Davey and Annie asleep in their rooms, and came upstairs to peek cautiously into the nursery. Four months old, Colin might drop his late-night feeding any time now.

In the crowded main bedroom, Julianne's ruined dress lay on the floor. Rob stripped off his confining jacket and the black satin bow tie and cummerbund, sighing with relief. She came out of the bathroom wrapped in a towel. "Could you do this necklace, hon?"

With difficulty he teased the clasp open with his work-thickened fingers. He could feel the tension radiating from her neck and shoulders as he touched them. She leaned back against him, and he drew her down onto the big bed, tossing the bath towel aside. Pearl shirt studs flew in all directions as he pulled off his shirt.

This was the place where all their difficulties vanished away: all the petty conflicts and fundamental disagreements and miscommunications, deliberate or accidental. When he made love to Julianne, everything clicked into focus, and Rob

knew that their marriage was as solid and well-founded as
the decks he built. And more—only here could he use the
weird mental powers without guilt. They were a huge
responsibility. He did terrible things with them. But to use
them for Julianne's delight made them okay. In the past
seven years he had learned more about her responses than
perhaps even she herself knew. Using that knowledge for her
pleasure was glorious, a never-failing well of satisfaction.

She fell asleep an hour later pillowed comfortably on his
chest. Rob could easily have dropped off too. But from the
baby monitor on the nightstand came a wordless grumble.
Colin was not going to sleep through. Rob slid gently out
from under Julianne's overlapping limbs and pulled the covers up over her bare shoulders.

Donning a threadbare red flannel bathrobe he went
downstairs to the kitchen. Only the tiny buzz of the fluores-
cent lights could be heard. He filled the big Pyrex measuring
cup with water and put it in the microwave. While it
heated, he went through into the toy-strewn living room
and powered up the computer in his office corner. It would
take Colin half an hour at least to tank up—plenty of time
to read the mail from the Moon. A few clicks of the mouse
got him logged on to NASANET for the preprogrammed
pass. Rob left the messages to download themselves while
he took the hot water out of the oven and stood a baby bottle in it.

Upstairs, Colin was just cranking it up. Julianne wouldn't
wake. As he climbed the stairs, Rob smiled with secret
pride—did he know his business in bed or what? He went
into the small nursery and lifted his son out of the crib. "Hey,
little guy, you're kind of wet." Colin, familiar with the routine, slowed down his fussing. Only a squawk every now and
then emerged to warn the world that a baby's patience has
limits.

Expertly Rob whipped off the sodden diaper and hitched
on a dry one. "Let's go downstairs and talk to Uncle Eddie."

The tiny body, so solid and warm in his arms, made Rob's heart swell with sudden misery. Those three junior rapists had been this cute once. Was a mother or dad waiting somewhere for a young man to come home?

He scooped up a burp cloth and the bottle as he went through the kitchen. He sat down in front of the glowing computer screen. Crossing an ankle over one knee, he set the baby into the angle of his legs and popped the nipple into the tiny questing mouth. Grunting with satisfaction, Colin waved his fat hands. Rob set them on either side of the bottle just to give him a hint, but Colin had no intention of doing any work. Rob continued to support the weight of the bottle with one hand while with the other he called up his e-mail.

Electronic communication is never perfectly private. E-mail to Moonbase was collected in Houston for inspection, and then squirted off-planet daily in one high-speed telemetry burst. Most of the other lunar colonists were resigned to their fishbowl existence. The first Moon settlement was an historic event. All transmissions including even the encrypted mail were eventually going to be fodder for analysis, research, and probably Ph.D. theses, so it wasn't unreasonable for NASA to keep an eye on it.

However, Edwin Barbarossa had cooked up an amusing private code. With it, he and Rob could discuss the single topic no one else could know about—their different but complementary supernormal powers. "We'll coauthor a sword-and-sorcery novel," Edwin had announced before his launch a year ago. "Maybe we'll set it in Mu, the mythical sunken continent. So you can be as up-front as you like about your weirdness, as long as it's the characters doing the weird." For a literary model he had presented Rob with a glossy paperback edition of *The Tritonian Ring* by L. Sprague de Camp, plus a list of further reading that Rob had avidly devoured: Howard, Silverberg, Tolkien. That and a simple one-letter-down-the-alphabet convention for names was all they needed.

So now Rob could understand Edwin's long e-mail with hardly an effort:

> But Rob—suppose we get King Severneth to visit a dictatorship, on his quest to keep Mu from sinking. Say he pays a state visit to the Pharaoh, who's pumping all of Egypt's money into building himself a pyramid. Don't you think it would be RIGHT for Severneth to tone down the Pharaoh's death fixation some? His gifts are practically wasted, otherwise. A little exertion of his "magic" and the entire country of Egypt benefits.

Rob paused to open a reply window on his screen and type,

> The whole thing buckles down to free will, Ed. Messing with a dictator's head turns him into a puppet. What right do I have to do that?

Quickly Rob backtracked and dropped *Severneth* in for *I*, and fixed the verb to match.

> What right does Severneth have to do that? He thinks he knows better, but the Pharaoh thinks he's right, too. To get onto a theological plane, the god of our made-up world knows what the Pharaoh's doing ('cause he's omniscient), and he can do something about it—have the Pharaoh choke on a chicken bone at dinner, or catch the flu. That the god HASN'T done so means that Severneth should think very carefully before charging in.

The issue of divine intervention versus free will should keep Ed, a sincere and intelligent Christian, going for a week. Rob typed quickly, because these were concepts they had been chewing over in fictional guise for months. But then he stopped to think. Edwin was the only person Rob could tell about what he had done tonight.

Suddenly Rob longed to tell, ached desperately to confide the entire incident to someone who would truly understand. His heart sank under the burden of the terrible guilty secret, a crushing weight that he knew he'd have to carry alone. There was no one he could tell. Julianne wasn't in on the weird stuff. The one time he'd confided in her at the very beginning had gone so wrong, he'd had to wipe the knowledge from her mind. That scalding memory, combined with his habitual reserve and the pressures of day-to-day living, meant that Rob had never arrived at exactly the right moment to take his wife into his full confidence. It was the same rationale he'd applied in his college days to an impacted wisdom tooth, postponing the inevitable until decay and pain forced an emergency extraction.

And though Edwin was in on it, he would never approve of casual murder. If he had somehow been present tonight at the bus stop, he would have argued that Rob could just as easily flush the muggers' brains like toilets—purge all the bad personality traits, turn them into decent upright citizens. Rob had done it before. And Edwin would have been perfectly right. Rob had drowned three men in a mere fit of rage.

Colin stopped sucking and batted the bottle aside. Rob draped the baby over his shoulder, shielding his bathrobe with the burp cloth, and patted the chubby little back. His hands were so big that Colin's diapered butt fit into one palm. The baby's feet dug into his chest hairs in an aimless climbing motion.

His mental turmoil was so great that Rob stood up and paced slowly back and forth, kicking the twins' stray toys lightly to either side. If there were only someone or some-place he could go to, to say, "I'm sorry—I wish I hadn't done it." But the entire beloved facade of normality was founded upon secrecy, layer upon layer of privacy veiling the inner furnace. He loved Julianne more than life itself, but he could not imagine telling her he was a casual murderer.

And Edwin had high standards and a sharply focused gift for discernment that Rob secretly envied. Edwin and that internal moral compass of his had guided Rob through some nasty dark places. No, Rob couldn't tell Edwin either. He was too ashamed to admit how badly he'd slipped up. Everywhere he turned, Rob seemed to confront No Entry signs, doors that he had crafted and carefully locked with his own hands.

Colin belched, a juicy resonant sound worthy of any beer-swiller in a bar. "Good boy." Rob sat down again and offered the bottle. "Top off the tank, fella. I don't want to see you awake again till morning."

Shifting back to Edwin's letter again Rob read,

> I know we've discussed this before, but I keep feeling that Severneth should think about telling Queen Kira about his magic.

"Kira," Rob said aloud, puzzled for a second. "*J* comes before *K* . . . Julianne. Damn!" Edwin's words marched inexorably down the screen:

> It's not like the secret's going to improve by keeping. Kira's going to be majorly confused and hurt whenever she finds out. And sooner or later she's going to, Rob. You know that as well as I do. She's married to poor old Severneth. How long can they go on like this? It's ridiculous. He has to open up and trust—

With an irritable click of the mouse Rob transmitted what he had already written. The nice thing about electronic conversation was that you could ignore what you wanted to. In Rob's opinion, his marriage was fine. He couldn't refer Edwin to his dynamite sex life even in fictional guise—it was too intimate. Besides, the nonexistent novel would become impossibly odd if an X-rated element crept in! But Edwin knew about the new baby: Do couples add to their families if the relationship is rocky? Rob could still laugh when he recalled the envious and lyrical congratulatory e-mail Edwin had sent for the occasion, complete with a virtual birthday cupcake. Regretting his impulse now, Rob read on:

> I know, we've argued this plot point before and you're sick of it. But think about it, okay? Carina sends some very roundabout regards, btw. She'll be in Peru digging up Moche skeletons for a month more, then she'll have some free time at last. Later, E.

Rob pulled open the reply window again and typed,

> Forgot to say, have Carina give us a call if she's in the D.C. area. Our sofabed is her sofabed.

No, he wasn't going to tell Edwin about tonight's incident. Edwin was a little too ready to adjust people's lives anyway—probably it came from being religious.

Rob clicked SEND again. Then he looked down at Colin. The budlike mouth had relaxed into sleep, and the milk drooled down Colin's chin unheeded. Rob powered down the computer, dried the baby's chin off, and carefully hoisted him over his shoulder again. Gently and smoothly he rose to his feet. He set the bottle down in the sink in passing, and climbed the dark stairs.

In the nursery, by the dim friendly glow of the Mickey Mouse night-light, he could make the confession. He held the small limp body to his chest, the fragile downy head tucked under his blond-bearded chin. "Colin, I did something terrible tonight. I'm very sorry about it. I don't know what to do."

There was no absolution an infant could offer, but Rob felt a little better for merely saying the words out loud. Deftly, with the feather touch of long experience, he lowered the sleeping baby into the crib without waking him.

✳ CHAPTER 2

$\mathcal{T}$ he recent regulations allowing the private sector to participate in and profit from federal programs had a number of downsides. For instance, as a condition of his PSPIP investment, Internet tycoon Burton Rovilatt had decreed that every astronaut had to keep up with his or her NASANET account. Each Moonbase colonist had come to an accomodation with the load. Edwin had found that if he answered his personal messages first, it was hard to get motivated afterwards to deal with all the public ones. Today in the comm dome he shuffled rapidly through the other boards first, saving his private friends-and-family box for the end of his daily pass.

Dressed in the blue NASA-issue T-shirt and loose pants, Edwin sat hunched above the keyboard in a posture endurable only in low gravity. His thick dark curls, unshorn for too long, were confined by a baseball cap. Through his featherweight earphones came Billie Holiday's smoky voice. Two more letters from science classes, all the standard questions including the ever-popular, "How do you use the bathroom in one-sixth gravity?" He inserted the boilerplate answers into standard school-letter reply formats and zapped them off. A long technical discussion about nuclear-electric rockets on the Propulsion topic, to which he posted, "I'm a humble microbiologist—don't ask me! Maybe Geena can say?" A few questions about his hydroponics garden, nothing new there. A possible interview, a magazine feeler, five photograph requests—all zapped back to Kennedy Space Center for handling.

Then, most annoying of all, the Personal Questions topic. PSPIP insisted that personnel be good sports about this. Tonight the perennial question about sex in space popped up from some adolescent kid in Tennessee. Edwin banged his forehead, gently, against the screen. "Do they never read the earlier answers in the topic?"

Lon came in, a tall graying Texan who oversaw both rock and water lunar mining. "Lemme guess. Bathrooms."

"No, zero-g sex. Again. Oh Lord, how long?"

Lon snorted, which was how he laughed. "Look, the badger's stuck on a rock again. You want to come help?"

Edwin jumped happily up, shedding his earphones. "You only value me for my pretty face, Lon." Some PR type at NASA had commissioned a detailed and humiliating Q poll of the moon colonists earlier in the year, with assistance from the staff of *People* magazine. Edwin now labored under the cruel label of "Cutest Dimples."

"Actually it's your back I covet. This time it's a monster."

Edwin followed Lon down the narrow hallway. This hall was the oldest part of Moonbase, the backbone of the settlement. The badger had excavated it three years ago, before any astronaut's arrival. The digging robot had arrived in its own lunar lander, and after camera surveys of the terrain, began scraping out a long trench. By the time the first team arrived, the trench was nearly three meters down into the regolith. All the astronauts had to do was unroll the first dome bag in the trench and inflate it. The laminated polymer of the bag was nearly three inches thick, but the sides of the trench supported the walls and the roof was reinforced with steel and plastic. Some lunar soil on top to shield it from solar radiation, an airlock at one end, and the Moon had its first building.

Now that the badger had excavated a half-dozen rooms, the original long narrow dome was merely a dim hallway and a conduit for cables. Their brightly adorned surface suits hung on racks at the far end. Edwin and Lon helped each other suit up, jostling in the narrow space. Then they cycled through the two-man airlock.

Edwin pulled both over-visors over his Lexan faceplate, but still the lunar day dazzled him. After the cozy dimness of the domes the moonscape always seemed immense. The harsh light confused perspective. He hardly recognized his own sharp black shadow over the rocky soil.

But all this he had learned to take in stride during the past year. They ran through their suit checklists, and then Lon said, "All set. Let's go."

Lon carried the toolkit while Edwin shouldered a folding shovel and a pry bar. In a slow bounding lope Lon led the way to the right, looping wide around the dirt-shielded oval bulges of two domes. Sound didn't carry in the gossamer lunar atmosphere, but Edwin could feel the badger's vibration through the thick soles of his boots when he touched down between every three-meter bound.

The excavation for the new dome was about two meters deep so far. It seemed big to Edwin, perhaps twelve meters in diameter, but after the dome and deck went in, the usable space remaining would be standard enough. The badger's slow, grinding progress around and around the oval had been disturbed by a large stubborn boulder near one edge. The robot was wedged helplessly between the rock and the dirt wall, tipped at an angle that lifted its treads off the ground. The rotating digging disc scraped agonizingly over the rock. In time the rock would be worn away into nothing. During the excavation of the first dome, the badger had digested three rocks bigger than this. But since this might take weeks, it was far more efficient for people, if they were available, to extricate the badger from its tight spot.

"Smile for the birdie, Ed."

They both turned to give the video camera mounted near the far edge a good view of them. "Very natty, your new soft-drink logo," Edwin remarked.

"I can't stand Mello Lite, that's the irony of it. But don't tell massa." Lon bounced stiffly down into the hole and aimed the red remote box at the badger. "Okay, Daddy's here. Pipe down."

Edwin hopped down too. The low gravity made jumps like this no challenge at all—he felt he hung in midair like a ballerina, coming down with majestic slowness. "How long are you pausing the digging program?"

"Fifty-five minutes. If we can't pry that rock out of here by then, we'll have ruptured ourselves."

"That'd be contrary to Pisspeep policy," Edwin said gravely. Lon snorted again as he Velcroed the remote to his hip.

The spinning blades slowed to a stop. Edwin helped Lon push and pull the robot backwards out of its tight spot. The robot was battleship-gray, the size of a doghouse, and very heavy even in the light lunar gravity. Its massive shielding protected it not only from radiation but from dust and falling rock. On Earth it would have been impossible to shift without a forklift. Lon said, "You want to start scratching around that rock? As long as we got the badger on its side, I want to look at the disc alignment."

"Sure thing." With the shovel Edwin began scraping stubborn regolith away from around the boulder. It was almost two meters long, scored and scarred from the badger's digging blades. The boulder was not very thick, though, and Edwin easily loosened it with the pry bar. "Ready when you are," he announced.

Lon rummaged in the toolkit. "Let me tighten—"

On Earth there would have been a roar from the engine. Here there was only a vibration and the sudden blurring of the digging disc as it began to spin. Lon spat a curse as he was flung back. A mist seemed to spurt from his body, a pink-and-white blur: blood and air. Edwin's years of training paid off. Without needing to think, he jumped forward and clamped both hands over the tear in the leg of Lon's surface suit. He pressed the emergency comm button on the inside of his helmet with his chin. "We got a problem out here by the excavation," he called. "Suit somebody up to help!" To Lon he added, "You hurt bad?"

Behind the shiny gold sun-visor Lon's face was invisible, but his voice was strong and steady. "It just caught me glancing. Oh, dammit to hell and gone, I've lost the remote!"

"I see it. It fell under the housing."

"I didn't finish tightening up the disc. The badger will tear itself apart!"

They watched for a second as the digging disc began an ominous wobble. Quickly Edwin reviewed the options. The spare remote was inside. A colonist needed at least a couple minutes to suit up. An overriding signal could be sent from the space station, but that also would take a couple minutes. In that time the robot could rack itself into a major repair job that would throw the colony off schedule yet again. *Time is money,* NASA always said these days. "The simplest thing to do is to just grab that remote," he said. "Here, Lon. Can you hold yourself together for a second while I slap on a patch? You feel woozy or anything?"

"I'm fine. But you can't reach under that blade! It's already loose. If it catches you—"

Fumbling in his heavy gloves, Edwin peeled the largest detergent logo off his upper arm. Doubling ads as emergency patches had been the easiest way for NASA to rationalize turning astronauts into walking billboards. He pressed the garish square carefully down over the tear in Lon's suit, and rose to his feet.

The remote lay just underneath the curve of the badger's housing. Even in the sharp-cut depth of shadow the red case was plainly visible against the gray soil. To reach it Edwin would have to lie down flat on his stomach, always a challenge in the bulky stiff suits. Their surface suits were the latest design, far more flexible than the old Apollo moonwalk suits, but they still weren't comfortable. If he was deft, the sharp cutting edge wouldn't catch his shoulder or head.

Edwin eased down joint by joint to sprawl in the dust. Once he was down, the grinding maladjustment of the disc was actually audible, vibrating through the entire length of his body. Lon yelled, "Forget it, Ed! It's not worth the risk! Geena, hurry up and stop him, will you?"

"You worry too much, Lon," Edwin said. He watched the wobble of the disc, choosing his time, and with a lightning snatch seized the remote.

Edwin pointed the remote and pushed OFF. "We'll have to reprogram the badger, but after this incident I don't trust that PAUSE feature anymore."

In another minute Geena and Mariko came bounding over the edge. "You must've been out of your mind!" Geena exclaimed. "What if it had cut your arm off?"

"It didn't," he said simply, dismissing it. "What do you think, Lon? Can you walk back, or do we carry you?"

Edwin's efforts to keep the incident low-key had some effect on base, but he had no control over the Earthside coverage. These days NASA was always on the lookout for drama. The footage of the badger's rescue ran incessantly on the Space Cable Channel that week. The detergent advertised on Lon's repair patch briefly swept every other laundry product off the market. Edwin's public bulletin-board topic exploded with inane adulatory messages. His Q rating soared, so that he briefly became the most well-known member of the Moon team. "At least it's no longer because you have dimples, right?" Charlie ribbed him.

"That poll was so unjust," Edwin complained. "You girls have dimples too, so why doesn't the public adore you for them?"

"Dimples are female standard issue," she said smugly. "On a guy, they're options, and therefore cute."

It was a relief very late the next evening to get to his personal e-mail. Rob had written:

> Firrin seems to have assumed that he could be useful with his specialty, without ever actually announcing it. Since his squadron doesn't in fact know about it, naturally there's a big hoorah every time he pulls a stunt. Can you say "wishful thinking"? I can. He's NEVER going to have any peace and quiet until he learns to keep it completely secret. What's so difficult to understand?

Even discussing his central dilemma in third person, with "Firrin" pasted on over his own name, was helpful. Edwin wrote back,

> But Rob, peace and quiet makes for a dull fantasy novel. Severneth reminds me of Mark Twain's cat—have you heard of her? She sat on a hot stove lid, and learnt her lesson so well she's never sat on a cold one either. I wonder if Severneth and Firrin aren't working towards two quite different coping mechanisms. When I get back in July we have to compare manuscripts. It'll be nice to get out of the fishbowl. Sometimes I feel like a performing animal in a very expensive zoo.

Edwin deleted that last sentence before sending the message—no point in provoking Houston. Then he moved to the last letter, from his wife Carina. As he read it his mouth opened in dismay.

The drownings didn't make the Sunday *Post*, but in the Monday Metro section there was a story about an elderly fisherman at Hains Point who had fainted dead away after reeling in the body of a young man from the Potomac. The next day the other two bodies turned up, discovered in midstream by boaters. The wrap-up story didn't run until Saturday. Deion Morris and Monte Timms had been sixteen, and Mark "Squeak" Ellison only fourteen. In their school photographs the three looked angelic, but the article hinted at gang involvement in their deaths. Sisters and mothers insisted in interviews that the boys were harmless. Funerals were scheduled for early the following week.

Rob knew it wouldn't help, but he clipped all three news stories and filed them in an old yellow file folder. Julianne ought never to have found out, but she came up from the basement on Saturday evening with the recycling stack to ask, "Davey, did you cut a piece out of today's paper? The other side has an ad about Pampers on sale, and I've got to see it."

Davey, a strapping nine-year-old, didn't look up from his comic book. "Naw, it wasn't me. Ask the dingbat."

"You don't call your sister names, Davey," Julianne said.

"I have it, Jul." Rob took out the clipping, resigned to his fate.

"I got this great idea, Mom! With the money you save on diapers, we could get a dog! Or a cat! Or an anaconda!"

"In your dreams, darling. The last thing this household needs is an animal." Julianne laid the clipping back into the cut-up page spread out on the dining table. "Oh, for dumb, this store is in Germantown. It's not worth driving that far." Then she turned the clipping over. " 'DROWNING VICTIMS POSSIBLE GANG SLAYINGS.' Do you know these guys, Rob? What are you saving this for?"

A number of possible lies flitted through Rob's mind. "They looked a lot meaner last Saturday night."

"Oh my god! You mean it's *them*?" Julianne dropped the clipping as if it burned her fingers. "How awful! And they got drowned? That's so weird—we must've been one of their last hits!" Rob was keeping busy, washing and cutting up some chicken for dinner, but she must have seen something in his posture at the kitchen sink. "Rob, is there something wrong?"

"No, no—I was just wondering whether I remembered to buy the tomatoes to cook with this." He was even able to rescue the clipping again, after she stuffed the newspapers back into the recycling bin.

But it was impossible to stay on guard every minute. In the small hours of Monday morning Rob had a fearful dream about attending fourteen-year-old Squeak Ellison's funeral. He stood in a big church at the end of a long line of sobbing relatives dressed in their Sunday best. All the way at the front of the line near the altar rail stood the open coffin. Above and behind it, suspended from the dim arched ceiling, was an enormous and outstandingly gaudy crucifix of some ethnic folk-art school, glittering with gold leaf and glossy primary colors.

More than anything in the world, Rob wanted to get out of that line. But other weeping mourners lined up behind him, and he was trapped. The organ played an old hymn, one that Rob recognized because Edwin occasionally sang it: "Lift Up Your Heads." And somehow this supplied the last touch of terror. Because Edwin wasn't supposed to know about this, there was no way he could know up on the Moon, and yet he was here, in the music he loved.

Spontaneously the congregation began to sing along with the organ. "Lift up your heads, ye mighty gates! / Behold, the King of Glory waits!" The organ hammered to the beat of Rob's heart, and the shiny painted eyes of the crude figure above looked down on him with wooden calm. And Rob knew beyond a shadow of a doubt that the dead teenager was waiting. When Rob got up to the coffin the dead boy would indeed lift up his head, to greet his murderer. And the hymn ground on and on, endless verses that Rob would have sworn he didn't know, laden with inexplicable dread: "Fling wide the portals of your heart, / Make it a temple set apart . . ."

He jerked awake with a shout of horror. Beside him Julianne clicked on the lamp, her eyes puffy with sleep. "Rob, what is it? Are you all right?"

"Just a nightmare." He sat up, shuddering.

"Oh, you poor thing, you're drenched. What was it about?"

"I . . . don't remember."

"You were saying something about Edwin," Julianne murmured sleepily. She clicked out the light again, and Rob flipped his pillow over to the dry side and tried to relax. Julianne yawned and said, " 'Ed won't like it.' "

"Huh?"

"That's what you were saying, over and over: 'Ed won't like it.' "

"Go to sleep, dearest, or you'll be exhausted at work tomorrow." He lay very still in the dark, waiting for her to drop off. When her breathing was deep and steady again he got up and went wearily downstairs. The air was cooler there—no amount of fidgeting with the ductwork seemed to get enough air-conditioning to the upper story.

Without thinking about it he sat down in the dark living room and powered up the computer for a pass. It was not quite dawn yet. The light coming through the patio doors was cold and gray. All he needed to kill was half an hour or so. Then the twins would wake, and he could dive into the morning routine.

To his surprise a red URGENT flag came up on the screen. He called the message up, and it was from Edwin:

Rob, I've just had a vexing e-mail conversation with Carina. The dig shut down early in Peru (some political hoo-ha) and she has an unexpected month free. She's determined to visit Central Asia and look up our old friend Gil. I CANNOT talk her out of it—Lord knows I've tried. Will you give it a whirl? She plans to come and pump you anyway. I know I don't have to tell you what a majorly BAD idea this is. See what you can do, please! E.

Rob replied immediately. How lucky he was awake so early! The upload went daily from Houston at six A.M., so Edwin would get the reply today.

You can count on me, Ed. I'll do my best to talk her out of it. Don't worry about anything. Oh, and back to the Mu novel—you can imagine there are times when it's convenient that Severneth plays his cards very close to his chest.

He hit SEND and leaned back, taking a deep breath. Gilgamesh had nearly killed Rob and Edwin both. He was the wild card, the unknowable Mesopotamian source of the powers that Rob fenced sternly in and that Edwin wore so lightly. Rob had defeated Gilgamesh and stripped him of all his power. But what had Gilgamesh been doing these past seven years? Mystically recuperating, perhaps?

Once, Rob had wanted to become a superhero. And what do superheroes do, but battle supervillains? Fighting Gilgamesh again, toe-to-toe, on equal terms, would be enormously destructive. Rob had only prevailed the last time by cunning and luck. The idea of even seeing the old monarch again gave Rob the willies.

And Carina wanted to pump him about his life as a heroic king in ancient Sumeria! It just showed you that the search for knowledge could be an unhealthy obsession.

From the two-bedroom addition at the back of the living room came the steady tramp of four heavy feet. Annie came in, her honey-colored hair in a tousle, and said, "You want my computer games, Dad?"

"No thanks, sweetie. I'm done."

Davey said, "He can beat you anyway." He resembled his sister exactly except for his eyes, which were gray-blue like Rob's instead of brown.

"Can*not*!"

"Let's eat breakfast," Rob interposed quickly. Nine was too quarrelsome an age. He poured their milk, looked over homework, and packed two bag lunches while the twins squabbled over their cereal. When a squeak came from the baby monitor, he sent Davey up with the bottle. Julianne always handled the morning feeding.

The phone rang while he was helping to find Davey's missing sneaker. He tucked the cordless phone between shoulder and ear. "Lewis residence," he said from his hands and knees, looking under the sofa.

"Hello, is that Rob? Carina Barbarossa here."

"Oh, hi! Where are you?"

"Miami, heading north. Could I spend a night on your couch?"

"Sure," Rob said, as heartily as he could. "When are you arriving?"

"Wednesday. Could we go out to dinner, just Julianne and you and me?"

Rob was cautious. "You want to talk about Central Asia, right?"

"Darn it, you'd think that it would take a little while for e-mail to get here from the Moon! That Rovilatt guy must keep all their noses to the grindstone, gossiping on his Net."

"Carina, first off, you need to know that only you and Ed know about Gilgamesh, okay? Julianne is not in on it."

"But . . ." Carina sounded astonished. "But shouldn't she know?"

"You're as bad as Ed," Rob said impatiently. "Look, I'll pick you up at the airport. Give me the flight and the time." As he wrote the numbers with a purple crayon on a fallen paper towel he saw little Colin valiantly trying to creep towards him across the carpet. He was so small, the most he could do was balance on his brisket and kick all four limbs into the air. Behind him stood Julianne, in high heels and a sharp sage-green Givenchy business suit. "Okay, see you Wednesday." He disconnected and said, "Is it time for the twins to catch the bus?"

"Yeah, we're just going. Who was that?"

"Carina. She's on her way from one project to another, and wants to stay the night Wednesday."

"I guess it's okay." Her hazel eyes narrowed a little, and Rob realized he didn't know how long Julianne had been standing there listening to his end of the conversation.

There was no time to talk about anything now, though. A wail—"Mommy! Jennie's already leaving for the bus stop!"—came from Annie on the front step. And Colin, distracted by a red Tinkertoy, was trying to lick it up off the rug.

Rob scooped him up. "Have a great day, Jul. I love you."

"Don't forget to put an extra stretchy into his bag. The standby outfit got messed last Friday." She gave him a peck and vanished out the front door to meet the school bus with the twins and then drive to work.

Rob stared around the messy living room. Tinkertoys peppered the room, Davey hadn't picked up his Legos, and some fallen purple Play-Doh had been trodden into the brown carpet and left to dry. Colin leaned over his arm, wiggling. He wanted that Tinkertoy. "Houseguests mean we have to pick up, little guy," he told the baby. "And I have to do two estimates today, and spend all afternoon getting a building permit. And you have a day-care date with Miss Linda. You better come help me dress."

✳ CHAPTER 3

*C*arina burst out of the airport gate like a running back breaking out of the line of scrimmage. Watching, Rob tried to see how the dynamic little figure worked her way steadily forward through the crowd of deplaning passengers. She didn't push or jostle, but somehow she passed people. Maybe it came of being so short—Carina was only about five-foot-two.

Rob felt no superiority from his own six-foot vantage. With her competence, energy, and striking dark beauty, Carina expected the world to be her oyster, and rarely had been confounded in that belief. Persuading such a strong-minded woman out of the Asia trip suddenly seemed much less doable. It's really not fair, Rob thought, waving at her. If Ed couldn't change her mind, how am I supposed to do it? Or—here was a startling thought—had he been hinting that Rob should do just that? Quietly fiddle Carina's brain so that

she forgot all about Gilgamesh? "Oh boy," Rob groaned
aloud. "I better ask him what Severneth should do."

"Never saw such a crowd," Carina greeted him. "It's a
wonder we weren't standing in the airplane aisle." She wore
a bush jacket, its multiple pockets bulging with oddments,
and a faded floral T-shirt underneath. Her jeans had red dirt
permanently ground into the knees. In one hand she had an
overflowing briefcase, and under the other arm she carried a
hemp tote bag bulging with what looked like yarn. She took
his hand in her own excavation-callused one and pumped it
briskly. "It's so great of you to meet me! Let's go get my
luggage."

With stunning fleetness she herded him through the airport, extracted her bags, and found the correct exit. The dark
cloud of her hair seemed to stream out behind with her speed,
like a comet's tail. Rob had never moved so fast through
Dulles Airport in his life. In no time they were rolling in the
truck towards home. "Now!" Carina said with determined
energy. "Where we left off: This mind-bending thingy of yours
is so major, I can see not telling any old body. But how can you
be keeping it from Julianne? It would be like you secretly being
Vice President of the United States. How can she not *notice*?"

"First of all, Carina, some ground rules. I'm doing it this
way because I want to live a peaceful and normal life. Please
accept my decision. I do not want to discuss my marriage
with you."

"And I don't want to hear arguments about how dangerous Gilgamesh is," she retorted, smiling. "So that takes care
of two major subjects. Shall we talk about baseball now?"

Rob had to laugh at that. "Well, suppose I tell you what
a king of Uruk wears? Ed didn't see Gilgamesh in his full battle armor, but I did."

"You did? You will?" When Carina turned her brilliant
dark gaze onto him, it was like being focused in a pair of
high-power searchlights. "That would be wonderful—oh,
I'm so glad I came! If I showed you photos of the bas-reliefs
could you choose the most similar one? Did you actually

touch or handle any artifacts? Did they look new, or well-worn? Start at the top, and work down."

Rob was appalled. "How long are you planning to stay, Carina?"

"Only till tomorrow—why?"

"Because if you keep this up for any length of time I'll be exhausted."

"Why have you been so cagey about this?" Carina demanded. "Edwin's been a honey about answering questions."

"Ed is an idiot." Rob scowled at a taxi passing too fast on the right. "He doesn't understand how mean people can be— He doesn't have a mean bone in his body. You can't have any idea of what a monster Gilgamesh was, because Ed couldn't tell you."

"Well then, you can do it," Carina said with calm triumph. "Give it your best shot. Tell me everything, and let me judge."

Rob had a sinking feeling he would either be outmaneuvered or worn down. The Barbarossa family must spend all their time together talking. At least it was a good mode of interaction for an astronaut's relationships.

They stopped at Miss Linda's to pick up Colin, and just beat the twins home. Carina frowned at the school bus. "I suppose the kids are in the dark too."

"Of course," Rob said, unlocking the front door. "You'll just have to control your passion for knowledge. Hi, Davey, look who's here! Annie, do you remember Aunt Carina?"

"No," Annie said frankly, but unbent so far as to accept a small Peruvian doll. Davey was much more openly delighted with his present, a wooden gun. It was fitted with a thick dangerous-looking rubber band for firing pebbles. Rob winced, foreseeing cracked heads, pelleted eyes, and visits to the emergency room. But Carina lectured Davey vigorously about weapons safety and responsibility, capping the lesson by showing the twins her .38 automatic.

"Good gosh," Rob exclaimed. "You travel with that?"

"I work in pretty wild areas," Carina said.

"You are the coolest aunt I ever met," Davey said in awe.

"Can we shoot it?" Annie begged.

"You know the answer to that! What did I just say, about being old enough?"

Rob retreated back into the kitchen, shaking his head. Sometimes Carina was terrifying.

By the time Julianne came home dinner was well under way—the pork chops in the oven, the potatoes frying. The twins descended on their mother, shouting, "Aunt Carina gave me a slingshot gun, they use them in Peru!" and, "Mom, Aunt Carina shot a coyote once! It was stealing her lunch!"

Julianne set down her briefcase and gave Carina an air kiss. "You're a hit," she said. "Boy, they're jazzed!"

"I'm afraid I've excited them a little," Carina said. "Maybe they'll cool down if we go into the yard. Rob, you can show me this new addition."

"You do that, hon," Julianne said. "Just give me ten minutes of peace with the baby."

"You got it." Slowly Rob followed Carina and the rampaging twins out back. The twins flung themselves yelling onto the elaborate swing set. "All my own work," Rob said. "I'm particularly proud of that crow's-nest arrangement up there. And the double swing, big enough for all five of us to sit. To your left, the new addition. Two bedrooms, a bath, and a hallway, substantially complete. I have to do some trim, and finish tiling the bathroom floor."

"It's lovely, but I didn't really want to hear about the bathroom," Carina said, with cheery single-mindedness. "I want to hear about Gilgamesh."

Rob had given this some hard thought while peeling potatoes. Describing Gilgamesh's artifacts would surely distract her from the more weird aspects. But hearing about armor wouldn't lessen Carina's appetite for a direct interview. In fact, it would increase it. He had to remember he had promised Ed to try and stop her. "Make you a deal," he said. "I'll tell you everything, a total data dump, if you give up on actually seeing the old guy."

"But I have to see him," Carina said, with the patience of a teacher helping a very stupid little boy. "How can I not talk to the man? You're only a secondary source. I have to get it from the primary source if I can."

"Then I'm on strike," Rob said coolly. "How about those Mets, huh?"

"You, you—" The color rose like wine in Carina's tanned cheeks. "Oh! Edwin told me a little about this weird thing of yours! Why don't you just use it to take over my mind or something?"

"Don't tempt me." It would be easy, so very easy. A minor adjustment of her memory, and she'd forget all about Gilgamesh. The entire problem would go away. "I only wish I knew what Ed would like," Rob mused.

The bulldog set of Carina's chin was utterly lovely, but her dark eyes had a glint very reminiscent of the .38. "You just try it!"

Rob shook his head. "More and more, I'm convinced it's wrong to make puppets of people. You're safe from me."

"Then you can't stop me," Carina said firmly. "I'm going to Asia." She turned and marched back into the house.

"Damn it," Rob said.

Dinner was a slightly tense meal. Afterwards Carina volunteered to clear the table while Julianne loaded the dishwasher. Rob seized this golden opportunity to send an urgent e-mail to Edwin:

You know that Lady Dorella is turning out to be a real stubborn opponent for Severneth. Were you envisioning a scene where he magically alters her opposition to his strategy for shoring up the foundations of Mu? Because it's really not like him, after all his agonizing about his subjects' free will. I don't think he can do it. It's all very well to talk about an abstract character like the Pharaoh, but Lady D is kind of integral to the story, don't you think? Tell me how you imagine this bit working out.

From the kitchen came the grinding sound of the garbage disposal digesting potato peelings. Cleanup was almost over. He had to wind this up. Quickly he added,

Carina plans to leave for Istanbul tomorrow. I doubt your answer will arrive before then.

He clicked SEND just as the women emerged. It was a school night, so everyone went to bed early. The twins promised faithfully not to jump on Aunt Carina in her sofabed until at least sunrise. Up in the master bedroom Rob lay beside Julianne, worrying. She shifted restlessly in the dark. "Rob?"

"What, Jul?"

"What were you and Carina talking about, out back?"

He turned onto his side, reaching for her. "Oh, she was telling me about the trip to Istanbul. And I talked a little about the time when Ed and I went climbing in Kazakhstan."

She touched his hand and held it. "Is that the truth, Rob?"

"Sure," he said, startled. "More or less," he felt impelled to add. He moved closer and ran a hand curving around her flank. "It was all unimportant—just chat." He realized he didn't want to talk, didn't want to lie awake fretting. He stopped her lips with his own before she could speak.

Edwin received the e-mail at the end of a long, trying day. The main hydroponics line had developed a slow mysterious leak. Edwin and Mariko spent hours crawling on their hands and knees through smelly puddles under the glare of the 400-watt high-pressure sodium-lamp sunshine, checking hoses and joints without result. The hydroponic garden was only one dome, nowhere near big enough to process the CO_2 the colonists exhaled. The vegetables it produced were mainly tasteless lettuce and cabbages. As a pilot project, though, the garden was vital—the forerunner of lunar agriculture, and all future space settlements.

Then the PSPIP liaison floated a new moneymaking idea: Moonbase doormats. The Cold War mind-set of the 1960s had carried the space program right through Apollo. But with the downfall of communism, NASA had gradually lost its way. Everyone acknowledged the need for a new paradigm, but the crew despised the PSPIP entrepreneurial template. "We already sell a catalogful of junk," Charlie said. "T-shirts, mugs, stickers, screen-savers, the works. Enough is enough!" Lon, who had a nicely acid memo style, undertook to express the opinion of the team.

The most worrying concern however was Phan. He'd been getting more and more withdrawn, until it was no longer possible to pretend nothing was wrong. For years the NASA shrinks had predicted that the psychological stresses of living on the Moon would be worse than the physical hardships, and it was annoying to find they were correct. It was difficult to discuss any one person privately in a small place like Moonbase. But Edwin had a good opportunity today while crawling through the hydroponics dome. Mariko had gone through the situation thoroughly with him.

Edwin was used to being a listener and confidant. The skill had, in fact, been one of the factors in his selection. But it was stressful, and he realized that he was getting tired. You can only dip so much from a well before it runs dry. He and Phan were the oldest inhabitants of Moonbase now, due to rotate back to Earth in six weeks. A year ago he never would have believed it, but Edwin knew now he was, like Phan, ready to go.

And now this e-mail from Rob. He had pulled it up first, knowing it would be important. He rubbed his temples, where a tension headache was beginning. Edwin regarded his marriage to Carina as a healthier one, on the whole, than the Lewises'. Rob's single-minded focus on his wife and family seemed a little excessive to Edwin, whose devout Baptist upbringing had advocated keeping God at the center of one's life.

But given that, how was it that Carina disagreed with him so vehemently on this Gilgamesh question? Edwin loved her dearly, but long separations were a given in every colonist's relationships. In fact, NASA made a point of selecting spacemen with high empathy ratings and good interpersonal skills, but also well-disciplined sex drives. Sending a bedroom athlete on a one-year lunar tour would be asking for trouble.

Edwin knew he fitted the NASA profile almost perfectly, monogamous by faith as well as by inclination. So did most of his fellow colonists—Geena was Jewish, Phan a Catholic, and Lon's father was the Episcopal Bishop of the Diocese of West Texas. The definition of "the right stuff" had changed yet again. Once, astronauts had been rocket jockeys, daredevils recruited from the ranks of fighter-jet pilots. Then they were engineers, piloting shuttles, building the space station. Edwin was of the new cohort, the colonists—a well-grounded, versatile crew trained to work and play well with others for years on end.

Automatically now, Edwin skirted around thoughts of how long it had been since he last touched Carina. Then a new, unpleasant idea occurred to him: Had he, in reality, been growing away from her? In a sudden panic Edwin tried to visualize his wife, the living woman.

The only face that came to mind was the one in the photograph taped to the wall near his bed: a good picture for once, of Carina kneeling by a Peruvian burial mound, holding a steel meterstick against what looked like a half-buried gunnysack full of bones—her first textile find. She smiled up at the camera, proud as punch of the mummy and its cerements, and her workshirt had slipped open without her knowing it just enough to show a tiny stimulating peek of cleavage. The combination of intelligence and cheesecake had been irresistible when Edwin chose this photo a year ago. But now this was all the image he had—a two-dimensional square of lines and colors. Somehow, everything else of Carina was gone from memory: her voice, the way she moved and walked, the texture of her hair. What was this between his ears, a sieve? There had to be a way to do better, to remember more thoroughly.

Instantly he got hold of himself. It was too easy, in the isolation and confinement of Moonbase, to let the imagination run wild and become cancerous. In no time he'd be as buggy as Phan. No, deal with the problem at hand. He'd have to ask Rob for help. Not adjusting Carina's memory— what a worrywart Rob could be! He'd never make it in the astronaut corps—but more practical assistance. Edwin bent over the keyboard and began to type.

In the morning, Rob fixed on a new tactic for his final try at derailing Carina. He couldn't make the attempt, though, until the house was clear. The twins had rousted Carina out with the larks, and she had made a luxurious breakfast: coffee, herbal tea, pancakes, and sausage. Davey in particular had no intention of losing Aunt Carina so soon. "I could go with you to the airport," he said wistfully. "I could carry your suitcase."

Annie hooted. "Dumbo, it has wheels!"

"Then I could push it!"

"Pipe down," Carina commanded. "Nobody carries my suitcase but me. And the taxi driver."

"I can drop you off," Rob said. "I have to take the morning off anyway, for Colin. His day-care nanny has a mammogram appointment."

"Ooh, he is a dumpling, isn't he? Let me hold him again."

Julianne came in, briefcase in hand, and shot the bunch of them a look. "Rob, if you could do the bus-stop run, I can get half an hour's jump on the day."

"Sure, Jul, if that would help."

"But wouldn't you like some pancakes?" Carina asked.

"I'm watching my weight," Julianne said shortly.

Rob got up to kiss her good-bye. "You've lost all the

Colin poundage," he teased her, smiling. "Are you going for the negative numbers now?"

She looked at her watch. "I'll pick up Colin, and Davey's going straight to science camp after school, and Annie's playing with Nona Gilberti—you remember her, she lives in the townhouses. So everything's cool for the P.M."

"Right," Rob said, disconcerted, and she was gone.

Carina poured herself another cup of tea with her free hand, supporting Colin with the other. He could just about sit up, the downy oversized head wobbling valiantly on his plump soft neck. "That is not a happy woman," she remarked.

"I asked you to stay out of it," Rob snapped.

"Get the twins off to school and we'll talk," Carina said. "Look at you, you hold up your head so great! Would you like this teaspoon? Yes? What a smart baby!"

Rob made the usual irritating morning push, scouting out mislaid shoes and socks, discovering that Annie was supposed to bring three egg cartons, Styrofoam, not cardboard, to class today, and inspecting a possible loose tooth in Davey's lower jaw. But at last he waved the twins into the school bus.

"I'm afraid the baby's messy," Carina greeted him when he got back. "You can change him, and I'll watch."

"Thanks a lot. You'll get your turn, when you and Ed start a family." When Rob took the baby, his fingers brushed her tanned arm, and through that contact—the weirdness was often linked to touch—he got a quick flash that he'd said something wrong. But she didn't pursue it, and the diaper couldn't wait. He led the way up to the nursery and attacked the problem immediately.

Colin's nursery was the size of a large bathroom, and crowded with baby paraphernalia. Carina dove in with her usual devouring curiosity. "What is this thing? A warmer for the baby wipes? My, my, that's decadent, Colin—I hope it was a shower present. Ooh, I like your rocking chair. Gliders are so soothing. Rob, why is this mirror in the crib so wavy? No, I get it, it's because it's plastic."

Colin burbled at all this talk, and Rob laughed. "Get a word in edgewise, champ—I dare you."

Carina laughed too. "Okay, you talk. Tell me something about ancient Mesopotamian monarchs who've mysteriously survived into the twenty-first century."

Rob put his new tactic into play. "Have a look at this, Carina. Right here." He pointed.

"Your eyebrow? That's only a little scar—you can hardly see it."

"Hurt like hell when I got it from Gil, though."

"You're kidding."

"He beat me up," Rob recalled, "and when I couldn't stand up anymore, he kicked me in the face." He stuck the new diaper on and wedged Colin's fat thrashing feet back into the legs of the stretch suit.

"Well, mores have altered enormously in five thousand years," Carina said, a little weakly. "You probably weren't sending the right cultural signals, you know? You should have had an anthropologist on the team."

"And that was just in the first couple hours of our acquaintance," Rob said. "It turns out that if you live long enough, you get a little crazy . . . There you go, big boy. Clean and dry. Let's go down and have a look at our toys."

Downstairs, Rob took the last of the coffee, and topped off Carina's tea. "You're trying to frighten me," Carina complained as she followed him into the living room.

"I'm reporting the bald facts to you, so you can make an informed assessment." Rob sat cross-legged on the rug, supporting Colin upright so that the baby could reach for his rattle. "Shall I tell you about Ed?"

"It's not going to change my mind," Carina warned.

"Gilgamesh forced Ed to step off a cliff. I think Ed might have survived the broken leg and the shattered pelvis— though that might have put paid to his astronaut career. But fracturing your skull in a primitive place is really dangerous. It was right here—" Rob pointed to his own head above the right ear. "A big dent, maybe four inches across. Probably he would have died in a couple hours."

Carina set her mug down as if she didn't want to drink any more. "But you did something. You saved him."

Rob nodded. "I gave him a piece of Gilgamesh's power. I still have the weird bit, that lets me do mental stuff—the piece that got Gil to the top of the heap in 3000 B.C. Ed has the undersea jewel of immortality, the pearl that let Gil survive for five thousand years. So we lived to tell the tale. Will you, with just your notebook and a .38? Carina, I'm trying to tell you that you're proposing to do a very dangerous thing. This guy is not like me, and even less like Ed. He is bad news, squared and cubed."

Carina sat on the sofa, staring at him out of huge dark eyes. For a moment Rob really thought he'd pulled it off. Then she said, "And now that Gilgamesh is no longer immortal, this priceless old guy, the last possible witness to the most formative era of human history, he'll die any day. There isn't a moment to waste! He's the last living speaker of Sumerian. I bet he can read cuneiform writing. He can tell about the politics, the agriculture, the art of his time—a living window into the past! Oh, can't you see how important he is?"

"I give up," Rob said in despair. "I will never argue with an archaeologist again. Just keep that gun ready to hand, okay? He's a psychopath. Did I tell you about the nuclear bomb?"

"I don't want to hear about it," Carina said, with decision. "I want to catch my Istanbul plane. It leaves in three hours. Give me five minutes to pack."

✳ CHAPTER
4

*H*e had done his best. Still, Rob felt uneasy enough to postpone his computer pass. Waiting until the following morning after six meant the new messages would have arrived. Sure enough, early on Friday morning was another URGENT-flagged letter from Edwin:

> Drat the woman. Couldn't she wait till I get back in July? Rob, I know this is a big favor to ask. But is there any way you could go with her? You're the only one who knows what Gil can do. She has no idea what she's getting into. I'm really worried about what could happen. Let me know, please. As to the book—I would not at all want magical tampering with Dorella. You are right, and I was wrong. (Why are you always right about these things?) Nobody gives a rush about the Pharaoh—he has no reality out there at the far right-hand corner of the map, and I never believed the Egyptians knew how to

keep Mu from sinking anyway. But Dorella is really important to my bit of the book. Severneth should let her do her thing—however aggravating or stupid!

When he read this, Rob sagged in his chair with dismay. The first thought that came to mind was that it would be a punishment to travel with Carina to the corner grocery store, never mind Central Asia. And he remembered the swing set he'd signed a contract to build at a church preschool, and the bathroom tiles still in their boxes in the downstairs shower stall. Only then did he picture himself facing Edwin when the space shuttle landed in July, and telling him that Carina had hared off alone to Central Asia and vanished. The frightful vision jerked him to his feet.

He ran upstairs as fast as he could. Julianne was in the shower, and he went in and sat on the toilet lid to wait for her to finish. She turned off the water and slid the steamy enclosure door aside, saying, "What you see is what you get!"

"You're beautiful, Jul," Rob said automatically. "But something's come up. Would you mind if I went to Central Asia?"

Julianne held a bath towel to her chin, her face suddenly taut. "With Carina?"

"Yeah. I figure a couple weeks will do it—"

She gave a huge gasping sob that filled the small bathroom. Then she slapped Rob hard across the face. Utterly astonished, Rob fell backwards off the toilet lid onto the tile floor. "You bastard! You have your *nerve*, telling me you want a fling with her! And at this hour of the morning, and while I'm taking a shower—" She began to cry, muffling her sobs in the towel and turning away to run into the bedroom.

Rob clambered breathless to his feet, his head whirling. "Jul—this is crazy! I don't even like her much!"

Scarcely dry, Julianne threw the towel down and began rattling the clothes hangers across the closet rail, tears pouring down her cheeks. "I do not have to put up with this," she wept. "This is not an 'open' marriage! I'd rather divorce you!"

"No!" This had gone far enough. Rob reached over her bare shoulder and pulled out the purple terrycloth bathrobe. "Put this on and come downstairs. I want you to see an e-mail!"

For a moment she fought him, struggling against the enfolding bathrobe he held around her, but then she gave in. Rob hustled her down to the living room, where Edwin's message still glowed unanswered on the screen. "Sit," Rob ordered. "Read that . . . You see? It's all Edwin's idea, not mine."

He went on one knee to scroll the letter down for her. She leaned against his shoulder, sniffling. "Oh, Rob . . ."

"You know I've never loved any other woman but you." He brushed the curtain of blonde hair back to kiss her clean damp cheek.

"Rob," she said, still reading, "who is Gil?"

The breath left Rob's lungs in a silent huff. Pure surprise held him immobile, and when Julianne turned to look him in the face she could see his turmoil. Her mouth trembled. "There *is* something. Something you aren't telling me. Oh, I knew it!"

Too late to dissemble. Rob knew there was no escape now except by force. He could wipe the question from her memory. It wouldn't be the first time he'd purged Julianne's head for his own convenience. But back then he had been younger, raw to power. He was sure now that crude meddling with a person's very self was wrong. He couldn't do it. He sagged forward until he could lean his head against Julianne's terrycloth bosom. "All right, Jul," he whispered. "I'll tell you all about it."

Julianne's fingers stroked the dark blond hair back from his brow. "Oh dear, there's red fingermarks on your face. I'm so sorry!"

At that moment the twins galloped into the room. Seizing the remote, Davey threw himself onto his stomach, turned on the TV, and zapped the volume all the way up. Annie said sweetly to Julianne, "Does Daddy have nits? Can I help to look?" Annie's own bout with head lice this year was still vivid in her mind.

Rob sat back onto the floor. Why had he ever sired children? "No, Annie, I have no parasites today."

"Turn that thing off, Davey!" Julianne commanded. "You know there's no morning TV on school days! Come and eat breakfast."

From the baby monitor came Colin's howl of hunger. "I'll get him," Rob said wearily.

The entire morning routine had to be gone through: cereal, milk, shoes, diapers, homework, bus stop. While Julianne saw the kids off, Rob made a pot of coffee and called the preschool to postpone the scheduled playground planning session. Julianne came first, and this time he was going to do it right.

"We'll sit on the sofa with Colin, and I'll tell you the whole story," Rob said.

"From the very beginning."

"Right . . . Do you recognize the name Gilgamesh?" He spelled it.

"A forward for the Chicago Bulls," Julianne suggested.

Rob laughed. "No. He was a king, in about 3000 B.C., in Mesopotamia. Gilgamesh had two things going for him: immortality and power."

Julianne moved restlessly beside him. "Rob, have you been watching *Xena* and *Hercules* too much?"

"No, no! This is real. Gil essentially could make people do what he wanted, forever. But his best friend Enkidu died, and then he got fed up and became a desert hermit in Kazakhstan—until about seven years ago. Then he decided to be sociable again, but he had no peers, no equals to talk to. So he divided his power in half and socked it onto me." Julianne sat so still beside him that he added, "You do believe me, don't you, Jul?"

"Of course not." She turned to glare at him. "This is that fantasy novel you're writing with Edwin. You know, Rob, I thought we were going to have a serious conversation, instead of all this ridiculous—"

Rob drew a deep breath through his nose, and concentrated on bouncing the baby gently on his knee. She always did this. This was the exact way she'd reacted seven years ago, the last time he'd tried to tell her. He couldn't let it upset him. And he couldn't let her wind herself up into a major mad. He interrupted her. "Jul. Let me demonstrate, okay? No, don't say anything more. Just come here, and watch."

He plopped the baby into her arms and drew her to her feet. Their suburban street was a quiet one once rush hour was over. Across the way a neighbor was backing out of her driveway. Rob stood at the living-room window and said, "That's old Mrs. Mickelsohn, right?"

"Yeah, but—"

"Just watch, Jul." The large blue Pontiac rolled slowly down the driveway into the street, swinging wide to clear the plastic recycling bins at the curb. "Now—she's going to continue to back up."

They watched as the Pontiac straightened up but went rolling on, idling backwards down the street for nearly a hundred feet. "Okay, now I'm going to have her go forward . . . and then back again, past her house one more time . . ."

"Rob, are you *doing* this to her?" Julianne's hazel eyes were huge, the whites showing all around as she clutched the baby tight. "Making her drive that way?"

"Yes, I am. That's what I'm telling you, Jul. I don't know what you call the ability, but I can do a lot of stuff. I—"

Rob realized that the Pontiac was still sitting at the curb, not moving. "Come on."

He hurried outside and across the street to the car. Mrs. Mickelsohn, plump and grandmotherly, sat at the wheel looking dazed. In the backseat, confined in a large plastic pet carrier, a surly white Persian mewed and scuffled. "Hi, Mrs. M.," Rob called, trying to sound casual. "Taking Snowball out for a spin?"

"Oh, hello there, Rob. You know, I think I may be having some kind of attack. What are the symptoms of stroke, do you know?"

Rob opened his mouth, but no words came out. Dumb with guilt, he could see it all now—Mrs. Mickelsohn off to her doctors, complaining about fits or strange mental afflictions. They would apply every test known to science and find nothing wrong, but would drain her meager health insurance dry on the way. The poor old lady would have to sell her house, or declare bankruptcy. Damn it, when would he learn to be *careful*?

But Julianne, bless her, was at his elbow. "Could it be something wrong with your car?" she asked. "It doesn't look like it's driving right."

"My goodness! Do you think that could be it?"

Quickly Rob picked up the ball. "When was the last time you had it serviced?"

"Why, I don't know, dear. Herbert used to take care of all that."

And Mr. Mickelsohn had passed away, what, five years ago? "I think you should take it to a garage, and get them to do the standard maintenance stuff," Rob said. "Change the oil, test the brakes, that kind of thing."

"Maybe you're right," Mrs. Mickelsohn said. "Oh, hush up, Snowball. We can go get our fur groomed after we drop off the car. Thank you so much, dears. My goodness, that baby of yours gets bigger every time I see him . . ."

She pulled away, down the street towards Fairfax City. Rob said, "Five years without maintenance—she must be buying her gas at a full-service station, and they're topping off the oil for her. I suppose that counts as a good deed. That was one of the things I wanted to do: good stuff, helping people. Like Spider-Man or something. But it's really hard— you'd be surprised. I'm always tripping myself up, like now."

"My god, Rob—this is so weird!"

" 'Weird' is the word for it, Jul." He tucked his arm through her free one, and strolled with her up the sidewalk. "Do you remember the latter half of '94 and into '95? That was when this 'weird' thing was driving me crazy, and I left home."

"You said it was your midlife crisis," Julianne remembered.
"I had to get this thing by the throat. Ed helped me—
that's when I met him. In the end we had to go to Asia and
take the other half away from Gil. And I gave Ed the immortality piece of it. So that's the story."

The front yards were full of late daffodils and tulips as
they went around the block, and the Bradford pear trees
bloomed along the curbs like white torch flames. Rob
waited, curbing his anxiety, giving her time to think.
Julianne could always be relied upon for good ideas. If only
she wouldn't suggest he run for President! He couldn't
remember if this was an election year, and it worried him.
But she surprised him by asking, "And where does Carina
come into it?"

"Gilgamesh is still alive, as far as I know. Carina wants to
interview him about Mesopotamia—the dumbest idea I ever
heard. Ed wants me to baby-sit her, and I think I have to go."

She looked at him narrowly. "And you don't find her
attractive."

"She's pretty, but she's a royal pain in the neck," Rob
said, with such heartfelt sincerity that Julianne laughed.

Confiding in his wife was a tremendous relief. He'd have
to admit to Edwin that he'd been right all along. And there
was something to be said for jealousy, if it distracted Jul from
political ambitions. Suddenly Rob felt great. "Would you
like to see a few more of my tricks? Let's go farther—it's a
fine day for a walk."

They loaded Colin into his stroller and walked arm in
arm. Their subdivision was an old, rather dumpy one, mostly
postwar Cape Cod houses crowded by mature trees. Rob
found its earnest middle-class mundanity endlessly soothing.
A man, even a weird one, who lived in such a relentlessly
modest neighborhood was really a regular guy.

Rob did minor things with the weirdness, flicking into
invisibility with his tarnhelm trick, coercing the local dogs
into barking in unison, making passing cars swerve in the
street. There was so little daytime traffic in their suburb that

briefly harassing drivers was perfectly safe. He was careful this time to target each driver only once.

"This is amazing, Rob," Julianne marveled. "You could do anything with this. Anything at all! You could rule the world, like in the cartoon!"

Rob twitched with involuntary alarm, but spoke up easily enough. "I had to decide what I really wanted in life. And I chose you and the kids. A nice normal family."

She laughed. "You know how some men are born to be wild? Or born to run? You were born to be a dad."

"That's true," Rob said, laughing too. "But it makes for a much less impressive rock lyric. Oh, and is it okay if I tag along with Carina? I have to let Ed know."

"I suppose so," Julianne said. "But don't be away too long, all right?"

So when they got back home Rob sent off a soothing e-mail:

No sweat, Ed, I'm on it. I'll leave this weekend sometime and try to catch up with Carina before she gets there. Everything will be fine. You can trust me to take good care of her. Oh, and I put some real solid work in on the Severneth-Kira relationship this week. He's told her everything about his magic, in a broad-brush kind of way, so the worst is over. A great relief to him, too, and I think the story will get on much better now—your advice was dead on-target. (What do you mean, "I'm always right"?)

That evening Rob lay on the bed wearing nothing but boxer shorts, watching Julianne's bedtime routine. Clad in black lace underwear, she was brushing out her blonde hair. The steady rhythmic motion was calm but sensuous, like a cat licking its fur. Rob reflected on his tremendous good fortune. Three kids, and Julianne still looked like a girl in a magazine. Carina's buxom brunette looks weren't his style at all. I was born in California, he thought, with drowsy lust. Give me a blonde any day.

Julianne set her hairbrush down and took up a jar of face cream. "I was thinking, at dinner," she said.

Rob contemplated the enchanting curve of her bra. "Oh? What about?"

"You were gone for a whole year, back in '95. And I don't remember worrying about you."

Rob sat up, his stomach twisting into a sudden nervous knot. "Jul . . ."

"It just seems kind of funny," she said. "I mean, a whole year of complete calm—that's not like me. I worried about the kids, about the bills . . ."

"Jul—I'm sorry. But I did that."

"What?"

Rob forced himself to meet her startled gaze in the reflection of the bureau mirror. "I—I didn't want you to be unhappy. So I told you not to worry about where I was or what I was doing. And you couldn't."

"You were playing your mind games? Like you did with Mrs. Mickelsohn? With *me*?" She set the jar of cream down with a clatter and turned to face him. "What else have you done to my head that I don't know about?"

"Well . . . Today isn't the first time I've told you about the weirdness. The first time was at the beginning. I wanted to be up-front with you, Jul, I truly did. But you frightened me—you developed all these ideas, for me to run for President, all kinds of things. And I couldn't handle it. So I—I edited your memory a little. That's all."

She stood backed against the bureau, her mouth slack with shock, staring as if he were something scaly from a horror movie that had dropped onto the bed. He jumped to his feet and seized her hands. "Jul, I apologize. I was young and stupid. I didn't know what I was doing. It's wrong to mess with people's heads in such a drastic way. I know that now, and I've stuck to it for years, even when it might be convenient not to. Like, it would have been miles easier to just make Carina forget about Gilgamesh. But I couldn't, not anymore. Do you understand? Do you believe me?"

"I . . . I guess so. Oh, Rob, this weirdness, I don't like it!"
She was shivering, and he wrapped his arms around her.
"I don't either, much. Let's call it a day, huh? I've thrown so
much at you, and you've been so brave." Her goose bumps
against his bare chest made his nerves hum with sweet tension. He kissed the top of her forehead where the pale silky-
fine hairs began.

"Wait, Rob." She twisted in the circle of his arm to look
up at him. "What about this?"

" 'This' what?"

"Here, in bed. Do you use this weird thing when we make
love?"

Rob couldn't speak, but she saw the truth in his face. She
wrenched away out of his embrace. "You— I thought this
was special! I thought this was *us*!"

"It is! It's—"

"And you've been steering me along all this time! Making
me do what you want and enjoy it! Oh, I never knew what a
degenerate creep you could be, Rob!"

"That is totally unfair! I have never, ever, forced you to
do a thing! In fact *I've* always done what *you* wanted—"

"And how can I know that, Rob?" she demanded. "How
can I know that any of this is real? When we touch, when we
kiss—for all I know, I really feel nothing for you at all. Our
whole life together could be fake. And there's no way I could
ever, ever tell!"

"It is not fake!" Rob yelled. "I tell you, Jul, if people lie to
me, I know it! And what we do here is real!"

"Well, if you're such a lie detector then 'read' this!"
Julianne's voice shook with rage. "You manipulative, lying,
sleazoid—I never want you to touch me again, and that's as
true as gospel! Get out of this room! Go away!"

"Jul, I—"

"Out!" she cried at the top of her voice. Stunned, Rob
retreated into the hall. She banged the door shut on him, and
locked it. He stood in the dark, listening to the stomp of her
angry feet and the creak of the bed. After a while he could

make out her muffled sobs. She wasn't going to change her mind. An interior lock is nothing much, he thought drearily as he went downstairs. You can pick it with a nail, a bobby pin, even. I can open that door. But what good would it do, if she doesn't want me to come in? Damn it, I'm in deep this time. Deeper than ever before.

He went down into the unfinished basement and got a blanket out of the cedar chest. It was too heavy for a spring evening, and smelled abominably of cedar. He lay down on the sofa and rolled himself in it anyway. He used to be able to sleep anywhere, but the knack seemed to have fled. He lay awake, his thoughts galloping around and around like a rat in a cage, until he suddenly dropped off near dawn.

Then he slept so deeply that it was a shock when Julianne called his name. He started awake. It was broad daylight. Julianne stood at the foot of the couch, dressed in her Saturday jeans, with a grim pinched expression around her mouth.

"You've been sleeping like an infant," she accused him. "I fed the kids and loaded them into the van. We're going to the store and to the dry cleaner's, and then to McDonald's. I think it would be better if you were gone by the time we came back."

" 'Gone'? Jul, this is ridiculous!"

"You were going to Kazakhstan to rescue Carina," she reminded him frostily. "She already has a big head start— you better get it in gear."

He had forgotten all about Carina. "Jul, I can't leave at a time like this!"

"I need the time, to think all this stuff over." She turned away.

Rob scrambled to his feet. He caught up with her at the front door. It was indescribably painful when she shrank away from his outreached hand. "Jul, I love you. You know that!"

"Call me when you find out what's going on with her," she said. "The twins will want to know when you'll be home." She stepped out the door and walked to the van without looking back. Annie had copped the coveted front seat, and waved frantically.

Rob waved back, and the van pulled away with Julianne's usual screech of tires. His brain seemed to be stuck in first gear, rolling around with stupendous effort and not very much speed. This couldn't be the end. He'd go and come back, and Julianne would have simmered down, and everything would be fine again. Already he was sick with yearning for it, that humdrum everyday stability. But first—damn it!— he had to go to Central Asia.

Rob couldn't leap tall buildings at a single bound, but modern travel came easy to him. He drove to Dulles Airport and got a seat on a flight to Paris simply by walking onto the jet. The gate attendant didn't see him, safely invisible behind his tarnhelm trick, and it really wasn't even stealing, with so many empty seats on the flight. Once on board, he let the invisibility drop so the stewardesses would feed him. He told himself that speed was essential—Carina had two days' start on him—but a familiar sense of black depression actually drove him. Without Julianne and the kids he'd go to hell in a handbasket anyway. Why not go in a 747?

Nor was it difficult for him to track down Carina. He could survey the entire panorama of human minds, every person on the planet, every brain utterly distinctive. To find a single specific one was only slightly tedious, no more so than searching out a specific magazine in a library stack. He traveled from Paris to Istanbul to Almaty, the capital of Kazakhstan, knowing that Carina was only a little ahead of him. Apparently she had laid over a day or two in Istanbul.

In fact, he got on the same flight with her to Qyzylorda, the Kazakh provincial capital. The empty seat he took was at the front of the plane and she was assigned a seat at the back, so he didn't speak to her until arrival. He let her do her salmon-swimming-upstream trick in the deplaning crowd until the bush jacket and dark hair passed him. Then he said, "Small world, Carina."

She whirled, shocked into unaccustomed silence for a second. When she caught her breath she said, "Whoa, you do have some talents!"

"Ed asked me to tag along."

"Edwin really takes too much on himself," she said, frowning, but then she smiled that absolutely confident smile again. "It'll be good for you to meet Gilgamesh again, maybe. Get off on a better footing this time."

Rob wanted to tear his hair out. "No way!"

"Don't be so negative. And you'll be very useful to me, too. Am I correct in thinking I won't need a translator as long as you're on hand?"

"Yes," Rob growled. "I understand everybody, and they understand me."

"Oh good, it's wonderful how things do work out! Because I need to save the money. Archaeologists never have enough funding, you know. You're going to be so handy! Come on, they're holding a car for me."

Rob had been to the Qyzylorda airport before, but wouldn't have recognized it now. Oil fields had been drilled in western Kazakhstan since his last trip. This was a brand-new terminal, ridiculously high-tech and spotlessly clean. He could have been in Denver or Tokyo. While Carina claimed her bags Rob went into a phone cubicle. This was the last telephone he'd be likely to see for some time. Today was Monday. Julianne's rages were like firecrackers, loud but short-lived. After an entire weekend to cool off, she might well be ready to make up.

The phone rang and rang. He looked at his watch, belatedly trying to calculate Eastern Daylight Saving Time. Then she picked up, her voice blurred with sleep. "Hello?"

"Good gosh, Jul, I'm sorry! I didn't realize it was so late over there!"

"Actually it's early. It's three-thirty A.M."

"I'm really sorry," he repeated. "But this is the last phone

I'll be able to get to for a couple of days, and you did say to call. We're just getting ready to drive into the desert." He paused, hearing only the hum of the overseas connection. "Jul? Are you there?"

The sound of her sigh came over the line in a rattle. "Rob, I think I want a divorce after all."

"What? But Jul, there's no reason! I swear, Carina means zero to me!"

"Oh, don't be silly. It's— I realized, you had this whole separate life from me, Rob. One that you didn't think I was *worthy* enough to know about. You didn't trust me. I don't have to take that kind of treatment."

" 'Worthy' had nothing to do with it—" But he couldn't continue. She was right. He hadn't trusted her.

"It's that you were able to do that, don't you see, Rob? That you felt you *had* to hold back so much. A whole chunk of yourself was locked away, closed off. And I knew it was there, but I could never open the door. We've never been a couple. We've only been a one-and-a-half. I've never had more than a piece of you."

Rob almost preferred the firecracker snap of her temper to this tone of reasoned grief. Julianne had really thought about this. And had he truly failed her as a husband? Failed to give her what she needed? Fear rose from his gut into his throat, choking his voice. "But all that's over now, Jul," he said breathlessly. "You have it all. Everything. And I love you, I always will. All I wanted, I swear, was to spare you pain."

A long pause. "Then we've got different definitions of love, Rob." Her voice was flat.

"Don't be hasty, Jul, please! Think it over some more, till I come back. Don't do anything!"

"Right now I don't think I'll ever feel the same, Rob. But we'll talk when you get back. Good night."

"Good-bye, Jul." The receiver almost slipped out of his sweaty grasp as he hung it up. He sank into a nearby seat and buried his face in his hands. Jesus, he thought. Oh Jesus. If I lose her I will have lost the best thing in my life. This accursed power! I'd drop it in the gutter in a second if I could get Julianne back!

Cool expert hands touched his forehead. "No fever," Carina decided. "Let me feel your pulse. Does it hurt anywhere? You've gone paper-white."

He jerked his wrist away from her fingers. "I'm not sick, okay?"

"If it's turista, I have Lomotil," she reassured him. "Don't be embarrassed to admit it."

"I am not embarrassed!"

She sat down on the seat beside him and stared thoughtfully up at his glowering, averted face. "Let me guess," she said. "You made a phone call. To home, shall we say? Not the children, but Julianne. You two are having problems."

"For the last time, I do not want to discuss my affairs with you!"

"All right, all right! Where are your bags? Let's get going."

"I don't have any."

She took this right in stride. "Okay then, you can help carry mine. Come on!"

The rented car was a jeeplike vehicle with a canvas roof and sides. Carina loaded in her luggage: a bedroll, a two-man yellow-and-orange nylon tent, a small pack of clothing, and the huge canvas briefcase bulging with papers, photos, and books. She also had an elaborate and battle-scarred camera kit complete with tripod, and the tote bag of knitting. Rob sat slumped in the passenger seat, immured in his misery, while she drove around town, packing the car with water, diesel fuel, and food. Finally, long after nightfall, she stopped and said, "All ashore that's going ashore."

"Where are we?"

"We're spending the night here," she said. "It's a student hostel."

It looked like a slum, a squatty gray concrete building looming out of the darkness—but what difference did it make? "All right."

"Hop out and register at the desk. Here, I picked up a toothbrush for you." She pushed it into his hand. "See you in the morning."

"Now, wait a second," he said, galvanized. "Where are *you* sleeping?"

"Right here in the jeep," she said with mild surprise. "This car only has canvas sides. If someone rips us off, I can't replace the gas or food. So I'll sleep here in the sleeping bag in the front seat, and everything will be fine."

"You can't do that!"

"Why not?"

Her dark gaze was genuinely questioning, and Rob clapped a frustrated hand to his forehead. "Because, from robbery to rape or murder is not a big descent, okay? No, don't bother to show me the .38. It's not possible. You can't do this."

"Then what do you suggest?"

Rob heaved an aggrieved sigh. "I will sleep in the front seat, and you sleep in the student hostel."

She didn't budge. "I can take care of myself perfectly well, you know. And what's to stop someone from robbing and murdering *you*?"

"Carina, nobody bothers me. Hasn't Ed told you? Okay, so you can take care of yourself, but it's stupid to run risks unnecessarily."

"I suppose you're right," she said. "Okay, I agree." She took her clothes pack and climbed down. "Oh, wait! Unwrap that toothbrush, will you?" He did so, while she bent to root in the pack. "Here you go." She squeezed half an inch of toothpaste onto the bristles. "I've found that if you can brush your teeth, everything else is optional. Now you're all set. Sleep well!" She flashed a dazzling smile at him and vanished into the hostel.

Snarling, Rob unrolled the sleeping bag and spread it out. It occurred to him that Carina might have engineered this entire thing, to get him to volunteer to sleep in the jeep. But perhaps that was too devious. The jeep had bucket seats, and he had to partially unpack the tent, extract the poles, and stuff the nylon cover between the seats to fill the gap. It was surprisingly uncomfortable. He did, however, brush his teeth.

✳ CHAPTER 5

*L*eft to his own devices, Rob would have sunk into a miserable and self-destructive lethargy. It became obvious next day, though, that lethargy could not exist in Carina's presence, any more than vampires can tolerate garlic. She opened the jeep door at an unearthly early hour, letting in the morning cold and allowing his head to fall jarringly back into unsupported space. "Good morning! Your breakfast, sir." She set an apple and a granola bar on the sleeping bag on his chest. "There's a samovar going in the common room—see you there."

Rubbing his neck, Rob sat up. The front seat of the jeep wasn't wide enough for a tall man to stretch out, so his leg had a cramp. His jeans and denim workshirt were grubby and rumpled from being slept in. The apple slid off his lap and rolled under the seat. Damn the woman. Still, it was easier to get up than argue with her.

After breakfast, the car had to be repacked. Rob wound

up heaving the heavy fuel cans into place and stacking the water jugs while Carina went off and bought some final items. "Chocolate," she said. "Not necessary but so nice. Milk, ice, meat."

"I don't drink milk."

"It'll be good for you." She climbed into the driver's seat and stuck the key into the ignition. "Okay—now, where to?"

"What? Don't you *know*?"

"Oh, more or less. South and west, into the desert. But you know exactly where Gilgamesh is. Or you can find out. So you do that."

"Why should I?" he demanded morosely. "Why should I facilitate a project I don't approve of?"

"Because it'll be faster." She spoke in the patient tone one used on pets. "I'll find him eventually by myself, but it might take a couple weeks. Don't you want to be efficient?"

Rob grasped the logic of this right away. If he could wind this job up fast, he could hurry back to Julianne. Surely, face-to-face, she couldn't stick to this divorce idea. "Right. It'll take me a little while, so you start driving. South and west."

"Will do!" She started the engine.

He leaned back in the seat and half closed his eyes. Seven years ago he had left Gilgamesh in the Kyzylkum Desert with some shepherds. Without money, friends, or language, he couldn't have gone far. And this area was sparsely populated. Rob reached out, searching.

When he opened his eyes again they were driving through farmland. The narrow road was lined with tall anorectic poplars. Studded with spider-legged irrigation derricks, the rolling green fields beyond stretched from horizon to horizon. "I can't find him," he said.

"Why is that? Is he dead? Too far away? Hidden?"

"I don't know. But if I had to bet, I'd say the latter. He's done that before, cloaked himself so that nobody could find him. Maybe I should find those shepherds instead. They'd be able to say where they saw him last."

"Good idea." She paused and added, "How *do* you do it? Do you, like, travel to an astral plane?"

"I've done that, but this is different," Rob said absently. "It's hard to describe."

"You really should be studied properly."

"That's what Ed always says. But I say no. Now, quiet, and let me work."

More time passed. Rob didn't often have to search for people, and he was getting tired. Finally he said, "Okay. Found them."

"Good, you're just in time!" She halted the jeep. They were at a crossroads. There were no road signs, only two ribbons of potholed asphalt crossing each other and flowing away across the steppe. "Do we turn right or go straight?"

"*I* don't know," Rob said.

"But you found the shepherds. How do we get to them?"

Rob sighed. "I can point in their direction. I can tell you a lot of minor facts: that they're at their summer settlement, five yurts, a stone sheep pen, and a corrugated-iron shed. There are two brothers, their wives, an unmarried sister, a grandma, a widower uncle, and about ten kids. They have one hundred and forty-two sheep, more on the way. But which way to turn here and now, I don't know. Because they didn't know—nobody there has a street map of Central Asia in their noggin."

"Okay, so point." Rob did, and Carina dragged on the wheel to turn right, more or less in the correct direction. "Lucky for you you're building decks," she grumbled, accelerating. "You'd never make a good private eye."

"No, I never would," Rob said fervently. "I'll never use the weirdness to make a living. Once Jul wanted me to run for President, but I wouldn't do it."

"That was good." Carina nodded her approval. "Strong silent men don't do well in politics. Although you'd shine in foreign affairs, I guess. Like Richard Nixon did. You have the paranoia, and a good, high deviosity quotient."

"I am not devious!"

"A man who lies to his wife for seven years must be devious," she reasoned. Outraged, he lapsed into seething silence. But she added, "I'm sorry—you did say you didn't want to talk about it. I didn't mean to bully you." The image of a five-foot woman bullying him was so comic he had to laugh, and then he couldn't be mad anymore.

They stopped for the night in a vest-pocket village. Out here in the boondocks there was not a single facility for visitors: no hotel, no restaurant, no stores. Rob persuaded a peasant to let them sleep in the empty schoolhouse, bribing him with chocolate and dollars. "You don't have a sleeping bag, so I bought you a blanket," Carina said. "Here."

Without discussion, they settled down on opposite sides of the tiny room. The hard wooden floor disturbed Rob's sleep, and he dreamed of Julianne, of her touch, and her smell, and the way the softness of her skin varied from place to place on her body. He woke far too early, before dawn, and lay huddled in his coarse scratchy blanket, sick with desire.

"You can drive some," Carina offered after breakfast.

"What are you going to do?" he asked, suspicious.

"Sort photos, and arrange my questions. I want to cover all the important ones first. I have a short list of fifty-seven queries, with four hundred and fifteen follow-up questions."

"Poor Gil! He's never going to forgive me after this."

"You can't believe the poor old man is really dangerous. I thought you and Edwin took all his magic away."

"It's not magic," Rob said. "Whatever it is, it doesn't come naturally, to Ed or to me. For Gilgamesh it does. Ed has this off-the-wall theory that Gil was born with the weirdness."

"I remember," Carina said. "It's in Genesis, the bit about the half-divine race who were the mighty men of old after the Flood."

"That's the one. The epic says that Gilgamesh is partly divine too. Who knows what happens when you strip a half-god of the power? For all I know, he's grown it back again."

The narrow road ran over shallow slopes of pale sandy soil. The thin stubborn wild ryegrass seemed feeble close by the road, but surveyed over a distance the empty land looked surprisingly lush. Among the stalks, poppies bloomed so vivid and piercing a red that the blossoms almost seemed to vibrate. In the late afternoon, a slow steady rain began to fall, and the grass almost visibly thickened and grew. When Rob wound down the window he could hear the green juicy sound of thirsty stalks reaching up towards the kindly sky. "It smells good enough to eat," he said.

"Well, we're going to have a few problems that way," Carina said. She had finished her paperwork. From the tote bag she now pulled a hank of blue yarn and two long shiny needles. "If this keeps up we won't be able to light a fire. And today's the last day on the meat in the cooler."

"Maybe it'll let up."

They drove on through the deepening twilight, hoping for a break. Finally the rain relented. "Only for a little bit," Carina said, scowling up at the low-slung clouds. "Let's hustle."

He pulled the jeep off the road. While she lit a charcoal fire and began toasting the lamb slices, Rob set up the yellow-and-orange nylon tent. There was no point in waiting to do it in the dark. Thunder rumbled as he worked, and before long the rain came pouring down again worse than before.

They dashed for the car. "Underdone, but better than nothing," Carina said, passing him a skewer. There was nothing to do but eat bread and meat and carrot sticks, and then sit in the dark, listening to the rain drumming on the canvas roof until it was time to sleep.

Rob sipped the last of his mineral water and stuffed the empty bottle into the recycling bag. "Where'd you meet up with Ed?"

Carina had looped her skein of yarn over the steering wheel, and was busily winding it into a ball. "At a pickup volleyball game in grad school. We were on the same team."

"You must have thrashed the opposition," Rob said, remembering Edwin's easy athleticism.

"Edwin's good, but I'm too short to do well in the front line . . . What I like about him was his laugh. It was a really happy sound."

Rob nodded. That was a good description. "He's a happy guy. Make a great parent." It was one of the highest compliments he knew. Then, sensing a change in the silence, he said, "Was that wrong?"

It was too dark now to see her face as she said, "We're having some problems."

Rob remembered that Edwin had planned to start a family years ago. "I'm sorry."

"I've had a full fertility workup, and there's no medical reason . . . Do you think, I was wondering—could the immortality have an effect on Edwin's system?"

"I never thought about it," Rob said slowly. "I don't know anything about reproductive medicine. But you know, I don't think old Gil left an heir to the throne of Uruk, even though he slept around a lot when he was king. So maybe you're on to something."

He felt rather than saw her springing upright. "That's a *great* idea! I could ask Gilgamesh about it! Let me write that down." She pulled a small flashlight from her jacket pocket and held it in her teeth while she scribbled query number 58 into the big loose-leaf notebook. Rob smiled, trying to imagine an ancient Mesopotamian monarch answering nosy questions about his reproductive history. He couldn't quite picture it. But Carina was a force of nature, unstoppable as a tornado. If anyone could do it, she could.

She clicked off the flashlight and sighed. "You don't know how much I envy you and Julianne sometimes. That baby!"

"He's the greatest." Unhappiness flooded through Rob as he thought of Colin. The sweet baby body, the energetic fat legs—if Julianne divorced him, he'd lose them. He'd be sev-

ered from all the day-to-day interactions of fatherhood, the
soccer practices and school assemblies and searches for Styrofoam egg cartons. If only he could take Julianne in his arms
and kiss her! He was sure all their problems would dissolve
there.
        Beside him Carina's voice quivered with sadness too. "It's
been so long! I miss Edwin a lot."
        Rob didn't think about it at all. He simply leaned over
and kissed her on the mouth. It was in no way a platonic kiss.
Instinct and habit took over in the warm drumming dark,
and it was as if he had Julianne beside him. And for a
moment the illusion was perfect, her lips parting hungrily
beneath his, her desire soaring under his unthinking manage-
ment to match his own suddenly raging appetite. The current
between them was like the crackling buildup of static before
thunder, and in a moment the lightning would strike.
        Then Carina broke away, gasping. Rob began to say
something, he hardly knew what, and suddenly cold metal
touched his nose. With a snap in her tone he had never heard
before, Carina demanded, "Do you want a third nostril?"
        The darkness was absolute, but she flicked on the flash-
light and Rob found himself looking down a long steel knitting needle. His mouth went dry as he imagined the damage
that point could do to cornea and eyeball and retina—
painful and permanent. The gleaming sharp needle didn't
waver in her hand, and behind it her dark gaze was hard.
"You are never, never going to try that again," she said
flatly. "Now grab that blanket. You're sleeping in the tent."
        Speechless, Rob obeyed. The night was stygian, and the
rain poured down. She slammed the door on him with a final
stinging comment: "I thought you were a friend!" The lock
clicked. He stood like a dummy, already soaked to the skin,
the sodden blanket weighing down his arm. Then he stumbled to the tent and crawled in.
        Like all of Carina's equipment the tent was practical and
efficient. Its weatherproof floor kept water out or, as in this
case, in. Rob curled up on the most uphill side so the water

would drip off his wet clothes and form a pool below. Of course he couldn't sleep. For a period of time he could hardly think coherently.

What was I doing? Why did I do that? The moment he could formulate the questions, the answers came, all different and all plausible. The entire horrible divorce question had upset him. He was dreadfully homesick. Lack of sex was warping his judgment. Jul had put the idea of adultery into his head in the first place with her suspicions. The weirdness had distorted his perceptions. Carina's own yearnings had blurred with his feelings for Jul. Edwin never should have raked him into this stupid expedition . . .

The endless array scrolled by on the surface of his thinking. But after a while, from some deeper level, Rob saw how all these answers were alike. They were excuses, every one. To try and seduce a friend's wife (a kiss, nothing more, the Excusenet said, and she was into it, for a second anyway) was despicable. There was no way to get around it. When trouble overset Rob's life, all the vile slimy things squirmed out from underneath into the light. He was so ashamed he felt scalded with it, even though it was freezing here in the wet tent.

And what would Edwin say? Rob forced himself to admit that this one stupid impulse endangered a friendship he truly valued. Somehow Carina had recognized Rob's instinctive use of the subtleties he'd perfected with Julianne. He could imagine how she might describe it to her husband: a psychic seduction, pushing the buttons to get her into bed. No man, however Christian, could forgive a breach of trust like that. It came to Rob that when they found Gilgamesh he should simply hand the weirdness back. In theory the power was as transferable as it had ever been. Fully empowered again, Gil would surely take up where he had left off, and beat Rob to death. All his problems would be over. The idiocy of this line of reasoning was so patent that Rob abandoned it immediately. He couldn't run away from his mistakes. He had to cope with them.

After a sleepless night of grinding misery, Rob worked the situation down to two major points. The first was that he had never really desired Carina for herself. He might indeed be devious and manipulative, living a lie with Jul for years, exterminating criminals whenever the mood struck him, locked in a perpetual and losing battle with the intractable baseness of his own nature. But at least he wasn't an adulterer. His mind and heart last evening had been full of Julianne. Carina was unlikely to be placated by this unflattering truth, but he had to tell her. The other was that, if he wanted to be able to live with himself, he'd have to confess the entire incident to both Julianne and Edwin as soon as possible. And, he told himself, if she divorces me on the strength of it, and if Ed never speaks to me again, then I'll contemplate suicide, but not before.

The rain blew itself away overnight, and the sun came up into a tremendous blue sky. Rob crawled stiffly out of the tent and tipped it to let the water drain out the zipper door. Emerging from its stuffy nylon confines into the clean sweet air was like being reborn. He propped the light structure against the tailgate of the jeep to dry, and spread his damp blanket out in the new sunshine. His jeans and denim shirt were also damp. He took a brisk walk down the road and back again to help them dry out.

The land was so flat he never lost sight of the car. He could see Carina moving around, fiddling with the orange-and-yellow tent and opening the back of the car, as he returned. "Let me help you fold it," he called as he came up. He didn't want her to think he was sneaking up on her.

"I can manage." She was watchful but not frightened—it was hard to imagine Carina ever being frightened. He noticed, though, that she wore the .38 in its holster on her belt now.

"Carina, I want to apologize. That was the stupidest thing I've ever done. But I wasn't thinking about you at all. It was Julianne on my mind, so much that—" He broke it off. No excuses. "I guess you don't believe me."

She stared at him without expression, weighing his words. "I'll think about it," she said at last. "If you'll spread that blanket over the load in back, we can get going."

He felt awkward now sitting next to her in the jeep, and they spoke of nothing but the barest essentials. By late afternoon they were nearing their destination. Rob took the wheel and drove slowly along a rocky trail that wound aimlessly across the landscape. The stony soil was poor, anchored only with goat thorn and dark green saxaul—a semidesert environment. They saw the pale shallow cones of the yurt roofs from miles across the valley.

In her mounting excitement, Carina forgot to be uncomfortable with him. "We can see the place—you mean you still can't tell if he's there? Oh dear, I wonder if he knows it's you that's coming. Perhaps he's gone on to live with other members of that family. If you kept on moving, from relative to distant relative, you could get a long way in seven years."

The moment the jeep halted at the settlement Carina was out the door. An old woman in a black headscarf and long black skirts came out of the nearest yurt to stare. "Rob, come and translate," Carina called.

Rob got out. The desert wind tousled his fair hair and plucked at his clothing. From around back came two men in round fleecy caps and worn, Western-style workclothes. He recognized them, and they knew him, too. Their sudden terror hit Rob like a bucketful of cold water. "Don't be afraid," he said quickly, but it didn't much help.

The older man, the uncle, poked his nephew and hissed, "Bow!" They bent almost double before Rob, and the old uncle said, "Great lord, we did not think to see you again."

"Ask him!" Carina urged. "Ask about Gilgamesh!"

"Quiet," Rob said. "We came to see the old one, the guest. Does he still live here with you?"

The old man's weathered Asian face twisted with fright. The nephew said bravely, "Forgive us, lord. But he was very old. He died three years ago."

Rob stood silent, stunned.

"What did he say?" Carina demanded. When he translated, she cried, "Oh no! How terrible! What a waste—I should have come years ago!"

The old uncle said, "He lived in peace here, and we treated him with honor. Would you like to see his grave?"

Unable to speak, Rob nodded. The nephew led them up the hill, Carina close behind. Rob and the two older people followed. On the other side of the hill was a shallow rocky valley, barren and dry. The desert wind blew strongly through it, nudging against them like a live thing. The grave was halfway down the slope. It was nothing more than a heap of tan rocks. But they had been chosen for roundness and size, and set carefully to pave a neat mound.

The uncle's voice was thin and grasshopper-dry. "When he was near the end, we asked him what ceremonies his own people performed for the dead. For he was not a Moslem, as you know. And he said he would not ask such difficult rites of us. But we pressed him, because everyone knows the final ceremonies are important. He would have made a fearful ghost. So he said, 'Bury me at sunset. In rock, not in the earth.' And this was the best we could do."

"You did well," Rob said. It was sunset now. The huge scarlet ball of the sun dominated the west, veiled only by a streamer of dusty cloud. He went down on one knee beside the mound, his heart swelling, and his shadow stretched out long and black over the grave. Somehow he was shaken to the core. Gilgamesh had been so terrifyingly alive when they met, it was impossible to imagine his death. And yet what could Rob expect? He had stolen the pearl of immortality from a five-thousand-year-old man. So that's four, Rob thought with anguish. Deion Morris, Monte Timms, Squeak Ellison. And now Gilgamesh. He just took the longest to die.

A drop of wetness fell onto the nearest round rock, and then another. With a kind of distant surprise Rob found he was weeping. Silent painful sobs shook him, hurting his throat, forced out not only by this defeat, but all the others.

He crouched by the grave of his mortal enemy and gave himself up to grief.

The old woman squatted beside him and patted his arm with a gnarled brown hand. "He was old, and content to go," she said in creaking Kazakh. "What would happen to the world if we old ones stayed on and on, encumbering the land? No, for the good of the younger ones, the old must die, and we know it."

Rob hardly heard her words, but her tone and touch were a comfort, and he began to recover. On his other side Carina bent to say, "Oh Rob, I'm so sorry. You didn't really want to do this at all. And you've been so unhappy . . . No, don't use your hands—you'll get your face dirty. Use this."

She pulled a large clean hanky from one of her capacious pockets. The old woman said, "You need tea. And food. My daughter-in-law is stewing some lamb. Come!"

The last of the day was dying in saffron and rose in the west as they made their way back down the hill. The felt yurt they brought him to was dark and smoky but warm, carpeted and ceilinged with rugs. Its high conical roof was supported by dozens of interwoven poles. Rob sat on a rug, exhausted, while Carina bustled back and forth, pulling food out of the jeep to share with their hosts. "These people are too poor to put us up, but we can't insult their hospitality," she said. "Here, you do this."

She dropped a slab of chocolate in his lap and pushed the nearest kid up. Instantly every child in the clan was on hand, watching. There was a teenaged boy, a toddler, and eight others in between, all dressed in threadbare shirts and patched pants or homespun skirts. Rob unwrapped the chocolate and divided it with his pocketknife. It wasn't a Hershey bar, but some Russian brand made in Gorky in a solid brick. It took some doing to carve it into fair shares. "Good gosh, I've just spoiled their appetites for dinner," Rob said, as the children licked up every crumb.

"Don't worry, they'll eat," Carina predicted. "These aren't snacked-out American kids."

The spices in the lamb stew tasted so foreign Rob couldn't enjoy it, but he ate the round hard bread. Carina contributed apples, granola bars, and canned peas and carrots. The entire family ate with them, scrupulously silent in case Rob should wish to talk. He didn't, but Carina said, "Ask them about Gilgamesh. Here, use this." She passed him a cassette tape recorder with a built-in microphone.

Obediently, Rob asked. The old uncle said, "At the beginning it was strange. I had a neighbor who was like him. He fell down in the pasture one day for no reason, and then he forgot how to talk. He had to learn the words again, like a baby. The old one was like that. He had to learn to talk to us. He had his own language, but it wasn't Kazakh, or Uzbek, or Russian. None of us could understand it."

When Rob translated this, Carina moaned in despair. "The last living speaker of Sumerian," she mourned.

"But once he could talk a little it was all right," the uncle said. "He took his turn with us staying up during the lambing, and he helped with the shearing. He was old, but pretty strong. And he build the new sheep pen."

Rob hid his surprise. "Tell me about the sheep pen," he said, at Carina's prompting.

"The old sheep pen was so small we only used it for pregnant ewes. So he built a new one beside it. We helped to carry the bigger rocks, and the children carried the smaller ones, but he fitted them all together himself. It was a mighty undertaking."

"I want to see it!" Carina exclaimed as soon as she understood this.

"In the morning," Rob yawned. His sleepless night and the long day made it impossible for him to keep his eyes open anymore.

They gave him some rugs to sleep on in his own yurt. He was too tired to object when an entire family vacated it for

him. Rob scarcely stirred all night. Its thick creamy felt made
the yurt darker than a tent or a jeep, and he slept dreamlessly
late into the morning. When he emerged at last, yawning, the
younger women shyly offered him green tea. He spotted
Carina with her camera down in the draw. His awkwardness
of yesterday had quite vanished, purged by tears and sleep.
The troupe of children trailed behind him as he walked down
to her.

Carina had found a couple of the older kids could speak
some English. Only useful words like "TV" and "movie," of
course, but that was enough for Carina. She was now sys-
tematically photographing the entire sheep pen, section by
section, and told Rob all about it.

"That oval rubbly section there is the original pen," she
said. "Zahni here says it was built in his great-grandfather's
day. This bit is Gilgamesh."

"Wasn't he the energetic one," Rob said. It was hard to
reconcile his memory of the solitary psychopath with the
silent testimony of the stones. Wood was Rob's medium, but
he could recognize a good drystone wall when he saw it. The
new walls extending from the old one were straight as rulers.
They tapered evenly from a wide base of big stones to a slim-
mer section at the top. Dry thorn bushes capped the chest-
high walls. The space enclosed was three times bigger than
the old pen, which looked shabby and haphazard beside the
precise new one.

"He had adventures, he ruled a kingdom, but Gilgamesh
was also a builder," Carina said. She quoted from what he
recognized as the epic poem:

" 'He had the wall of Uruk built, the sheepfold
Of holiest Eanna, the pure treasury.
See its wall, which is like a copper band,
Survey its battlements, which nobody else can match.' "

Carefully she focused the camera and took the picture.
Then she moved the tripod a yard or so down and focused

again. "This was a master builder's last creation. Isn't it exciting?"

"Without the living witness to back you up, what can you do with these photos?" Rob sat down on a rocky outcrop, inspecting it first for sheep dung. The children clustered around him like hopeful puppies. "You can't publish them."

"I can study them, can't I? Who knows what insights I might get into Sumerian construction techniques? Stand over there by the gate, will you? I want a human figure to give an idea of the scale."

Rob hesitated. "I don't want any solid evidence to exist that I was ever here."

"What is it with you, with this privacy fetish?" she grumbled.

"It's a coping mechanism, okay? I need all the help I can get."

"I'll say." She grabbed one of the children instead. The grinning kid mugged happily for the camera.

"If it ever gets out that I can do stuff," Rob said, "my quiet life will be history. Anonymity is my only refuge."

"I was thinking we can leave after I finish this roll," she said. "You want to get home, don't you . . . Look at this bit. Gilgamesh fell ill before he could finish the wall, so the family built this corner themselves. Doesn't it look good?"

Rob got up to see. The final angle didn't have quite the nice touch of the main section, but only a zealous eye could spot the difference. "It's miles better than the original small pen. Maybe it did the old guy good, to live here."

"Yeah. Zahni says next winter the family's going to stay with some cousins and help build them a sheep pen just like this one." She carried the camera to the last position.

Rob followed with the camera bag, tripping over closely following kids. "I think this is cupboard love, Carina. Is there any more chocolate in the jeep?"

"In the green paper bag behind the driver's seat."

He fed the children the last bar, to their great satisfaction, as Carina packed up her photo gear. The entire family came out to see them go. She thanked them politely in English for their hospitality, and Rob said, "Thank you for taking care of the old one. You did a good thing."

"We were glad of him," the nephew said.

As they drove away, Rob looked back at the settlement. It was strange to think of little truncated Sumerian fortresses sheltering the sheep of Kazakhstan. But perhaps it was no bad legacy. With a vehemence that surprised him, Rob hoped that Gilgamesh was reunited with Enkidu now, his stormy heart at peace at last.

Carina said, "I was looking at the map, and we could save ourselves miles by driving due north to Tyuratam. That's the city where the Baikonur Cosmodrome used to be, when this was all the U.S.S.R. and there was a Soviet space program. They must have an airport, so you could leave from there."

"If there's an airport, what about this car?"

"I can drive it back to Qyzylorda by myself on the main highway. Your job was just to defend me from that big bad Sumerian, not to chaperon me all over Central Asia."

She was trying to help him home faster, he realized. "You are a kind person."

"About time you noticed. I figure we could get to Tyuratam as early as tomorrow night, depending on road conditions. You could be in the U.S. by early next week. Would that help you?"

He stared out the window at the rolling dry scrubland. "I don't know if anything can help me," he said in a low voice. "Jul says she wants a divorce."

"Really? Oh no, how sad!" But then Carina added, "Any woman with self-respect would, you know."

"Thanks a lot."

She unclipped a plastic water bottle from the holder on the door and sipped. "NASA has this really thorough marriage-awareness seminar," she said cheerfully. "Every astronaut and their spouse has to take it. It turns out that communication is what women demand. And trust. Guys, on the other hand, have to have sex and fidelity. We can't stand it when you lie to us, and you go nuts when we sleep around. It's a wonder anyone ever stays married."

"I did communicate," Rob retorted. "I opened everything up just before I left. And she hit the ceiling."

"After seven years you finally get around to it. Good for her!"

Behind his beard Rob ground his teeth. Women! "I did tell her at the beginning. But she ran amok with it, wanting me to get into politics, and kick her boss around. I had to push the reset button."

"And you, of course, have never done anything ill-judged with your funny talents."

Rob couldn't say anything. Deion Morris, Monte Timms, Squeak Ellison. Which is a worse crime, to off three people or to steal a national election? Maybe Edwin would know. But Rob might never get a chance to ask him. How had his life collapsed so fast, at the slightest stress? The mystical realm of Mu in the novel was no better, with that same ongoing tendency to slump helplessly beneath the waves. Foundation and framing, he must not have built properly. A deck this ramshackle would be a blot on Lewis Home Improvement, never to pass building inspection. Didn't his own life deserve at least as much care in construction? But it was a botch now. If only he could begin again!

After a long time he said, "My family is the linchpin of my existence. If I lose the ones I love, I go to pieces. I'd do anything to keep it together. Anything."

"You tell Julianne that," Carina said instantly.

"What will she say?" As if, Rob noticed with irritation, any woman could speak for any other woman.

"Well, probably she won't believe you'll change," Carina admitted. "But what the heck? At this point you have nothing to lose by making good resolutions."

Pickings were slim for supper that night. Carina had been a little too open-handed with the shepherds. Eating from the last can of peas and carrots, Rob was astonished at how easy the atmosphere was. Only the day before last she had been carrying a gun. Nevertheless he took care to sit well away from her. She still had that knitting.

In the morning he said, "I trawled around, and there's a government plane leaving Tyuratam for Volgograd at six P.M. You think I can make it?"

"We can try. But will they let you onto a—oh, never mind. Dumb question."

They took turns driving, to make the best possible time. Once in Tyuratam, Rob was able to direct them straight to a decrepit military airport west of town. The barbed-wire perimeter fence was in rags, but the gate was manned. Carina halted the jeep by the side of the road. "Do you do magic to get us through?"

"It's not magic. And no, I think I'll walk from here. You just drive on into town. What are your plans?"

"I think I'll go back to Istanbul and spend a few days with some archaeology friends. They have some clay Hittite tablets at the university I'd love to see."

He got out of the car and stared back at her, trying to decide what to say in farewell. It seemed idiotic to thank her for offering to put his eye out, but in fact he was grateful.

But she spoke first. "Now you remember—tell her exactly what you told me."

"I will," he said. "And I have my toothbrush."

"Then everything's under control!" A final dazzling smile, and she was off in a cloud of dust.

Rob adjusted his tarnhelm trick and walked to the gate.

✳ CHAPTER 6

*V*ery early Tuesday morning, Rob arrived on the red-eye from London. He wasn't sure whether to go straight home or not. After ten days in the same jeans and shirt it might be smarter to take a shower someplace before greeting Julianne. But all his clean clothes were at home, and he was frantic to see her. So he drove the truck straight back. Rush-hour traffic delayed him, and he didn't actually pull into the driveway until eight A.M. The van was gone, the house empty. *Jul is never out the door so early*, Rob worried. *Unless she has a breakfast appointment?*

He consulted the calendar that hung from its magnet on the refrigerator door, and felt the blood sink away from his cheeks. *Lawyer, 9:15*, it said on today's date, in Julianne's pointy handwriting. "Oh my god," he said out loud.

He could find her, of course. But sifting out one person in the teeming population of the D.C. suburbs was slow work. It would be easier to find the lawyer—Jul's secretary would have the name in her Rolodex. The Association of Garment Design didn't open until eight-thirty. Rob had half an hour to kill. He decided to take a shower and trim his beard. And dress not in work clothes, but something more respectable. He needed every tiny factor in his favor if possible.

At eight thirty-one he phoned Julianne's office. "Stephanie? This is Rob. Could you give me the name of the lawyer Jul is seeing this morning?"

"Oh no, I don't think so," Stephanie said, flustered. She must know what Julianne was seeing the lawyer about.

But a phone contact was enough for Rob. He could reach right into her head, guided across the miles by their phone connection, and scoop the data out. "Never mind, I have it," he said, and hung up. Philomene Beckley, attorney, he said to himself. South Arlington. I can make that in forty-five minutes if I hurry.

He made it in forty. The law office was a big one, in a large glass office complex like a beehive. The secretary said, "Ms. Beckley will be here any minute, if you'll have a seat."

"No." At this distance, only a room away, Rob couldn't miss. He strode over to Ms. Beckley's office and yanked open the door. And there was Julianne, dressed for a business day in a crisp taupe-striped linen suit and a flowery silk blouse, sitting in a leather wing chair. "Jul!"

Julianne started. "Rob! What are you doing here?"

"You have to wait your turn, sir," the secretary insisted at his elbow.

"Go back to your work," Rob commanded her. He gave his words the push, the muscle. He couldn't worry about petty free-will questions now. The girl spun on her heel and went straight back to her typing. He shut the office door on her and turned back to Julianne.

She had risen to her feet, clutching her handbag. "Rob, you're not going to do anything desperate?"

"What are you imagining, Jul?" Rob said, angry and hurt. "Knives? guns? I would never hurt you, never. You can't believe that."

"Well, no," Julianne admitted. "It's just the way you came bursting in like an angry Viking. I'm only here to talk to the lawyer, okay? An informational meeting. We're not discussing specifics at all."

With a fierce effort Rob kept his hands back. She had told him not to touch her. Grabbing would be disastrous. "Jul, I love you. I don't want a divorce. I'll do anything to keep this marriage together. Counseling, therapy, psychiatrists, you name it."

Julianne groped angrily in her bag for a tissue. "All I really wanted was your trust, Rob. That's what hurt so bad. Being shut out." Her voice quavered, and she wiped her eyes.

Fleetingly it came to Rob that Carina had been right—she always was. "You have it, dearest. I promise to keep the door open, if you'll give me another chance. Let's try again—please?"

In spite of himself his hands were outstretched, pleading. Julianne muffled a sob in her tissue and then threw it down. "I do love you, that's the hell of it. Oh Rob . . ." The hand-bag went flying as she reached out to him, and then it was all right again, her blonde head resting on his shoulder and her tears soaking into his clean white shirt. He held her next to his heart, pressing her up against the tall bookcases packed with fat law books, and kissed her. Impossible to believe that he ever could have pretended other lips were hers, even for a second.

She stiffened in his grasp. "Rob—you aren't, you know, doing weird stuff, are you?"

"No!" Rob struggled to control his voice. "I would never manipulate your feelings for me, Jul! What good would it do me, to make you into a puppet? I've had your freely given love, and I'll never be satisfied with less." She relaxed again, and he stroked her hair, murmuring, "All I've used it for these years is to learn a little. Like the way you like your neck rubbed. And this . . ."

His hands knew their way so well over her body, even encumbered by the linen jacket. Everything was right now.

The world was perfect, with the two of them united at the center of it. The silk of her blouse whispered under his palms as he caressed her, and the faint aroma of her temples under his mouth excited him unbearably. They were sliding together miles deep into passion when someone cleared her throat and said in a rich contralto voice, "So, you have your second lined up, Mrs. Lewis. That's all well and good, but it might give you some legal hassles."

Ms. Beckley, a beautiful black woman, went across to her desk and sat down, smiling. Rob blushed so scarlet it felt like his hair would ignite. He jumped back from Julianne, acutely aware that his light dress pants did nothing to hide his arousal. "I'll wait outside," he muttered, and stumbled out to the waiting room. He sat down in the nearest chair and snatched up a newspaper from the coffee table for a barricade. At her desk the secretary choked with laughter.

From the inner office Ms. Beckley's beautiful bell-like voice was intermittently audible: "Your *husband*? Mrs. Lewis, I clearly understood that . . . wasting your time and mine . . . Think it over carefully, maybe get some counseling, and then come back to me if you're really sure . . ."

Julianne burst out of the inner office, her high heels tapping her annoyance. "You have my address," she said to the secretary. "Send me a bill. Come on, Rob. Did you bring the truck? I took the Metro here."

Not until they were safe on the road did Rob dare to glance at her. "To the office, right?"

"Yeah. Is marriage counseling going to bother you, Rob?"

"My only hope for a regular life has been secrecy, Jul. The more people who know, the more risk I take. But you're more important than all that. I'll tell everything, to any shrink you like. Set it up, and I'm in."

"Hey, what have you done to this cab? I can actually see the vinyl."

"I didn't actually tidy it," Rob admitted. "Just shoved all the papers and stuff behind the seat. But I know how it peeves you to sit on hex nuts and oil rags."

"You are so sweet sometimes!" She snuggled up against him, and he hugged her shoulders with one arm. When he pulled the truck into the dimly lit parking lot deep under Julianne's building, it seemed entirely natural again to kiss her.

". . . Do people come down here a lot?"

"Only at the beginning and end of the workday . . . No, don't pull this blouse—it's a Missoni. Let me unbutton it."

The bench seat was not really wide enough, and the steering wheel kept on catching Rob in the shins. Still, it was a homecoming he had not dared to dream of, a rapture that pierced like pain. Weak with happiness, he sprawled exhausted on the seat as Julianne stood outside and pulled her pantyhose on again. "I thought things like this only happen in porn videos," he said. " 'Beautiful blonde seduces construction worker in his truck.' "

She laughed. "One more kiss, and then I fix my makeup. We missed you a lot, especially at mealtimes. I had to do carryout twice!"

"And I missed you . . ." Guiltily he sat up, pulling his shirt together. "Jul, when I was driving Carina around Kazakhstan last week, I—I missed you so much, I kissed her. She got pretty mad."

"I'll bet she was—if you told her it was because of me! She probably doesn't get a lot of that." Julianne giggled, sleeking her hair in the side mirror.

Rob blinked in astonishment. Jul wasn't going to hit the ceiling. She thought it was funny. Unbelievable.

Julianne stepped into her high heels again. "Okay, I think the major damage has been fixed. I have a travel steamer up in my desk to get the wrinkles out of this skirt. Pick up some milk on your way home, don't forget today is Scouts, and I'll get Colin on my way back. Oh dear, now look! You have lipstick on your face. Good-bye, hon, see you this evening!"

Rob watched her walk into the elevator and drew in a deep contented breath. Forgiven, reconciled, his world on track again, Rob could put his finger on the error in his previous thinking. Jul hadn't really been worried about adultery.

Trust, the open doors between them, was the central issue. He found it difficult to believe he had been so stupid.

There was only one more hurdle to clear. He drove home, not forgetting the milk along the way, and powered up the computer. He'd been away so long a lot of messages had piled up, mostly on the public board. He saved these to look at later, and pulled up Edwin's note.

> Just a short one to say thanks, bud. You're a true friend. We're getting kind of busy here so I'll wait for your mail when you get back, okay? E.
> P.S.: I'm delighted to hear that Kirra (did we say Kira or Kirra, I can't remember) is taking it so well. Told you so!

Rob sighed. Edwin's letter was more than a week old. He pulled down a reply window.

> The entire trip was a bust, Ed. Old Gil passed away in 1999. Carina will tell you all about it, I'm sure. I feel terrible about the entire affair now. If it weren't for me, the old codger'd still be hale and hearty.

He paused, and then began typing the next sentences steadily.

> Ed, I shuffled Severneth off on his quest to save Mu, and he got himself into real trouble. It turns out that Kira didn't take it well at all. The whole situation blew up in his face before he left. And because his marriage hit the rocks (he seems to have a gift for digging himself in deeper and deeper) one evening he gave Lady Dorella a kiss. That was all it amounted to, because she got real mad at him, but he's been miserable about it ever since. I really apologize for the stupidity of this bit. I'm ashamed of it.

Rob sat for some time, staring dissatisfied at the screen. If only he could tell Edwin about it face-to-face! E-mail was so easy to misunderstand, so impersonal and juiceless. But this would have to do. There is no good way to tell a man you've made a pass at his wife. Shaking his head, Rob clicked SEND.

✳ CHAPTER
7

$\mathcal{E}$dwin leaned back, staggered. He could hardly believe it. In fact he scrolled back to the beginning and read Rob's message again. For a moment he was tempted to break his own rule and print the message out. But that would attract notice here in the crowded comm dome, and he didn't want that. Bad enough that it should go out on the net. He clicked the mouse and the e-mail vanished—forever, he hoped.

It passed belief that Rob could have acted like that. Edwin would have sworn that Rob was incapable of unfaithfulness to Julianne in thought or deed. It just showed that you could never really know a person, know what they were like inside.

Except Rob—Rob could know, of course. Had he read Carina's mind? What had she been thinking or doing, to encourage or deter an advance? Married for seven years now, Edwin knew that a kiss was neither a starting point nor a conclusion. What exactly had happened out there in the desert? Could he trust Rob to be up-front about something so explosive? Rob's gift for cunning had never seemed so ominous before. For the first time, it was forcibly borne in on Edwin how many crucial emotional systems in his makeup depended, absolutely and in totality, upon the trustworthiness of other people. Was he building on sand? If Rob was Judas, if Carina had played fast and loose—

With a start Edwin recognized his trend of thought as clearly as if it bore a label: This Way Madness Lies. After nearly a year on Moonbase, even his famous resilience was getting tapped out. If he let it, this thing would drive him buggy. But he wasn't going to let it. He was on the last lap now. In three more weeks he'd be home, and he could sort it out then. He squared his broad shoulders and clicked a few more keys. Deal with all the bulletin-board messages, then exercise, then check on the bacterial colonies . . .

During those final weeks Edwin drove himself steadily and hard. There was no lack of work to keep him busy. The Lunar Transfer Vehicle *Benjamin Franklin* would be bringing three months' worth of supplies as well as two new base members. Elaborate preparations had to be made. Old CO_2 and water filters were bundled together, broken and worn-out hydroponics equipment packed for vacuum transport. The new dome, four months in the digging, had to be smoothed and sealed by hand to receive the new polymer bubble that would be delivered. The channel linking the new dome to the hallway was dug by hand also—the badger couldn't be trusted so close in.

Still, the team noticed something was wrong. "You're the one who always eats his full share," Geena complained. "Now you're throwing the inventory off. It's too late to start turning your nose up."

"It just doesn't taste right anymore," Edwin said. "Hydroponic cauliflower is beginning to pall."

And once, Phan, who rarely spoke these days, surprised Edwin by saying, "You can't fool them, Ed. They'll get you sooner or later."

Edwin slid his test tube carefully back into its rack. "Who, Phan? Who are 'they'?" But Phan turned away.

Somehow he had never answered Rob's last e-mail. A week or so later, Rob wrote again, a very short hesitant note:

How are you doing, Ed?

Edwin exerted all his diplomacy to reply,

You've probably seen on TV we're very busy here getting ready to shuffle personnel. So I haven't had time to think about the latest plot developments. When I get back we'll talk, okay?

After Edwin sent this, he found himself thinking about his great-grandfather. The old man had emigrated to the U.S. before the First World War. Family folklore had it that Kemal had fled his native village in Macedonia after stabbing his young wife and her lover. Three generations and a hundred years—how interesting that some touchiness about women still runs in the family, Edwin reflected calmly. We've advanced a lot since those days. I would never murder a faithless woman . . .

The team went on a twenty-four-hour schedule as the *Franklin* arrived. The automated Lunar Landing Shuttle's accuracy had improved in two years, and the first load touched dirt only a hundred meters away. But it was still grueling work—unloading supplies from the LLS onto the lunar rover, and then loading on all the things to go back, all within the tight confines of the launch window. Then, while the LLS made its trip back up to the *Franklin* in lunar orbit, all the new supplies had to be hauled back to the base and stowed away.

The personnel exchange was scheduled for the final return trip. The idea was to have the seasoned lunar astronauts doing the hard work. When the very last moment came in the crowded hallway just before they sealed down their helmets, Edwin found he was extremely reluctant to say good-bye. The mixture of emotions was unsettling for everyone. Mariko wept, and Charlie gave him an unexpected juicy kiss on the forehead. "Give my regards to the lone prairie, pal," Lon said, wringing his hand through the gauntlet. Geena said, "If your replacement is half so nice, Ed, we'll all be happy!"

The spidery shape of the LLS dropped silently out of the black sky, and the two new colonists climbed out. The logos and brand names glittered bright and new on their surface suits. A flurry of confusing introductions by the rover as the incoming astronauts greeted them, and they were out, on their way. Edwin bounced over to the LLS, saying, "You know, now that it's over, I'm going to miss the place." Phan as usual said nothing, but Edwin didn't mind.

They had to fit themselves into their seats like puzzle pieces, but the awkward head-downward angle was tolerable in one-sixth grav. This is how they did it in the beginning, Edwin thought. Shepard, Glenn, all those early spacemen, rode wedged in little tin cans like this. In fact, this was an even smaller and more simple machine, because it wasn't pressurized. The LLS trembled as its rocket booster kicked in, the vibrations sinking right into his bones, but the sound came as scarcely a murmur. There were no video monitors for the passengers—another economy move—but Edwin could see the stark lunar landscape in his mind's eye. This past year could well be the pinnacle of his professional life. How could you ever top being one of the first pioneers of a new planet? But life is long, Edwin reminded himself. I have time the way nobody else has time.

There was nothing to be done on their short shuttle flight. For ten minutes they were just passengers, Spam in a can. The LLS was fully automated, and Anna up in the *Franklin* would handle approach and docking. Edwin could hear the faint scrape of the grapnel arms, pulling the LLS into the *Franklin*'s tight embrace. The READY lights blinked on, and Anna's voice came through their Snoopy caps, saying,

"You're rigidized, boys. Come on in." They unclasped their seat-belt harnesses and drifted free, weightless at last.

First Edwin and then Phan floated up out of the LLS and into the *Franklin*'s cramped airlock. There was just room in the little cylinder for them to stand back-to-back, boots wedged into the foot restraints. Edwin pushed the repressurizing switch. It took three endless minutes for the pressure to cycle up to 10 psi. At last the hatch swung open and Owen's handsome dark face peered in. Edwin popped the locking ring on his helmet and let in Owen's voice: "How are ya, Ed? Phan, you look good! Let's get you out of these suits. Anna is rarin' to go."

Designed for deep-space work only, the *Franklin* was a cramped, unstreamlined cylinder, bigger than the old Apollo lunar command modules, but much less roomy than a space shuttle or Independence Moonbase. Edwin didn't care. He had flown in on the *Franklin*, and its cluttered battleship-gray interior held no mysteries for him. At the front, near the curving windows, the commander and pilot seats faced a huge semicircular console solidly paved with switches and digital displays. Four other passenger seats folded away to increase cargo space. Retaining straps, coiled and Velcroed into neatness, bobbed like gray grapes from every surface including the ceiling and floor. There were no bunks, again to save space, but sleeping bags could be attached anywhere.

Edwin settled in immediately. In astronaut training down in Houston, their acquaintance had merely been professional, but now talking to Anna and Owen in person was ridiculously pleasurable. Even Phan began to thaw. "So it was tough," Anna said.

"I may be too gregarious to be a Moon colonist," Edwin said.

"Six is a real small number," Anna pointed out. "When the colony's a little bigger it'll be more fun for everybody. Enough people to have amateur theatricals, for instance."

Edwin laughed at this absurdity. "Dear girl, when is there time?"

"There ought to be time," Owen said. "Problem now is, there's no slack in your schedules."

Everyone fell silent for a moment, thinking about the economic factor. *Time is money,* the PSPIP people were fond of saying. "I'm really getting tired of Pisspeep," Edwin mused.

"You aren't alone, brother," Owen said. "It's like having half a dozen bosses, all with different agendas. If only we had somebody like Deke Slayton in the old days—an advocate who'd go toe-to-toe against the brass for the crew."

"It's not too many bosses, it's too few," Anna said shrewdly. "The PSPIP isn't set up right."

Edwin said, "You know, I think you have it? Five hundred investors would spread the load out more. They'd have to come to a consensus before hassling us."

"Moonbase is a little isolated for this kind of thing," Anna said. "It's not like we could send you subversive and incendiary memos on NASANET, if you know what I mean! But you'll find there's a feeling on the NASA side that Pisspeep has grabbed too big a slice of the pie."

"You give that dude Burt Rovilatt an inch, he'll grab a mile," Owen noted. "You don't get that rich without being mighty pushy."

Anna grinned evilly at her reflection in the window. "Maybe we should start a union. Imagine the headlines, if we carry picket signs that say, 'LUNAR WAGE-SLAVES ON STRIKE!' Oh yeah, it's definitely time to start pushing back."

"Amen to that," Edwin said happily. "I and my dimples will be right with you." Everyone laughed at that.

A midcourse burn was scheduled for plus-20 hours. As commander and pilot, Anna and Owen did all the work. Edwin lay strapped in his seat listening through his headset to Joni Mitchell in her jazzy phase, and paging through the *Journal of Microbiology.* He could have read every word of the text on-line at Moonbase, but there was more to a magazine, to any publication, than just the words and pictures. The ads for lab equipment, the gloss and heft of the paper, even the faint smell of the ink—all this was part and parcel of reading a magazine, and he hadn't known he'd missed it so much. He let the publication float a foot from his nose, not reading but simply enjoying it.

A sudden shrill noise split the air and made him jump. The fire alarm! Instinctively Edwin clawed at the belt releases, tossing his music headset aside. Since the days of the tragic *Apollo One* test launch, every spaceman dreads fire. Anna snapped, "Owen, scope it out. The detectors say Storage Bay Two. Ed, Phan, POS—now!"

Everyone scrambled. Owen bobbed up out of his seat and kicked gracefully off down the small cabin towards the storage bay. The crew's Personal Oxygen Systems were stowed in a locker behind the flight seats. As Phan reached to unlatch the door there was a sharp popping sound, and Owen exclaimed, "Jeez!"

All the cabin lights blinked out. Right away they came on again, as the backup power distribution system kicked in, but in that instant a black cloud of searing acrid smoke ballooned out into the cabin, and the lights shone yellow and dim. Other alarms blinked or screamed their warnings, adding to the chaos. Edwin could hear Phan coughing, and Anna gasped and swore like a sailor. In a matter of seconds it was impossible to see or breathe.

But Edwin didn't need to do either, although his eyes streamed and his throat burned. By touch he found the fire extinguisher and unclipped it. He dove through the thick greasy air, visualizing the storage-bay layout. He collided with something soft but bulky in midair. Disoriented, he clutched it. It was Owen. "Medical kit!" he called, and the necessary intake of breath to speak set him coughing too.

But the fire was the first priority. Edwin caromed off a wall, groping to where the smoke was thickest and hottest. He could just make out the blown access panel through the scorching black soup. Bracing his feet against a bulkhead he squirted a stream of sticky chemical foam into the hole.

Immediately the heat and smoke diminished. Edwin hardly noticed, shouting, "Owen! Owen, are you okay?"

The other man didn't answer. A blob of shiny wet blood expanded steadily on the side of his head. Without gravity it wouldn't drip.

The poisonous cloud hovered in the middle of the cabin now, like a weightless and obese octopus, the tentacles drawn slowly into the vents by the cabin circulation fans. Phan came diving through it, his face obscured by his oxygen mask. In one hand he had his POS pack, and in the other the bulky gray fabric cube that held the medical kit. Between the two of them they pulled Owen over and Velcroed him to the wall.

Anna was there now, wearing one POS and carrying another. "No, not me, put that on him!" Edwin exclaimed. He ripped open a packet of gauze with his teeth. Important to slap something on that gaping head wound before it was covered by the oxygen mask. Phan pressed the disc of the stethoscope to Owen's chest. "Ed," he wheezed. "There's no heartbeat."

"Impossible!" Edwin seized Owen's wrist but couldn't find a pulse. "Oh Jesus . . ."

The cabin seemed full of greasy black dishwater. Anna coughed through her oxygen mask, saying, "It might've been the head blow, or that first blast of smoke and flame . . ."

Phan crossed himself, and Edwin said, "God have mercy on his soul."

Anna looked at him. "Ed, where's your air mask? How can you be breathing this crap?"

And out of the closet we go, Edwin told himself. "I'm a tougher cookie than you know, Anna," he said wearily. "Kind of an exception to the rules. Tell you about it later. Let's get Owen wrapped up first." For the look of it, though, he put on the POS. The oxygen smelled of plastic.

The simplest place to put the body was into Owen's own sleeping bag, which they then Velcroed to a bulkhead. Phan and Edwin did this while Anna talked the disaster over with Houston. The *Franklin* had lost more than half its electrical power. This was not a disaster, because there was triple battery redundancy, except that the fans would need more power than ever to vent the entire main cabin. Still, Anna began emergency power-down, turning off nonessential equipment to save electricity. There was no telling what other, hidden damage the electrical fire had done.

Edwin pushed Phan gently into his chair and fastened the seat restraints. One of them would have to help Anna pilot the *Franklin*, and without modesty Edwin knew he was better-qualified. When he set the POS pack beside Phan's seat he suddenly noticed the younger man's wheezing gasp through the mask. "Phan, how do you feel?" he demanded. Phan shook his head. The cold of space seemed to blow through the cabin onto his spine as Edwin saw an even more acute danger—that the fumes had damaged Phan's lungs. What had burned back in the storage bay—insulation, plastic, wires? The toxic brew floating in the air was a killer, and they had all breathed it.

How far will Gilgamesh's immortality carry me? Edwin wondered. How long can I go without breathing properly? He wasn't invulnerable like Superman—bullets didn't bounce off his skin. He merely had preternatural recuperative abilities. For years he had idly considered conducting some good airtight experiments on himself, but nothing as horrible as this.

He slipped into the pilot's seat beside Anna and said, "I did this in a sim once. We're supposed to depressurize the cabin—sweep all the crap out into vacuum."

"Only two suits," Anna said from behind her mask. To Edwin's horror, he heard the labored wheeze in her voice, too.

"One for you and one for Phan," Edwin said. "I don't need one." She gave him a look through the visor of the mask that spoke volumes. "I'm not kidding, Anna," he insisted. "Did inhaling the smoke bother me? Shall I take off my POS and show you?"

She shook her head. With an exasperated click of the tongue Edwin began to pull off his face mask. Her hand was suddenly tight around his wrist, and she wheezed, "No, and that's an order."

"Anna, I can survive vacuum!"

"Don't you dare go buggy on me!" she whispered. Her voice was thin but steely. Not only did she not believe him, he realized, but there was no way to convince her now, in the middle of a crisis, while she was frantically saving the *Franklin*. If only he'd told everybody months or years ago!

The only option left to him was to help her with the tremendous job at hand. "I'll take over anything you say," he said, defeated. "Any of the low-tech stuff."

Anna nodded with satisfaction behind her air mask. From an elastic pouch above a console she took a blue looseleaf binder and held it out to him. He took it and read the label: LTV Earth Orbit Insert Procedure 14-A. Startled, he looked at her. "This you call low-tech?"

She nodded, shrugging one shoulder in apology. "If you have to," she said in a strangled whisper.

Edwin nodded too, understanding at last. The vital thing was to get the *Franklin* back into low Earth orbit, however inexpertly, even if they all died in the attempt. The *Franklin*'s sister ship, the *Benjamin Harrison*, was still undergoing testing at KSC, not due to come on-line till the end of the year. Losing the sole Lunar Transfer Vehicle would maroon everyone on Moonbase. He opened the binder to the first page and began to read, blinking through the greasy haze.

The cabin's air improved too slowly as it cycled through the scrubbers, and the personal oxygen systems had never been intended for long-term use. They were trapped like bugs in a killing jar, inhaling poison with every breath. Edwin switched his scarcely used POS for Phan's, to see if that would help. With ventilators and oxygen tents and a fully equipped intensive-care unit, Edwin knew he could be saved, but the LTV's medical equipment could be nowhere near that level.

The only aid Edwin could offer was his presence. Nobody should have to die alone. Phan was unable to speak, choking and wheezing. Edwin rooted through the sick man's personal pack and pulled out rosary. He had never seen Phan use it.

But it seemed to comfort him now in this final extremity. Edwin held his other hand in both his own, offering his own silent prayers, until it was over.

"It wasn't lack of oxygen," Edwin said, looking down at the dead man. "His lungs gave out—from the smoke, I guess. Damn it." Researchers in the biological sciences necessarily know death well. Edwin had presided over the demise of billions of bacteria, thousands of fruit flies, hundreds of white lab mice. But this was the first human being. And Phan had been a friend. Edwin set his teeth, swallowing tears.

Floating in the soupy air beside him, Anna shook her head. She sagged against him when he guided her back to the command console. Under the blue T-shirt her rib cage heaved as she fought her own damaged lungs for air. The sound was horrible, a slow agonizing wheeze. But she pulled away from him and bobbed slowly into the pilot's chair on the left. Mute, she pointed with authority at her own empty commander's seat. Edwin sat in it. Everyone who went through astronaut training knew the theories and principles, but Edwin himself had never piloted a spacecraft before. He was trained as a Moon colonist, not a pilot. There was no point in wasting Anna's waning energy telling her this.

He fastened her seat restraints and then his own. She was blue around the lips, but her long clever hands made an imperious "Give me" gesture. "Okay," Edwin said. "Capcom will give me the Go / No go. I begin by entering the 622 command code on the computer . . ."

There were over four hundred items on the EOI checklist. Through sheer force of will she took him through the entire procedure before she passed out. Edwin felt her pulse. It was weak and thready, and there was still two hours to go. Houston had simplified things tremendously by launching a shuttle to dock with the *Franklin*—it was utterly beyond his skill to pilot the LTV to rendezvous with the space station—but Anna might not survive until then.

Edwin closed his eyes, praying hard. Then he gently unlooped the headset from around Anna's neck and

unclipped the throat mike. It felt presumptuous, wrong, to plug it into his own comm unit. He wasn't breathing now of course, but he made the mental gesture of taking a deep breath. He'd done the same thing in sports, and before exams, and at the door of his orals for his Ph.D.—a gesture of fierce focus, of mental preparation, igniting the furnace of the will. All the extraneous stuff, friends, family—yes, even Anna and Phan and Owen—had to be excluded if he was going to pull this off. In a sense he'd been doing this for more than a year. Now was the final white-hot push, truly the last lap.

Finally he spoke. "Capcom, *Ben Franklin*. This is Lunar Specialist Barbarossa. Anna Pontipp is unconscious. You're getting down to the bottom of the barrel here."

"Don't say that!" Capcom responded, in a surprising breach of protocol.

But Edwin was already in tight focus, safely armored from even kindly distractions. "Anna's walked me through the burn procedure once. Let's go for two."

Back in Fairfax, Rob was prey to every emotion Edwin had to exclude. The story broke over the radio while he was setting the posts for the preschool playground, and he was too upset to continue work. Luckily it was summer vacation, and the pupils wouldn't need the swing unit until fall. He drove straight home and planted himself in front of the TV.

There were no cameras working in the *Ben Franklin* anymore, so the TV newsmen were forced to play and replay Anna Pontipp's hoarse announcement of the "anomaly" and the deaths of Owen Mahomet and Phan Li. In the latter, she was almost inaudible, struggling to force every word out. It was a jolt, after a long excruciating radio silence, to hear Edwin's voice. Not until he heard those disciplined but audibly healthy tones did Rob relax a little. "Gil would never have believed it," he said.

"Why are you worried?" Julianne asked. "Edwin's immortal, right?"

"That doesn't mean he doesn't get hurt," Rob said. "It just means he doesn't die from it. And I'm sure Gilgamesh never pushed the envelope like this."

"How is he ever going to explain it to NASA?"

"God only knows," Rob said grimly. "This is just about my worst nightmare."

They were playing the transmissions live now, while the TV anchors flashed up photos of the *Franklin*, the Freedom Space Station, computer animations of the Earth-orbit maneuver, and the most recent PR picture of Edwin flashing his broad grin from under the brim of a NASA baseball cap.

"What if the spaceship crashes or something?" Julianne picked at a cuticle until it was raw. "Could he survive that?"

Rob felt a thousand years old himself. "I don't know. Nobody does. That's the devil about immortality. You can't experiment with it, except by risking your neck."

Julianne got up. "I'm going to phone Carina."

"Good idea, the poor girl. If you can get through."

Rob channel-surfed. All the networks had preempted evening programming to cover this. He skimmed past discussions about the Private Sector Profit Investment Program's influence (benign or bad?) on the space program, and safety factors in space travel, and the Moon colony and the long-postponed Mars venture. Particularly chilling was the review of past space tragedies: the deaths of Grissom, Chaffee, and White in the 1960s, and the tapes of the unlucky *Apollo 13* mission, and the *Challenger* disaster. Most of all, they discussed Edwin himself—his résumé, his space career, his daredevil rep, his astonishing hold on life so far under killer conditions. There was no way under the sun that Edwin could hide his gift now, Rob realized. And once they were on to Edwin, they'd be very close to Rob himself.

Julianne came back. "Why can't men just choose a channel and stick to it?"

"Sorry." Rob set the remote down. "What did Carina say?"

"She wasn't picking up, so I left a message. Just to let us know if there was anything we could do at all to help."

"Good."

She sat beside him on the sofa and leaned her head on his shoulder. "I'm so glad you don't do dangerous stuff."

"Don't you believe it. If I don't get moving on that playground unit tomorrow, Mrs. Flowers will impale my head on the tire swing."

But Rob couldn't bear to go to bed yet. Julianne fell asleep against him, her feet tucked up under the edge of her bathrobe, while he watched and waited. All this power, Rob reflected sadly. I have the power to become a superhero, even god-emperor of the planet, if I were stupid enough to want such a thing. But I can't do a thing for Ed. He's alone.

NASA had made a stupendous effort to move up the launch of the space shuttle *Atlantis*, the oldest space shuttle in the fleet. The networks all switched over briefly to show its midnight launch from Florida. Tiny on the TV screen, the clumsy four-part ship rose on a thundering plume of flame and smoke into the night sky. With luck, the *Atlantis* could dock with the *Franklin* in a couple hours. If Edwin was clumsy, and inserted the *Franklin* into an eccentric Earth orbit, it might become impossible.

Rob knew he had nodded off when he jerked awake after one A.M. The TV showed row upon row of tense NASA flight controllers presiding over glowing high-resolution screens and computer keyboards, but the voice was Edwin's. "Good to go, Houston," he said.

"Is it happening?" Julianne asked, yawning.

"Yes." Rob took her hand in both his own without looking away from the screen.

Edwin was hoarse but calm as he went through the labyrinthine command sequence: "Timing program running as of now. Guidance control set, thrust control to auto. First firing phase commencing . . ."

The jargon was opaque, as mysterious as the lost Sumerian language. The anchorman had a tame space expert on hand to translate for the viewers, but Rob hardly heard them. His stomach, always his weak spot, ached with ten-

sion. For the first time in his life, he wanted to pray. The feeble armor he had collected around himself all these years was
useless when things fell apart. But he felt too inexpert to
begin now. Edwin knew people everywhere, all over the
world, and some of them were good at it. Rob could safely
leave the prayers to them.

A computer-generated animation of the *Franklin* on its
course filled the screen now, with a clock counting in one
corner. The expert said, "Barbarossa has to bring the engine
up through three firing phases to full thrust. The computer is
programmed to initiate and terminate firing but he has to
manually control the throttle."

The anchorman said, "This NASA animation is in real
time, so you're seeing what we hope is the actual motion of
the *Franklin*."

"You're squeezing me," Julianne complained, tugging at
her hand.

Rob let go. "I'm sorry, dearest. God, I'm so scared for
him."

The clock ticked on and on while the expert became mad-
deningly involved in discussing all the horrible things that
could happen. "And it would be almost as bad if the *Franklin*
went into an end-over-end tumble," he said. "It does him no
good to be in Earth orbit, if he's spinning so fast the shuttle
can't dock—There! Shutdown! It's finished, he did it! That's
a good burn, beautiful!"

The picture switched to the NASA control room, where
shirt-sleeved controllers leaped up from between the rows of
blue computer monitors to clap each other on the back. With
a toothy smile the anchorman said, "He did it! Astronaut
Edwin Amadeus Barbarossa, last survivor of a tragic fire on
board the lunar transfer vehicle *Benjamin Franklin*, has
brought his ship into Earth orbit, within reach of the space
shuttle *Atlantis*. It's hard to imagine how he can hang on for
the hour or two it will take for them to dock with him, but
his heroic sacrifice won't be wasted . . ."

Julianne yawned again. "Hon, let's go to bed. I'm

exhausted. He's safe now, right? The TV guys don't know it yet, but he'll come out safe and sound."

Reluctantly Rob clicked off the TV. "Everything's going to be different, Jul, from here on in. Really different."

"If Edwin survived this," Julianne said, "he can survive anything."

Rob had set his alarm, so he was up even earlier than the twins the following morning. Foggy after only a couple hours of sleep, he staggered downstairs and turned on the TV again. He had missed the rendezvous and the docking. The picture was coming from the *Atlantis* now. Shuttle astronauts were bobbing in zero gravity and occasionally blocking the picture. At the far end of the cabin, a spaceman fiddled with a hatch, and two others were in vacuum suits, ready to board the *Franklin*.

"No transmission from Barbarossa in forty minutes," the anchorman said. "This is going to be a tragic scene, folks."

The expert said, "There's an airlock on this side, and an airlock on the LTV side and of course a hatch between."

"Three doors, and there goes the first one," the anchorman said. "And the rescue team goes in, I understand they're trying to keep the two atmospheres separate . . ."

Annie appeared at Rob's elbow. "Can't we watch cartoons instead of this?"

"No cartoons," Rob said, so sternly that she flounced off in a pout to pour some cereal. An endless wait, and why hadn't they put a TV camera in the airlock? A tremendous flurry of zero-grav activity, weightless bodies surging back and forth, and there he was! Grimy from head to foot, coughing so that he couldn't stand up—but Edwin was alive.

Rob grinned, even as he fought down a treacherous urge to weep. "Jul!" he shouted. "He made it!" From upstairs came a sleepy mumble.

Davey came in and, with the deep satisfaction of someone repeating back a parent's admonition, said, "You're gonna wake the baby, Dad."

"He's even got his baseball cap," the anchorman marveled. "It's a miracle. A genuine, deluxe miracle!"

The words brought Rob back to reality with a thump. "You're in real trouble now, Ed," he said out loud.

Davey said to Annie, "Ours is the only dad who talks to his TV."

CHAPTER 8

$\mathcal{F}$or the next few days Rob was on tenterhooks. The *Atlantis* landed in Florida, and Edwin was hospitalized under a total press blackout. A day of mourning was declared for the three dead astronauts, and they got a heroes' funeral at Arlington National Cemetery, complete with jet flyovers and a eulogy from the President. PSPIP set up memorial scholarship funds in their honor. The *Franklin* was ferried to the space station for repairs. Not a word was said about immortality, and Rob tried to relax. Perhaps Edwin had somehow fudged NASA completely?

There were so many messages on all Edwin's boards on the Net that Rob didn't bother to download them. To read them all would take years. He did send Edwin another e-mail, a short "glad you're back" message, but received no reply. Surely he couldn't still be ill. He must be busy being debriefed by NASA. Or probably he was still angry about Carina. Rob tried to reverse the situation. How would he feel if someone made a pass at Julianne? He was sitting in his office corner, thinking this, and instantly his eye was caught by the old yellow file folder, now buried under some papers and boxes towards the back of his desk. Deion Morris, Monte Timms, Squeak Ellison—they could tell how Rob would react.

July was winding down. Swim team was over at last. Annie and Davey tolerated day care only because Julianne promised to take an entire month off. "We'll go to Uncle Ike's cabin in the mountains and have fun," she told them as she set paper plates on the picnic table. "Right, Rob?"

"You'll have fun," he said with amusement. "I'm going to clear brush and redeck the boat dock, remember?" Julianne's oily brother Ike had a sweet deal going—Rob did repair and maintenance on the cabin in exchange for vacation time.

Julianne said, "Promise me you won't commit to some last-minute building project, Rob, okay? I don't think I could face driving alone all the way to West Virginia with these three wild Indians."

"My calendar is clear for August."

"If I catch a fish, will you cook it, Dad?" Davey asked.

"I'll catch two," Annie said.

"I'll cook everything, okay?" To prove it, Rob neatly flipped all the hamburgers on the grill and dropped the kettle lid down again. "Dinner in five, Jul."

"The telephone!" Annie yelled. "I got it!"

"No, me!"

They wrestled for the cordless phone until Rob plucked it away. "Hello?"

"Hello, Rob? Carina here."

"Carina?" Rob handed Julianne the spatula and stepped into the house. With the sliding door shut, the kids' uproar was barely audible. "How's Ed? The newspapers don't tell you anything."

A soft quacking noise came out of the phone. It took Rob a second to realize that Carina was crying. The very concept was shocking. "There's something—something terribly *wrong* with him, Rob."

"What? That's impossible. He can't still be recovering. It's been weeks now—"

"Be careful what you say," she cut in sharply.

"Who's paranoid now?" Rob tried to joke.

"I went to see him today. It's the first time they let me in. And he's different, Rob. He hardly recognized me. He's like a zombie."

"This is unbelievable, Carina. That doesn't sound like Ed at all."

"Can you do something, Rob? You know, check it out? Please?"

He knew exactly what she meant. But Rob felt he had to say, "You know, Carina, it's possible that Ed wouldn't want me to butt in. We haven't communicated in months."

"*I* want you to butt in," she cried. "Rob, I'm afraid he's lost his mind. Is that . . . possible? For him?"

"You remember Gil?" Rob said reluctantly. "I always thought he was missing a microchip. It was only seeing his drystone wall that made me think different."

Carina blew her nose. "Julianne left a message on my machine. She said if there was anything you two could help with, to call. Well, I'm calling. I need help, Rob."

"If you put it like that, of course I'll try," Rob said. "But it might take awhile. Do you have a pencil? Write this number down." He was pawing through the files on his desk as he spoke. He read a Virginia phone number off one of his home-improvement contracts. "I'm going to be building a front stoop there the day after tomorrow. You call me, any time between nine and four."

She sighed. "You have no idea how good it is, to talk to someone who believes me. Thank you, Rob."

They hung up. Rob went out to the patio again, where Julianne was shifting hamburgers onto plates. "Take these," she said, handing him the platter.

The twins were already bolting down their share. At the

head of the picnic table Colin sat in a clip-on high chair, gumming a hamburger bun. "Is that gross," Annie said with delight. "He's slobbering it all down his front. Eeeew!"

"Eat, Annie. Davey, you want tomato? Don't make a face like that, say 'no thank you.' Jul, that was Carina on the phone."

"Oh? How's Edwin?"

"Still in the hospital."

"Daddy, I'm finished," Annie interrupted, "can I go see if Jennie can play?"

"Phone her first. She's very worried about his health."

"I don't want my bun," Davey said, "can I give it to the lamprey here instead?"

"No, stick it in the bird-feeder." Distracted at last, Rob had to ask, "When did Colin become a lamprey?"

"When the twins saw that nature show on PBS about sucking fishes," Julianne said reasonably. "But shouldn't Edwin be better by now? I thought bouncing back fast was his whole stock in trade."

"She's afraid he's mentally ill. So she asked me to look into it."

Julianne stared across the picnic table at him. "Rob, can you do that? Make diagnoses? I thought you just ran around trying not to force people to do stuff."

"I don't plan to diagnose anything. I just want to pop into Ed's head and look around. But it'll take some doing because I'm trying to find out something fairly subtle. So I wanted to warn you."

"Oh boy." She scowled at her hamburger. "You know, this stuff makes me really nervous. What is it going to entail?"

Rob had thought about the most innocuous way to put it. "I'll go to bed this evening, and start. If I'm still asleep tomorrow morning, don't worry about it. Just carry on with your day. It will be totally unremarkable, Jul. I'll just lie there. No fireworks, nothing to see."

Julianne got up and began stuffing used paper plates into

a garbage bag. "I saw a T-shirt the other day—I really should go back and buy it. It said, 'My NEXT husband will be *normal.*' " Rob laughed, and reached to help her with the plates.

To minimize family disruption, Rob kept carefully to the summer evening routine: a bath for Colin, bedtime stories for the twins, the final drink of water, kisses all around. Only after everyone was asleep did he begin. The simpler stuff he did was pretty straightforward, but complex tasks with the weirdness got odd. Rob knew this was a signal-processing problem. The power was too strange for a normal person to handle directly. His brain had to manage it at one remove, as metaphor or symbol.

So when he lay down on his pillow and set out to assess Edwin's mental health, Rob was not surprised to find himself in a forest. Huge towering trees formed a rustling green canopy high over his head. They weren't oaks. He had worked enough in carpentry and construction to know that. But they were oaklike trees. At his feet, strong gnarled roots bulged out of a deep velvety carpet of moss. Not a sign of human habitation marred the forest. There were no roads or paths, no gum wrappers or empty soda cans, no distant engines roaring or airplanes buzzing by above. It was a forest from a fantasy novel. "Very appropriate," Rob said. "It was Ed who got me into them."

Rob set out in a direction that felt right, untroubled by his bare feet and boxer shorts. He could hardly have climbed into bed beside Julianne wearing jeans and workboots. The trees were people, of course. This was the forest of humanity, every person a green and growing member in it. He was used to it now, walking through a living metaphor.

When he touched the rough lichened bark of a tree in passing, the tree said, "Hey, watch it with the fingers, buster." Able to walk and talk and act, these trees could have been taught by the Ents. But mostly they talked, a steady murmuring chatter: "Is it ever going to rain? I'm sick of dry soil." "Look at this guy, over here!" "Where ya going, man?" "So then I said to her, I said, 'What do you mean, those are my roots?'" Trivial, but not unpleasant—like eavesdropping on a crowd at a shopping mall.

But there was always more to this inner place than Rob could fathom. In this case, for instance, what did the birds stand for? They flitted everywhere, jewel-bright as birds rarely are in northern Virginia, but too high up for Rob to glimpse distinctly. It was a mystery.

He walked a long way, but a dreamlike telescoping of time occurred, so the length of the journey didn't weigh on him. In this place, whatever aspect it took, he never got tired or bored. He listened to inane tree chatter, ate a wild strawberry, and watched birds. Somewhere high above the leaves the sun reigned in an endless noon, but down here it was shady and cool. He almost forgot why he came, in the pleasure of rambling up and down the mossy green valleys.

But then in a low place the forest opened out into a glade. Rob recognized it immediately as an old beaver pond. The beavers had dammed a creek, backing the water up into a pond that had gradually silted up. Now only a rather swampy meadow remained, closely surrounded by the sort of tree that likes the wet. "Not willows, but very similar," Rob said, examining a long trailing branch.

He pushed through the tangle of twigs into the open. After the cool forest shadows, the sudden glare made him squint. His bare feet squelched into warm muddy water. Immediately he tried to step back, to go around, but somehow the branches behind him were tightly intertwined and he couldn't get through. He could only go on.

But there on the other side of the water meadow was a tree that didn't fit in—not a sort-of willow, but one of the tall quasi-oaks from farther up the hill. There was nothing to distinguish it from a thousand other oaks, but Rob recognized it instantly. He ran to it, splashing through the rank reedy grass. "Ed?"

He pushed past the strong green willow shoots and touched the oak's rough trunk with both hands. "Ed, it's me, Rob. Talk to me." Nothing. Edwin wasn't talking. And all these trees talked a blue streak. Or was it that he couldn't talk? Rob leaned his forehead against the trunk, feeling, searching. Edwin was there, deep inside, but he was in trouble. Suffocating in quicksand. Drowning in muddy water. Buried deep under dead leaves. Of course, this tree shouldn't be here. It should be growing farther up, in drier terrain. Was this distress only the tree's? What did this imply for Edwin? "Ed, you're being cryptic," Rob said in exasperation. As if in response the branches above him rustled, though there was no wind. This was all the data he was going to get.

The branches grew quiet, but still there was a rustling noise, stealthy at first and then bolder. The muddy water around Rob's ankles quaked. Alarmed, he turned. The willows were shuffling their roots through the soft marshy soil. Slowly they closed their ring tighter around the oak and around Rob. And now their whispery voices could be heard in the rustle of their long boughs: "He's staying, you stay too." "You seen *The Wizard of Oz*? Read Tolkien? That was us." "Closer, boys, closer!"

Hastily Rob shinned up Edwin's tree. A big branch forked off above and he clambered onto it. The willows crowded close around, jeering. When they interlaced their branches, almost all the daylight was shut out. In the cruel twilight Rob could feel the oak trembling under him. Something had to be done. Oh, for his gas-powered chain saw!

Rob stood on the branch and leaned his back against Edwin's trunk. He was master here—he had to remember that. A long willow whip slid casually around his neck, and he tore it away. "You are making a big mistake," he said.

"Ow, that hurt!" one willow complained.

"He's threatening us," another one giggled.

"Let's hear your defiance, little one," a third willow whispered. "Before we pluck you apart."

Rob smiled. "You can't hurt me. This is my place, my country. You are within this land, but I contain it."

The willows shuffled their roots, unbelieving. "Aah, let

him show us." "Oh, but we have this oak—that will be almost as much fun as a meat person."

"Don't count on it," Rob said. "Do you think I'll leave Ed to you?" The power answered his will, boiling up under his hands, surging through the muskeg. This was his country, every bit of it, and though he couldn't fathom everything, his power was invincible here. The land rose at his silent command like a cake in the oven, up and up until the marshy dip became a tall hill crowned by the oak. The willows slipped helplessly downhill with the water, tumbling over to show their roots.

Behind him a voice said, "Rob? Rob, are you there?"

"Ed?" Rob turned and almost fell out of bed. Julianne bent over him, dressed in her purple terrycloth bathrobe. "Jul—shouldn't you get ready for work? What time is it?"

"Rob, I've *been* to work. Are you all right? It's ten o'clock at night. You've been lying there without moving for twenty-four hours. I couldn't stand it anymore." She was trembling, her hands clutching at the lapels of her robe.

He jumped up and hugged her. "Poor girl, your hands are like ice! There's nothing to worry about. I feel great."

"You were in the exact same position I left you in this morning, like a Crusader carved on a tomb. It was creepy. I didn't want to get into bed with you."

"We certainly can't have that!"

From across the hall came a sleepy squeak. "Colin's lost his pacifier again," Julianne said.

"I'll fix it. You hop into bed and pull up the covers."

It was always tedious restoring the pacifier, because Colin would wake up unless somebody held the thing in his mouth for a minute or two. A good recipe for a backache, but Rob was glad to see the baby for a bit, and to think. He untangled the pacifier from a bumper pad and popped it into Colin's questing mouth. Only half-awake, the baby sucked energetically, making a rhythmic rubbery squeak.

He had done a number on those willows, but that might

or might not have any effect on Edwin's real-life situation, whatever that was. Rob's inner space was a living entity, with a kaleidoscopic quality that often precluded plain answers. There was no point in going back—he hardly ever got back to the same place when he went in. I found out all I could there, he realized, but I still don't have any hard data. Something's definitely wrong with Ed, but I don't know what. And there's something wrong with his situation, but I don't know about that, either. Carina is not going to be satisfied with this. I have to find some other way.

The frantic sucking slowed down as Colin drifted deeper into sleep. Rob let go and tiptoed out. Back in the main bedroom Julianne turned on her pillow to watch him come in. She said, "I wish I'd known that being in on this weird stuff was going to be so scary."

"There's nothing to be scared of, Jul." Rob climbed into bed beside her and turned the light out. "I'm a very powerful person—you have no idea how powerful. I can never get hurt doing stuff. In fact, my biggest job is not to hurt other people by mistake."

Her hands were warmer now between his own. "As long as you're sure you're okay."

He smiled down at her. "What can I do to show you I'm fine, huh?" She laughed, and returned his kiss.

In spite of the financial hit, Rob had never regretted his switch from a white-collar job to carpentry. Working with his hands was more real, more satisfying. And he could think while working. The next day he used masonry bolts to attach beams to Mrs. Zwingle's old concrete stoop, and thought hard.

Shortly before lunch, the front door opened. Mrs. Zwingle looked through the screen door and said, with profound disapproval, "Mr. Lewis, someone's on the phone for you."

He wiped his workboots carefully on the mat inside, and

followed her into the kitchen. Silently she pointed at the phone and then sat down at the counter with the *Post*. Rob sighed, but there was no help for it. Mrs. Zwingle was an old-fashioned prune who kept a sharp eye on workmen. Probably she was worried he'd steal her silverware. He picked up the receiver. "Hello?"

"Rob, Carina. I'm calling from a pay phone in a mall. What did you find out?"

"I think you may have the right idea," Rob said carefully. "I want to do something about it."

"Oh no! someone's listening at your end, is that it? Darn it, we've got to talk properly! You have to tell me what's going on with Edwin!"

"I don't really know about that, but I know how to find out. Look, do you have a pencil? I want you to come up to visit, and bring some stuff. Okay—the tent. Swimsuit. Hiking boots, maybe. Oh, and a sleeping bag or two. You won't need any cooking stuff—the cabin has a kitchen. You just need a place to sleep."

"Rob, what are you hatching? What cabin is this?"

Behind him Mrs. Zwingle rustled the newspaper sourly. Rob quickly dove down this conversational byway: "You know Julianne's brother Ike? He's out of drug rehab now, and dating a rich girl. Her dad's a real-estate developer and he has this cabin, on a lake site he's planning to turn into a resort someday. But until he does, we have this deal with Ike to use it. Two bedrooms, two baths, which is why you need the tent, because nobody in their right mind wants to sleep with the twins."

"But what about Edwin?" Carina wailed.

"Come up anytime it's convenient," Rob said, ignoring that. "If you want a pickup at the airport, just phone. See you in a couple days, okay? Then we can really talk." Mrs. Zwingle gave Rob a distrustful look as he hung up. "Thanks," he told her.

Rob had forgotten about Carina's gift for speed. The doorbell rang that very evening during shampoo time, before he had a chance to bring Julianne up-to-date. "I want to be a South American tree sloth," Davey announced in the tub, "and have green mold growing in my hair."

"Not while I'm living here you're not," Julianne said, shuddering. "Now tip your head back. Let the water wash your forehead."

"Is green mold more bad than head lice?" Annie asked Rob.

"Good gosh, who knows? Here, you comb for a while. I'll get the door."

"No, I will!" Clad in nothing but her underwear Annie galloped down the stairs.

"I want to!" Davey yelled, but Jul had a tight hold on him and shoved him under the gushing shower again.

"When you're dry," Rob said. He tucked Colin like a football under his arm and followed Annie.

"Whoa, you look like a wet mop!" Carina said at the door. She wore her usual khakis and bush jacket, but her brown eyes were smudged underneath with worry.

"It's Aunt Carina!" Annie shrieked, at a joyful pitch that made Rob's ears sing.

"Yow!" Stark naked, Davey tumbled down to see. "Where's your gun, Auntie?"

"Did you bring us a present? Why don'tcha bring us a puppy, huh? Or a llama!"

"Lookit, I lost a tooth!"

Julianne came downstairs, her hair straggling and towel in hand. "Carina? What are you doing here?"

"Rob told me to come," Carina said. Both women glared at Rob, who groaned. A reputation for deviousness had its downside.

"Here, you hold the little guy. I'll get your bags."

Ignoring the kids' hoots Carina said, "That was a pretty dirty trick, Rob, hinting around like that!"

"And how come I never get told about things around here?" Julianne demanded.

"I'm sorry, Jul—there hasn't been time. I've told you

essentially all I know, Carina, but we have to put the kids to bed now."

"I never sleep," Davey declared.

"Me neither!" Annie cried. "I want to stay up with Aunt Carina! We could eat popcorn and watch videos!"

"How can you ever get anything done?" Carina asked in despair, clutching Colin.

"You get used to the uproar." Rob came up the steps with a bedroll and a bag. "Let me through, Annie. Aunt Carina's going to stay a few days."

"I am not," Carina said mutinously. But the kids were screaming with joy and didn't hear.

✳ CHAPTER 9

With great difficulty all three children were put to bed. Julianne and Carina sat on the dark patio, ostensibly admiring the fireflies. Rob gathered up some glasses and a pitcher of iced tea and went out to join them.

"—when Rob gives you that *look*," Carina was saying. "Edwin says it's like looking up the back end of a solid-rocket booster—you don't want to be there when the countdown gets to zero."

"Just a minute here." Julianne turned slowly to stare, not at Carina, but Rob. "She knew, and I didn't?"

In a sudden sweat, Rob set the tray down on the picnic table so clumsily the glassware tinkled. "Jul, I—"

"So she's known about your weird tricks for years? Who else is in on it?"

"Only Ed, but—"

"And Edwin tells me everything," Carina said helpfully.

"So of course I knew about Rob." Rob shot her a scorching glare.

Julianne grabbed him by the front of his T-shirt. "How come I'm always the last in line to find out about the important stuff?"

She was mad all right, but how mad? "Jul, I hadn't gotten around to the minor details—"

Carina mused, "People who are really devious know to tell the same story to everybody."

Rob ignored her. "I just didn't want you to worry, Jul."

"Oh, for god's sake!" For a moment he thought she would sock him again. "How often are you going to tell me that?"

"Overprotective," Carina prompted.

"That's right," Jul said. "I don't want to be in a glass case. I don't want to be protected, not if it means being lied to."

"I did tell him once," Carina said. "We can't stand it when they lie to us."

Damn it! The effort made his eyeballs feel hot, but Rob held on to his temper. The last thing he needed was Carina as a cheerleader and coach. But to quarrel with her would distract him from what was really important. If Julianne really hit the ceiling, if she felt this was the last straw . . . "I will never lie to you, Jul," he said. "That's a promise."

"Not even by omission," Julianne insisted. "No more of this *Father Knows Best* stuff."

From the sidelines Carina suggested, "The sexism latent in American society today."

Julianne blinked. "What?"

"Oh, you know. Seventy-five cents on the dollar, the glass ceiling—all the lingering inequities that still hinder gender parity."

On this point, at least, Rob felt sure of his ground. "Jul makes twice what I do," he said.

For a second the silence was frightful, but then Julianne snorted with laughter. "This is so ridiculous."

Carina began to laugh too. Seizing the opening, Rob said, "It's not a crime to want the people you love to be happy and trouble-free, Jul. And I love you. I'll do anything to make you happy, and if it's worries you want, I'll share."

"As long as you'll try." She hugged him with one arm. "Basically you're a nice man, hon. Any other superpowered guy would have blown his top just now. Carina, the way he glared at you! If looks could kill, you'd go out in a basket."

Carina nodded. "Like the back end of a solid-rocket booster."

Rob realized Julianne was right, as ever. All his titanic self-discipline must be having a good effect. Seven years ago if browbeaten like that, he would have flailed around pushing reset buttons. He was actually improving! The realization gave him a little thrill, rapidly swamped in self-consciousness. He sank into a plastic deck chair and wiped his wet forehead on the shoulder of his T-shirt to hide his embarrassment. "Can we quit discussing relationships, and talk about Ed now?"

Carina squeezed her hands together. "Please, let's!"

Julianne poured iced tea for everyone. "You were going to look into Edwin's mental state."

Carina seemed to coil like a spring in her chair. "And what's the story? What's wrong with him?"

"I don't know," Rob had to admit. "That's all I can tell you—that there is something badly amiss, with him and his situation. It doesn't work like a candy machine, pumping in the coins and getting what you want out the slot. It's more like, like . . . Anyway, I have no specifics. It just didn't turn out that way."

"What? I came all this way at the drop of a hat, and you can't be *specific*? What good is this thingy of yours, anyway?"

Julianne leaped to his defense. "Rob spent twenty-four solid hours finding that out for you. The least you could do is be grateful!"

"It's okay, Jul," Rob interposed. "I knew you wouldn't be happy with that, Carina, so I developed another plan."

She wasn't listening to him. "You were my last hope, Rob." In the humid summer darkness her face was invisible, but her voice shook with tears.

Julianne stirred her iced tea so that the ice cubes clinked. "I don't like the idea of *my* husband being *your* last hope."

"Oh, don't be so juvenile! Rob, Edwin told NASA. About being immortal. And they didn't believe him. They think he's insane."

"Oh my god." Rob slumped in his chair.

"But that's nutty," Julianne protested. "He can prove it. He already has. How do they think he survived the *Franklin* fire?"

"They're saying he murdered the other three. To save all the air for himself."

For a long moment the only sound was Carina's muffled sniffs. Then Julianne got up and fetched a box of tissues. She turned the yellow patio light on, pulled a chair up beside Carina's, and held them out.

"How can anyone believe Ed could kill?" Rob's thought processes staggered in their tracks as if he'd been sandbagged. "He wouldn't hurt a fly. You can see that in five minutes' acquaintance."

"But it does make sense, sort of." Carina blew her nose on a tissue. "If they can't believe he's immortal, it's perfectly sensible. How else would he have survived without air? It'd be easy to suffocate somebody whose lungs were already damaged. Probably it wouldn't even leave marks for the autopsy."

"Oh Jesus." Rob leaned his face on his hands. The fearful logic of it horrified him. "What will happen? Will they jail him? Send him to the electric chair?"

"It'll never come to a court trial." Carina's voice wavered as she fought for control. "NASA can't afford to have a murderer-astronaut. The PSPIP money guys would never stand for it. Can you imagine the headlines, the TV coverage, the trial? It would be worse than O. J., worse than McVeigh." She swallowed hard. "I'm terrified—that they'll just lock him in a mental ward. Forever."

"Forever is what it would be," Rob said grimly. "Oh my god, poor Ed."

Carina broke down completely, leaning on Julianne's shoulder and sobbing. Julianne held her hand and looked across at Rob. "You had another plan, right, hon? You said you were going to do something. Oh, Rob, what *can* be done?"

"I couldn't tell you on the phone," Carina choked out. "Or on-line. They're not going to let Edwin go. They're not going to let any of this come out. Oh God, I sound so crazy myself. But they're all in league against him."

"If they're all out to get him, Carina, then paranoia is a reasonable reaction." Rob dragged his chair across and sat down again. He took Carina's other hand and patted it. "Look. I was thinking about just driving down in the truck to talk to Ed, face-to-face. There are things I can do a lot better when I'm close to a person, touching him. But now, listening to you, I think it's time to get tough. I'll break him out."

Carina gave a little hiccup of astonishment. Julianne said, "You can do that?"

"Nothing to it, if I'm careful. I'll bring him up to West Virginia to the cabin, and then we'll think about what to do next."

Carina sat up straight. "I want to come!"

With dismay Rob recognized that bulldog glint in her eye. Julianne said, "If she's going, I want to go too."

"And then we bring the kids as well? Why not invite Mrs. Mickelsohn, drag the whole neighborhood along? No—I'm doing this by myself. You two will drive to the cabin with the children, and I'll meet you there with Ed."

Carina jumped to her feet, the tears forgotten. "He's my husband. I ought to be there!"

"Let me make this clear, Carina," Rob said as firmly as he could. "Under no circumstance will I bring you. The way I'm going to work this, I have to be alone."

Her natural curiosity won out. "How *will* you manage it?" Carina demanded.

Rob stood up. "Mainly with my tarnhelm trick. Watch—you don't see me."

Both women's eyes widened in surprise. Carina reached a hand out, and Rob stepped out of the way and sat down softly on the patio step. Julianne giggled. "I remember this one. It's cute."

Carina's dark eyes narrowed. "Tarnhelm, he said. The tarnhelm was the dwarves' helmet of invisibility in the Norse legends. He's not gone. He's here someplace, probably real close." She swept a searching hand around again.

Rob dropped the trick. "You know, you are too smart for a girl."

"What a sexist thing to say!" Carina said. "You wouldn't tell Annie that!"

"I take it back, I take it back!"

Luckily, or not, Carina was still concentrating on Edwin. "I bet you can do that trick on two people as well as one," she said. "So you can bring me."

"No way—absolutely not. Remember I have to get Edwin out, too. It's going to be dicey enough, without an extra person to worry about. Don't make this difficult, Carina. Besides, it's essential that you drive with Jul to West Virginia."

Carina looked at Julianne. "Really? Why?"

"This is news to me," Julianne remarked.

"Jul, I promised you wouldn't have to drive to the cabin alone, remember?"

"Oh, for Pete's sake!" Carina blew her nose again in frustration. "All right, we'll do it your way. But I don't have to like it."

Once her consent had been secured, Carina applied her full horsepower to the plan. Early Saturday morning she was up, cleaning out the front seat of the truck. "Papers are in this bag, parts in here, and tools are in this pile," she informed Rob cheerfully at eight A.M.

Still in his red bathrobe, Rob picked the newspaper up off the driveway. "How can you do this so early, without coffee?" he asked, yawning.

"Herbal tea is better for your system. But I did make coffee already. It's in the kitchen."

"I helped Aunt Carina find the paper bags," Annie told Rob.

"We're going to vacuum next," Davey said.

"Good, good." Rob retreated into the house, but very soon Carina came in to demand the keys.

"I want to clean out the back, too."

"I can do that, Carina. There are some things I want to take with me."

Her brown eyes sparkled with excitement. "Like what? You want the .38?"

"After all your law-abiding lectures to the twins? I'm not licensed to carry a gun, and I don't need one. I need to bring the chain saw and the machete. And maybe the shorter ladder."

"A machete!"

He was both amused and annoyed to see that she was impressed. "Carina, I am not Rambo. I need the tools to clear brush at the cabin, not to hack my way to Edwin."

Saturday was laundry day. Rob had envisioned a leisurely morning with the family until his clothes were dry enough to pack. But Carina had other ideas. She marked the best route to Florida with a highlighter on an AAA map, packed him a lunch, and would have run all the wash through if Julianne hadn't grabbed it first. It became apparent that he was going to depart for Florida very soon. When Rob went down into the basement to find a pack, Julianne was there adding fabric softener to the load. "She's like a chain saw herself," he grumbled very quietly to her, and Julianne giggled.

In the end, he was able to stall until after lunch, mainly so that the dryer cycle could finish. It was a breathlessly hot, still day, but in the shade of the backyard the morning cool loitered. There was time to sit with the twins out on the big swing. He was careful not to mention his destination to them, and he warned the women about it. It wouldn't be fair to count on the discretion of nine-year-olds. All they knew was that Rob was taking a trip. "But you won't forget to come to the cabin," Annie said. "It's very important for your mental health to have a vacation." She sounded so much like Jul that Rob laughed.

"Aunt Carina says she knows how to build a birchbark canoe," Davey said, on his other side.

Rob put an arm around each kid and set the swing in motion with his toes. "I'll be there before it's done. I promise." Sitting here, in the swing that he had deliberately designed to take a grown man's weight, Rob felt lightheaded with happiness. How fragile all this is, he thought. My life is founded on sand. These kids, the little guy, Jul—is it reasonable to love mortal things so much? A breath, a touch of power, and they're gone. Was it possible to teach the heart to be wise? He wasn't sure he wanted to. For these loved ones he would kill and die, counting no cost, accepting any pain. And somehow Edwin came under this rubric too, and even Carina, to some extent. He was going to pull out all the stops to rescue Edwin, and there was no internal debate, no doubts about it at all. Other decisions came hard sometimes, the ones that poor Severneth got to wrestle with, but this was so easy.

Carina stuck her head out the sliding patio door. "Soup's on, kids. Come on, Rob, time's a-wastin'."

The twins ran in, whooping. "Don't you ever give it a rest?" Rob asked, following. But she had already darted inside to start the kids on their food.

After lunch he carried little Colin to the truck, letting Carina bring the pack. "Take care of him, Jul," Rob said, handing him over. "Little guy, ride herd on these dames. Don't let them run wild."

"Tell your dad not to be so silly," Julianne said, and Colin obligingly gurgled. "Rob, please, please be careful, okay?"

He kissed her. "Don't worry, dearest." It was not a command.

Carina took his hand and gave it a brisk pump. "You be as devious and paranoid as you ever can, you hear?"

He laughed. "Count on it. Okay, clear the driveway. I'm outta here. Davey, that means you!"

As he drove away he looked in the rearview mirror and saw all of them on the front lawn, waving. He waved back.

The trip down was straightforward. Rob drove south on 95 for nine hours, taking only a few breaks. He spent the night at a motel near Fayetteville, North Carolina, signing his name as J. R. R. Tolkien. As he threw his pack into the passenger seat early Sunday morning, a further devious thought came to him. From the back he fetched a screwdriver and a paper bag. Carefully he unscrewed the neat white Lewis Home Improvement signs from either door of the truck. Why offer any observers his name and phone number?

Another long day's drive brought him to Florida. Again he stayed in a motel, paying for his room near Titusville in advance in cash. He caught up on sleep the next morning, not rising until ten. Let the clinic staff get through their first flurry of Monday-morning work. With her usual thoroughness Carina had described the place for him in minute detail. In fact he needed no directions. As in Kazakhstan, he could find anyone he wanted to. He drove to the Kennedy Space Center and straight to the secluded clinic building, threading the maze of roads on Merritt Island without difficulty.

The clinic building was a four-story concrete office block, completely unremarkable. He parked as far out as possible in the parking lot, but close enough to the other cars to be inconspicuous. August in Florida was brutal. Even his T-shirt and shorts felt too warm. The sun blazed down on drainage ditches and acres of tall marsh grass, raising the humidity to the strangling point. Adjusting his tarnhelm trick, Rob went into the clinic building and gratefully breathed the air-conditioned coolness. The security guard at the desk didn't look up from his newspaper as he passed.

Up the elevator to the third floor. In the elevator hallway was another uniformed guard. If NASA thinks Ed is murderously insane, this isn't excessive, Rob reflected. He loitered until he could slip through the double doors behind a janitor. Nothing even mildly unusual, not even doors apparently swinging open by themselves, was going to occur if he could help it.

The space beyond had a curiously jury-rigged air for a medical facility. Bottles and jars were organized in shoeboxes on tables, instead of in cabinets. Charts were stuck to the walls with pushpins or drafting tape. Several folding tables were arranged into a U-shaped nurses' station, flanked by a coffee machine and a photocopier on a cart. A nurse sat typing on a keyboard. Beyond were a couple of doors that opened into doctors' offices, and a third, to Edwin's room.

Rob slid quietly through that door, his heart in his mouth. The doorway was screened on the inside by a folding partition made of green cloth over tubular steel framing. The room had its own bathroom and was furnished with an anonymous gray steel institutional wardrobe and nightstand. Blazing Florida sunshine streamed through venetian blinds onto a high hospital bed. Rob stared, shocked beyond words at the motionless figure propped on the pillows. Pale and still, Edwin was almost unrecognizable. Without its usual animation and life his face seemed to belong to another person.

Rob tiptoed closer. "Ed?"

Edwin's eyes remained half-closed, focused on something a million miles away. His strong square hands lay slack, striped with light, on top of the brown hospital blanket. He wore a green hospital gown and an unremovable plastic ID bracelet locked around his wrist. His spaceman's pallor made him look like a corpse. Only his hair seemed to retain his old vigor, curling with its own wiry life over forehead and pillow.

Rob pulled up a metal folding chair and sat down, racked

with doubt. Could it be that Edwin was actually ill? He
looked like hell warmed over. Suppose he was? Removing
him from medical care might kill him. Nobody knew a
thing about how Edwin's immortality operated. Perhaps sur-
viving the Franklin fire had overloaded it, used it up, even.

Or he might be genuinely mentally ill. The orbiter ordeal
was enough to send anybody around the bend. Rob could
never believe the murder part. But looking at Edwin now, it
wasn't beyond the realm of possibility that he was temporar-
ily unstable. And in that case too, removing him from the
clinic would be stupid.

Rob reached and picked up Edwin's limp left hand.
Against the dead-white skin, the strong dark hairs on the
knuckles and wrist looked painted on. A long thin red line
ran ruler-straight up the inside of his forearm from the base
of his thumb to the bend of the elbow. It wasn't a needle
track or the imprint of a blood-pressure cuff. Puzzled, Rob
licked a finger and rubbed the line, but if it was ink, it didn't
come off.

Rob dismissed it. There were ways to resolve his doubts,
and the sooner he got moving on it, the better. He got up and
shifted the folding screen slightly, so that it stood in the path
of the door's inward swing. It would never do to be surprised
in here. He sat down and took Edwin's hand again. This
close, touching Edwin, he could evade many of the confusing
images. He could dive right into Edwin and confront him,
mind-to-mind, wherever he was in there. Rob closed his eyes
and plunged in.

In the course of their friendship, Rob had rummaged
around a little in Edwin's head before. Now he went deep,
down to the central stronghold. Everybody had one, and
every one was different. Edwin's appeared to him as a long
wide warehouselike room, not very high-ceilinged, but pleasantly lined on both sides with broad deep-silled windows.
Tables were ranged in rows and aisles, filling the entire space,
so that it had the look of a sewing factory or a sweatshop

loft. Each table was laden with a bewildering assortment of stuff.

Cobwebs covered everything, thick ropy strands like an effect in a cheap horror movie. Rob poked gingerly at a looming spiderwebby mound. Under the cobwebs was an electron microscope. He picked up a yardstick from another table and began sweeping cobwebs away, moving methodically from table to table.

Here were maps, papers, and hundreds of books; the skull of a toothy dinosaur; sheaves of electron micrographs; an elaborate and detailed diagram of Moonbase and its environs; a globe of Mars. On one table, an eerie and familiar pearl the size of Rob's head weighted down a stack of notes. It was the pearl that Gilgamesh had brought out of the waters of the abyss, that Rob had given to Edwin—the jewel of eternal life. Everything Edwin was interested in was represented here. No wonder the room was enormous.

Rob couldn't resist wandering around a bit. There were areas that seemed fairly well-organized, especially around the electron microscope, but many of the tables seemed to hold a random assortment of items flung together. How could Edwin ever find anything? Perhaps it was just the way a Renaissance man's head worked.

When Rob looked at the notes under the pearl of immortality, they were illegible—probably only Edwin could decipher them. But the books were fascinating, table upon table heaped high with language texts, science fiction, theology, history, and computer tomes intermixed with the inevitable microbiology. There was a stack of *Car and Driver* and *Autocar* magazines, and more scientific journals than he could count. And here was an upright black Yamaha piano, with sheet music in an overflowing heap on the bench, and a glittering green electric bass guitar leaning to one side. In his wildest imaginings Rob could not picture Edwin playing bass in a rock band. But here the instrument was, sparkling under its cloak of cobwebs. Maybe a garage band in high school?

But he's not here, Rob told himself. He hasn't messed with any of this stuff in a long time. Where was Edwin in all this? He prowled the perimeter of the room until he came to a door. It was a plain, paneled wooden door with a brass knob. The knob turned easily enough, but the door stuck in its frame. Without considering it, Rob pushed the door at the stuck place, thumping with his shoulder and lifting it at the knob. Florida humidity, he thought.

The door flew open, and there was Edwin at last. He wore his white lab coat and sat in a desk chair at an empty desk, looking so much like his old self that Rob blew a long sigh of relief out through his mustache. "Ed, how are you doing?"

"Rob?" Edwin looked up, unsurprised. His formerly cheerful face was now abstracted, tired and a little sad. The epic had described Gilgamesh with "the look of a man who has gone on a long journey." Now Rob saw what the poet had meant. "I had a dream about you the other night."

"Yeah?" Rob came around the desk and perched on a corner—there were no other chairs. "What was it like?"

Edwin shrugged, unsmiling, staring off into the distance. "Just your usual odd dream. I was weaving myself a crown of green leaves, like the Greek statues, you know? And you turned up with a chain saw."

Startled, Rob said, "Were they oak leaves? Or willow?"

"I can't remember. Laurel is traditional, the favorite of Apollo. The god of music, and artistic achievement."

"They were oak," Rob insisted. It occurred to him that he was going to have a problem here. If Edwin was mentally ill, he wouldn't be able to tell Rob about it. Certainly he wasn't reacting now like his old self. "Ed, are you all right in here? Would you like to, well, maybe come out into the main room?"

"No can do, bud." Edwin nodded absently at the door.

Turning, Rob saw that the wooden door was tightly shut again, though he had left it ajar. "I can open that door—if you want to come out."

"There's nothing I'd like better."

His tone was so remote and sad that Rob exclaimed, "That's all I needed to hear! It'll take a little while, Ed, but I know from doors. I promise I'll fix it." He reached out to clap Edwin on the shoulder, and to his shock his hand slipped right through, as if he had become a ghost.

Both men stared at the sight. Startled into animation again, Edwin said, "That's right, you're a carpenter!"

"Wait, Ed," Rob interrupted. "I'll get back to you." There was something going on outside, out in the real world. Quickly he stepped back into his own body.

The door was jostling the folding screen. Finally a nurse stumbled in past it, saying, "The darn thing, how did that happen?" She stared accusingly at Edwin, but he obviously wasn't responsible. Secure in his invisibility, Rob rose softly from his chair and backpedaled as the nurse rearranged the screen to her liking. Then she fetched an instrument tray in and set it on the table, rolling it up to the bedside. "Time for your shot, dear." She anointed Edwin's arm with alcohol and held up the loaded hypodermic.

Was it benign, or malevolent? God, I hope I'm guessing right, Rob thought fervently. With a tiny mental gesture he redirected her aim. The needle sank deep into the pillow beside Edwin's arm, and the plunger went home.

"There you go, that's a good boy." The nurse made a note in her file and closed it. She swabbed Edwin's arm again and picked up the tray. "Lunchtime in twenty minutes, dear."

That file, Rob thought. Suddenly alert, he followed the nurse through the swinging door and back to the station. She stuck the file into a larger, hanging file folder labeled with Edwin's name. As soon as she walked away with the tray, Rob lifted the entire hanging file out.

He ducked into an office and sat down in the doctor's leather chair to page through the file. "This is beyond me," he muttered. Why did doctors write such cryptic abbreviations in such abominable handwriting? He had no idea what

the papers meant. It would take an expert, an M.D., to say
what was really going on.

But here was the sheet the nurse had marked—a checklist
of medications and dates. Scopalamine. Heroin. Haldol/Ati-
van. Thorazine. Droperidol. Morphine. Dozens of them, different ones every day. Was this scattershot approach usual in
psychiatric medicine? It didn't seem right to him, but then
Rob's knowledge of medicine had been garnered mainly
from watching *ER* and *Chicago Hope*. He had the answer
here in his hands. He just didn't have the training to understand it.

The door opened and the doctor came in, a thin Asian
man with glasses and receding gray hair. He took his white
coat from a rack in the corner and put it on over his polo
shirt. Rob stood up, unseen, as the doctor approached his
desk. Now, a person with the answers, Rob could handle
perfectly. "Hi, Doc," he said softly. "Time for a data dump."

It was easy to turn Dr. Nakamura's head inside out, but
not very informative. There were lots of basic questions that
the doctor didn't know the answers to: Edwin's diagnosis,
for instance. With a slow, mounting rage Rob realized that
this doctor was a jailer, not a healer. He'd been told off by
someone on the PSPIP side merely to keep Edwin immobi-
lized. He didn't know whether Edwin was really ill, nor did
he care.

"You swine," Rob whispered. Fury flooded into his veins
like ice. A doctor has a thousand doors to death—acciden-
tally getting infected with AIDS, swallowing poisons from his
own medical supplies, a slip of needle or scalpel or laser. For
a long luxurious moment Rob reviewed these vicious possi-
bilities. Then he got control of himself. He was not going to
force this poor little jerk to commit suicide too. Dr. Nakamura was just a pawn. There were other people responsible.

Besides, there were more productive ways to use this
knowledge. Rob took the file out to the photocopy machine.
There was nobody in the office now. He copied both sides of
every page, the entire file, before returning the file to the hang-

ing rack. He stuffed the photocopies into a big interoffice-mail envelope filched from a nurse's box of supplies, and went back to Edwin's room.

Edwin didn't look any better. Who knew how long it took for his enhanced recuperative powers to throw off psychoactive drugs? Quickly Rob searched the room, opening and shutting the metal nightstand drawers and wardrobe doors. No clothes or shoes—Edwin would have to abscond in a green hospital gown and paper slippers. Even his gold wedding band and watch were gone. The only personal item here was the famous red NASA baseball cap, hanging on a hook in the bathroom cubicle. Rob folded it flat and stuffed it into the envelope with the xeroxes. "Not even a toothbrush," he told Edwin. "Your wife would be shocked. What do you think, Ed? Can you stand up and walk?"

With gentle encouragement, Edwin could sit on the edge of the bed, but no more. Frustrated, Rob tucked him back in again. The nurses would bring him lunch in a couple minutes. Better to steal him after he was fed. In the meantime Rob could scout around for a wheelchair. Surely there was one somewhere in the building.

"Lunchies," the nurse said cheerily, bumping in with a tray. Rob slipped out and left her to it. It took him nearly an hour to find the wheelchair, folded in the back of a supply closet. He rolled it back in triumph.

Edwin was a couple inches shorter than Rob, and had lost both muscle and bone mass in low-grav life. He was perhaps twenty pounds lighter than a year ago. But he was still a heavy man, barrel-chested and wide in the shoulders. Rob hoisted him clumsily to his feet, not knowing the knack of handling bodies. Edwin's knees seemed to be loose and wobbly, unable to support all of his weight. Then the wheelchair skittered away when Rob tried to maneuver him into it. He had to set the brake and start over again. "Some rescue," he panted. And what about fingerprints? He spent a couple minutes wiping down the doorknobs and nightstand drawers with a wad of toilet tissue. He tucked the interoffice-mail

envelope beside Edwin, and readjusted the tarnhelm effect.
"Nobody sees either of us," he said aloud. "Okay, Ed.
You're now a fugitive."

They wheeled without incident out into the hall, down
the elevator, and out to the far side of the grilling-hot parking lot. The light-blue truck was like an oven. Rob ground
down both windows before hoisting Edwin into the front
seat and buckling him in. "You'll have to put up with it while
I bring the wheelchair back," Rob said. "This is part of the
devious bit—leaving nothing unusual." Edwin merely closed
his eyes. In the harsh brilliant sunshine he looked ghastly.

*E*dwin sat like a dummy while Rob drove all afternoon. The old truck's air-conditioning, broken two years ago, had never been worth the cost of compressor repair. The humid air swept in through both open windows, filling the silence with its thunder. Rob avoided the interstates now, striking west instead across the flat hot country to Orlando and then north to Ocala on 441. There was no hurry, and he wanted the freedom to pull over at any time. This precaution bore fruit near Tavares when Edwin suddenly mumbled, "I have to get out."

"You do? Oh no, I get it. Right you are." Rob pulled onto the gravel shoulder and reached across to open Edwin's door. Edwin tumbled out just in time, and vomited into the marshy drainage ditch. Rob fetched a water bottle and a roll of paper towels from the back. His years in the parenthood trenches had eroded any squeamishness. "That's probably a good sign," he said, inspecting the results. "Your system's throwing off the drugs . . . That's right, rinse and spit . . . Holy mackerel, Ed, you're not decent. We've got to get you some pants. Seat belt okay? All right, let's go."

They spent the night in a small motel outside Ocala. Edwin slept without stirring late into the morning, so Rob went out shopping. When he came back laden with bags, Edwin was just sitting groggily up in bed in the dark room, knuckling his eyes with both hands. "Rob? I thought I was dreaming . . ."

Rob pushed the curtains open, letting in a flood of tropical daylight. "Nope. It's your superpowered buddy to the rescue. You feel like a shower?"

"Would I! I haven't had one since I don't know when. Lead me to it!"

He was unsteady on his feet, though, so Rob helped him to the bathroom, and adjusted the temperature of the water as he would for his own kids. You couldn't count the oddly slow-motion bathing facilities on the Moon, which would put Edwin's last decent shower at more than a year ago. When Edwin emerged at last, wrapped in a towel, Rob had his purchases all laid out. "Jockeys. Shorts. T-shirt. Socks. Sneakers. And here's some doughnuts and juice, for the inner man."

Damp, Edwin looked like a dog drowned after a long bout with the mange. The dark hair furring his chest and arms lay plastered flat against the slack ashen skin. He sank weakly into a chair and took a doughnut. "Holy Mike, you're efficient."

"We'll take your hospital togs with us."

"Where are we going?"

Rob doubted Edwin could handle a full explanation yet. "To Carina," he said, and Edwin nodded his acceptance.

Rob knew he should have expected Edwin's physical weakness. Enforcing bed rest on a man newly returned from one-sixth gravity was probably responsible. The plastic bag containing the athletic socks utterly defeated him, and Rob had to thread the new laces through the sneaker eyelets and tie them for him. Nor could Edwin climb into the truck cab without a boost. "Sunscreen," Rob worried, stuck in daddy mode. "You're going to fry in this sunshine. Sunglasses. A hat."

"I have a hat," Edwin said sleepily. "A baseball cap."

"Did I tell you you're in disguise, Ed? What do you say to a cowboy hat? Oh, and let me use the tin snips to get that ID bracelet off."

Still, Edwin recuperated almost as Rob watched. Rob drove north on 301 to Jacksonville and on into Georgia. He deliberately chose a small-town diner for lunch instead of a fast-food restaurant. They took a booth furnished with a sugar shaker, an individual jukebox, and a giant bottle of ketchup. Rob passed Edwin the handwritten and mimeographed menu. "What's your fancy, Ed?"

"I haven't eaten like this in a year!"

Rob grinned but warned, "Keep your voice down, pal."

A man who believed in meals early and often, Edwin revived visibly on fried catfish and homemade buttermilk biscuit, with a huge salad, and pecan pie for dessert. Afterwards they walked across the street to a five-and-dime to pick up sunglasses and a straw cowboy hat. Edwin declined the sunscreen—"I don't burn, you know." Rob had to admit the truth of this. Edwin's ghostly pallor had already warmed into his more usual olive color. By tomorrow he'd be as tanned as any Southerner.

Conversation languished in the truck as they drove north. Rob respected Edwin's unusual quiet. It was what he himself would have wanted. After nearly two hours, Edwin suddenly said, "So, Rob. How do you come to be busting a murderer out?"

"There are habeas corpus laws in this country, Ed. Whatever you may or may not have done, you haven't been tried or convicted. What those doctors were doing was illegal, and you can nail them on it. No conviction, no commitment hearing—where do they come off, doping you up like that?"

"It was Pisspeep," Edwin said bitterly. "God, I trusted

those guys. I even told them about the immortality. And Burton Rovilatt swore he'd take care of everything."

"Burt Rovilatt?" Rob was impressed. Burton Rovilatt had the biggest stake in the NASA PSPIP.

"And the next thing I know, they lay this murder scenario on me, and everything went down the drain."

Rob wondered how accurate Edwin's recollection was, after all those psychoactive drugs. "You've gone through a bad time," he said neutrally.

Edwin hunched up in his seat as if his stomach hurt. "They died in my arms, you know. Owen and Phan. Oh Jesus . . ."

Rob kept his eyes on the hot sunny highway while Edwin struggled with his grief. You don't treat employees this way, he thought angrily. Granted, the *Franklin* disaster was an accident. But after Edwin had saved their ship so courageously, the last thing he deserved was accusations and betrayal and Haldol. I don't care if PSPIP is scared rigid. This really stinks. Aloud he said, "Whatever happens, whatever they say, I'll never believe you'd hurt another person, Ed. It's impossible."

"How do you know that, Rob—even you?" Edwin's voice and face were expressionless now, as if he had fallen back behind some inner fortification. "How does anyone know what they're capable of? Sometimes I think the doctors were right. I didn't kill Owen and Anna and Phan, but I'm capable of it."

"No, Ed," Rob said, suddenly bitter himself. "You know nothing about it whatever."

Behind the aviator sunglasses Edwin's gaze was unknowable. He said, "Do you read the Bible, Rob? Listen: 'You have heard that it was said to the men of old, you shall not kill, and whoever kills shall be liable to judgment. But I say to you that every one who is angry with his brother shall be liable to judgment.' By that rule, Rob, I've murdered you a couple times over."

It was so sudden that Rob's nerves jangled with alarm.

But the issue had to be resolved. It had festered far too long already. He kept his foot steady on the gas, his hands relaxed on the wheel, and said, "You mean, about Carina. In Kazakhstan."

"You know they had the dickens of a time drugging me," Edwin said in a bloodless voice. "This condition of mine makes me resistant. I had a lot of time to think. I realized I'd never be sure of the truth about that incident. Never. You have too much power, Rob. You could seduce my wife, rape her even, and wipe the experience from her mind. No one would ever know. She hasn't spoken to me about it. She might even have asked you to do it. She's anxious to start a family—I see you know that."

"No, Ed!" To hear a good man suggest such horrors, and so calmly, sent shivers down his back. Unable to bear it, Rob pulled over onto the shoulder and cut the engine. "We're not driving another inch," he panted, "until I tell you what happened that night."

"Don't you see? It doesn't matter, Rob. Anything's possible." Immobile as a statue, Edwin stared out the windshield at the semis whizzing by.

Rob wanted to yell at him, strike out with fists or mental bludgeons, anything to break through Edwin's stoniness. Stones? he thought wildly. I'm no stonewright, like old Gil. I need a door. Shaking, Rob said, "Listen to me, Ed. Before we drove off into the desert I phoned Jul, and she said she wanted a divorce. By the time Carina and I got out into the middle of nowhere, I was a wreck. I would have kissed the jeep. And she was thinking hard about you, missing you, so there was this overlap . . . Carina only let me get away with it for a second. Then she offered to impale me on a steel knitting needle."

Slowly Edwin turned to look at him, the sunglasses masking all expression. "You're joking."

"Her exact words were, 'You want a third nostril?' "

His unnatural calm shattered as Edwin began to laugh. "Oh Lord, that's just like her!" He leaned back and guffawed, brushing the sunglasses off and slapping his forehead.

Rob relaxed, grinning. When Edwin laughed from deep down in his chest like that, nothing could be wrong anymore. Rob started the engine again and eased back into traffic. "That's right, amuse yourself at my expense . . . Your wife terrifies me, Ed. That knitting is camouflage for carrying a deadly weapon. And when Jul was yelling at me, she was coaching her—it was horrible. You know she bullied me into this entire rescue expedition."

"Now, *that* I do not believe, Rob. Oh, you poor devil, ha ha! And I never said thank you. I'm still in major Dutch, but nothing like I was yesterday morning."

"We'll sort you out, Ed. But not today. All I want today is to get into South Carolina. If we crash in Columbia, we can make the cabin by tomorrow night."

From that point, everything was fine. They ate dinner in perfect harmony in Orangeburg at a seafood restaurant. Over conch soup and clam fritters, Rob explained about Ike's girlfriend's father's cabin. "A jailbreak, a cure, and now a hideout," Edwin said. "There's nothing beyond you, Rob. You even got my shoe size right. These sneakers fit me fine." He scraped the last of his soup out of the bowl.

"Measured your foot while you were asleep," Rob said. "With the steel tape measure in my toolkit."

Edwin laughed at this. "You're so together, there can't be anything wrong between you and Julianne. No divorce, right?"

"She knew I was hiding something from her." Rob buttered a roll and bit into it. "You were right about that. I don't know how women know, but they do. And weirdness is not the first thing that leaps to mind when you know your man is lying—she thought I was having an affair. We were going to go in for counseling. But who knows whether she'll ever get around to finding a therapist."

A couple more hours on the road after dinner got them past Columbia to a motel. The following morning dawned clear and hot—a good highway day. Rob grinned at his friend over his first cup of coffee. "You want to drive?"

Edwin's eyes shone. "Would I! I haven't driven in a year!"

"Not a car, anyway."

For the first few miles up I-77 Rob was watchful, but he soon relaxed. Edwin had been an excellent driver for as long as Rob had known him and, like all spacemen, excelled at tasks calling for good hand-eye coordination. "You remember your old car—the Mazda?"

"Sure do. I had to sell it—Carina couldn't take a sports car to Peru. Now I'm back, I should buy another. A man's got to have wheels, right?"

"What kind of car could ever keep an astronaut happy? You'll need a pocket rocket."

"It will take serious research." Edwin leaned one tanned elbow out the open car window, tipped his cowboy hat down low over his aviator sunglasses, and began to laugh. "A pocket rocket—I'll remember that."

It was wonderful to see Edwin blossoming into his old confident self again. Already he looked to have gained ten pounds or so. The immortality had helped him throw off the drugs, but his spiritual rebound was entirely Edwin's own doing. Such valor was enviable, the stuff of heroes. From personal experience, Rob knew that he himself was far more brittle.

After lunch, Edwin surfed the crackly radio offerings and found perhaps the only station in the Carolinas that broadcast classical music. Rob leaned back in his seat as the torrent of muscular, disturbing music engulfed him—very different from the sixties rock he usually stuck with. Edwin kept the truck spinning down the highway at precisely five miles per hour over the speed limit, and sang along at the top of his lungs: " *'Und der Cherub steht vor Gott'!*"

Rob was sure he had never heard it before. It wasn't even in English. But the melody was powerfully familiar, tugging at the shirttail of memory. "How do you know all the words? Don't tell me you speak whatever that is."

"To Beethoven's Ninth? The Schiller poem was originally

in German, but there's a loose English translation in the
hymnals. Classical music was a family favorite when I was
growing up. My father even named me after Mozart."

Rob shook his head at the idea of loading a oddball name
like that onto a baby. "At least he kept it to your middle
name. And 'Amadeus' is better than 'Wolfgang.'"

"Yep, I lucked out there! Ah, the chorus again—you want
to hear the English? Bet I can remember the words . . . *Joyful, joyful, we adore Thee, God of glory, Lord of love; /
hearts unfold like flowers before Thee, praising Thee their
sun above! / Melt the clouds of sin and sadness, drive the
dark of doubt away'* . . ."

Edwin insisted on driving all the way to West Virginia.
They left the interstate at the state line and took narrow
mountain roads north, deep into the Alleghenies. Once past
White Sulphur Springs, Rob had him halt the truck in a heavily treed picnic area. "Time to be devious again, Ed," he said.
"Hop on down." From the back he took out the paper bag
and the screwdriver.

"Very natty," Edwin said of the home-improvement
nameplates. "Why reattach them now?"

Rob tightened the screws while Edwin held the plates
lined up against the rust-rimmed holes in the doors. "You
wouldn't have noticed, Ed. But I've been very, very careful
this trip. No phone calls, no faxes, no logging-on. I've paid
cash for everything, and I never once used my own name. I've
fidgeted with the heads of every waitress and motel clerk we
dealt with—they forgot our faces the minute we walked out
the door. There isn't a piece of paper or a person from here
to Florida that can identify us. Your NASA bosses have no
trail. For all they know, you sprouted wings and flew away
to Bermuda."

Edwin nodded in appreciation. "So why is West Virginia
different?"

"Because here, I'm known. I am a respectable carpenter
and home improver. I can't afford to be seen lurking with a
fugitive spaceman. I want people around here to be able to

swear that I drove up to the cabin alone. And that means, Ed, that you're going to have to ride in the back for a while, out of sight."

Edwin sighed. "Well, it can't be as cramped as the LLS."

Rob raised the back hatch and lowered the tailgate. Carina's tornadolike tidying had made the rear area unrecognizably neat. The short ladder hung on hooks over one wheel well, and on the other side narrow shelves held toolboxes and bags of nails. The low dim center aisle was covered with a clean but balding strip of gray utility carpet. With a martyred air Edwin crawled in and lay down. Rob unhooked one end of the ladder. "Now if I wedge the ladder diagonally like this—just push that chain saw aside—and then drop this tarp over your legs, you're hardly noticeable."

"Can't you just tarnhelm me?" Edwin wheedled. "Then I could sit in the front seat."

"That would lack the James Bond touch." Rob slammed the tailgate up. "Besides, I want to put groceries in the front seat. We're stopping at the farm market stand for tomatoes and corn."

Edwin groaned, but Rob ruthlessly shut the hatch on him. The truck cap had no side windows. A little light struggled in through the dirt-filmed glass of the rear hatch. By craning his neck, Edwin could just glimpse the back of Rob's dark blond head through the front panel. Riding in back was surprisingly noisy, what with the tools jingling and the parts rattling back and forth in their boxes and bags. The ladder shifted alarmingly as the truck bounced over a pothole, and Edwin braced it against the wheel well with his knees. The ride to the farm market seemed eternal. Then, when the truck pulled into a gravelly space and stopped, the shopping seemed to take hours. The truck was very stuffy, and the tarp smelled of paint thinner.

At last he caught the sounds of footsteps on gravel, and conversation. Rob opened the passenger-side door of the cab, saying, "But you want to be sure the first layer of shingle is hanging on tight. No curling ones, for instance. Otherwise your new layer won't hold."

An older woman's reedy voice said, "When George climbed up there on his ladder to look it over, I thought I'd swoon. That's one steep roof we got, specially the bit over the bedrooms."

"You better hire a pro, then. George isn't getting any younger, you know . . ."

The speakers moved around to the back. Rob startled Edwin by lifting the hatch and setting a whole Sugar Baby watermelon by his feet. Edwin kept perfectly still under the edge of his tarp, and held his breath. ". . . in this climate I'd go with asphalt shingle," Rob said. "Cedar shake'll just go mossy on you."

They stood by the open hatch and thoroughly discussed roofing options, with frequent detours into George's state of health. The old lady would certainly be able to testify that the truck was empty, front and back. Edwin mentally cursed Rob's daring with all the fluency Lon and Geena had taught him, hoping Rob would read his mind. Finally Rob slammed the hatch down and got moving. The truck lurched rattling and clanking uphill, and then down onto a rough road, and at last came to a stop. Edwin flung off the tarp and sat up. "You enjoyed that," he accused when Rob lifted the hatch.

Rob grinned, not denying it. "Get a move on, Ed. The ladies are waiting for us. And don't step on that melon."

In the gathering twilight they shifted the groceries to the back, and Edwin took the front seat. Rob drove slowly because of the ruts and potholes. The gravel road wound up over the steep saddle of a thickly wooded ridge and then down. Far below through the trees, Edwin caught glimpses of the lake glowing rosy in the last of the sunset. He blinked at it. Suddenly the significance of Rob's words sank in. He didn't have to avoid yearning for Carina anymore. She was down there by the lambent water, only a mile away. "How much longer?" he demanded.

Rob laughed at his eagerness. "We have to go right around the lake, and it's getting dark. A quarter hour, at least."

It was fully night by the time the truck came to the cabin. The A-frame was lit up like a Christmas tree in the deep velvet darkness. When Rob cut the engine, the only sound was cicada song and the tentative hoot of an owl. He set the hand brake. A deep calm satisfaction filled him, the same joy he got from completing an ambitious building project, a two-level deck or a gazebo. He watched Edwin scramble out of the seat and run towards the house before getting out himself.

The crunch of their tires on the gravel must have alerted the family. Carina's short, shapely figure appeared, silhouetted in the light of the screen door. Then she vanished, flying across the deck and down the steps to leap sobbing into Edwin's embrace. Edwin hid his streaming eyes in the dark cloud of her hair for a long moment, before the first kiss. Averting his gaze and tactfully stepping around them, Rob went up the steps himself. Julianne came out to meet him, carrying Colin. Rob took both of them in his arms and gave Julianne a long leisurely kiss. "A good job well-done," he told her. "I'm so happy."

"You should be. My god, what a stunt. I can't believe you did it! How is he?"

"Healthy as a horse. Is Carina staying in the tent?"

"Yeah, halfway down the hill. She has her own sleeping bag and both the twins'."

"Good. Then we can leave them to bill and coo. Come on, little guy. Your daddy could use a beer."

✻ CHAPTER
    11

*I*n the morning, Rob waded carefully down the hill through the cool dewy grass, balancing a laden tray. It was strange to see Carina's yellow-and-orange tent set up under towering pine trees instead of on a poppy-strewn steppe. The silence was complete, cool and thin and bright like champagne. Rob set the tray down on a stump and tapped a coffee mug with a teaspoon. "Ed! Breakfast is served!"

After a long time Edwin emerged, clad only in jockey shorts. His long curly hair was tousled with sleep, and he had a replete air of utter content that Rob recognized instantly. All the ugly fantasies of adultery and betrayal had evidently evaporated in Carina's presence, like the phantasms they were. Edwin yawned. "What are you doing up so early?"

"It's nine in the morning, Ed. The twins have been on the go since dawn. I wanted to warn you to lie low until noon at least. Children have no discretion. It may be very useful

someday, for the kids to believe that you and I arrived here
separately."

"You're getting too fanatical about the caution and cunning, Rob." Edwin sipped his steaming coffee. "Shouldn't
you relax?"

"All in your service, pal. And speaking of which, this mug
is Carina's herbal tea, and this tureen is oatmeal, her
favorite. You'll have to share it. I told the twins Carina was
sleeping late. I'm sure you can keep her entertained for a couple more hours." He laughed out loud at Edwin's sudden
blush.

The twins had discovered a creek with a small waterfall,
and the entire family hiked out to see it. After lunch Colin
had his nap, the twins went swimming, and Rob set about
clearing the brush around the trail to the lake. Edwin found
him wielding the roaring chain saw on a tangle of thorny
trees. The sight chimed oddly in his memory, and he sat
down on a fallen log to watch.

He had not had a chance to see Rob at work in years.
With his sun-burnished fair hair and heavy tan, Rob looked
every inch the outdoor worker. What struck Edwin today
was his easy skill. Rob handled the heavy gas-powered saw
effortlessly, attacking the tree trunks with the economical
grace of long experience. Competence was one of the cardi-
nal virtues in Edwin's book, as it was in every astronaut's.
And physical fitness, too—Rob's arms were as big around as
most spacemen's thighs. Sweat gleamed on his shirtless body,
heavily sprinkled with sawdust, leaves, and bits of bark spat
out by the saw. Edwin watched the shift and play of muscles
on Rob's mahogany torso—the kind of bulk and mass
achieved by actually doing heavy labor, not working out on
machines—and flexed his own flaccid biceps. He had to start
exercising again!

Rob looked up and let the saw sputter to a halt. "So here
you are," he said. He pulled the safety goggles with their
attached ear protectors, off and wiped his forehead with the

Hitachi Power Tools T-shirt hanging from his belt. "You look great—completely recovered." With a twinge of envy Rob realized that Edwin looked exactly as he had seven years ago, when they had met. His hair was thick and dark, only very slightly thin at the crown. It would never fade into gray as Rob's was doing. Nor would his round-cheeked face ever weather into lines, or his waistline sag, or his vision dim. Rob flexed his wrists and fingers, which still buzzed with the vibration of the saw. The joints were starting to give him trouble after a day's work, or on cold mornings—the fore-runner of arthritis, of age and senility and death. But Edwin, Fortune's favorite, would never know them. Body and mind, his prime would last for centuries. Immortality means that age passes you by.

The two men stared rather self-consciously at each other. Then with a thrashing and crashing like stampeding buffalo the twins came roaring up the trail. When their taffy-colored hair was wetted down from swimming, the two looked like mirror images. "You said we could come when the chain saw stopped," Annie shouted.

Davey yelled, "Dad! Dad, I saw a pelican! Unless it was a stork. If we catch it, can we take it home?"

"Are there freshwater pelicans?" Rob asked Edwin. "Kids, do you remember Uncle Eddie? Aunt Carina keeps him as a pet."

The children gave Edwin a fleeting glance. Annie, who disdained the social niceties as lies, said, "No."

Davey tugged at Rob's hand. "Dad, you have to come down to the lake! Maybe it was a hawk!"

"Okay, okay!" Rob set his gear down on a stump.

The path to the lake was steep and overgrown, but the kids barreled heedlessly down the hill. Edwin set a slower pace. Rob brought up the rear, reflecting that such a hike would have been beyond Edwin's strength only a day ago. "You have the right name," he remarked.

"Yeah?"

"I'm almost jealous. It comes so easy to you, Ed, it's unfair. Just like Mozart."

"You must've seen that movie! You know, you should never count on Hollywood for reliable data."

"Well, I feel like what's-his-name, the second-rate musician, at the moment."

Edwin stopped and looked back over his shoulder, grinning. "Nonsense, Rob. You, as Salieri? There's a much better analogy in classical music. If I'm Mozart, facile and fast and brilliant, you're Beethoven. Troubled, hardworking, and shaping great art with labor and pain. What do you think?"

Caught by surprise, Rob said, "I listen to the oldies station, mostly."

From below came a double wail: "Daddy!"

Edwin began to laugh, and galloped downhill to the shore. "Look at that, a diving platform! Come on, last one there's a rotten egg!" He kicked off his sneakers and jumped in, clothes and all, with a bellyflop splash. The twins yelled with joy and followed, cavorting.

Rob sat down on a rock to shuck his workboots. Beethoven? It was just like Edwin, to open a door and give a tantalizing glimpse of new realms beyond. There were sure to be books about the composer at the library back home.

Very little happened for more than two weeks. Carina and Julianne had come to a rapid meeting of minds on the drive up. They decreed that, if possible, nothing should disturb the vacation. The men were too sensible not to align themselves with this policy. So by common consent, all Edwin's problems were tabled for future consideration, and everyone got involved with innocent and mundane recreation.

With his happy gift for living in the present Edwin took the lead on this. He began jogging again, and swam across the lake twice a day. Rob finished barbering the underbrush and began prying the old rotten boards off the dock, preparatory to installing new ones.

Carina's birchbark canoe had run into difficulty. It floated perfectly well empty, but when a twin sat in it—it was too small for an adult—the craft slowly filled with water. "I made it exactly the way the Huron Indians did," Carina complained. "Except that it's not hunting season, so I couldn't get deer sinew. I used binder twine instead."

"Marine caulk," Rob proposed.

"Not historically correct!" Carina's tone suggested that he was proposing sacrilege, and Rob beat a retreat. But Edwin laughed so heartily at the debate that Carina admitted that perhaps modern caulking polymers were not so bad. Rob promised to pick up a tube of marine caulk in town.

Colin was big enough now to sit up in an inflatable ring with a seat. Rob took him swimming, which meant floating in the gravelly shallows within arm's reach while Colin splashed around, unable to drown himself. Dressed in a pair of tiny blue swim trunks hitched under his soft baby belly, and a T-shirt embroidered with a whale, Colin was unendurably cute. He had two teeth now, and a tuft of colorless fair hair. His Aunt Carina spoiled him rotten.

The bigger kids discovered that their Uncle Eddie was a sucker for exhausting water games of every sort—water tag, Marco Polo, duck and chase, chicken fights, water jousts. Rob was perforce drawn from his peaceable wallowing into these contests. "You go right ahead, hon," Julianne said helpfully.

"I'll watch the baby," Carina volunteered.

"Thanks a lot!"

"The unfairness of it," he complained that evening by the rustic fireplace, after the kids were in bed. "Pitting me against someone like Ed. Davey pulled that standing-on-my-head trick and almost drowned me. While you, Ed, just burble along under the surface."

Edwin laughed. "You should borrow it." He chose the

reddest apple from the bowl on the fieldstone hearth and buffed it on the front of his faded gray T-shirt.

Carina looked up from the knitting in her lap. "You can do that? Just hand the immortality over like a hot potato?"

"Oh yeah. It looks like a pearl, Rob tells me. But I understand that's just an image, a construct. Like the picture of Pavarotti on the label of his CD. In fact Rob's promised to take it away anytime I'm bored with it. The pearl, I mean, not a CD."

Julianne took a bite of her own apple and said, "Then what, hon? Would you keep it? Become immortal yourself?"

"Not me. With any luck I'll predecease Ed and he'll be left holding the bag. Today I'm sure I lost a couple years off my life span. Davey must be heavier than Annie."

"Yesterday you said the opposite," Edwin said. "The only solution is to weigh them both."

"Wait a minute." Carina let the sweater sleeve on its needles fall, the bulldog gleam glinting in her eye. "I think Rob should take it away. At least for a while."

"You're serious?" Rob frowned. There were reasons why that was a bad idea.

Before he could bring them up, Carina continued. "Say a year. Until I get pregnant."

Julianne squeezed Rob's arm, to indicate that she knew what Carina was talking about. "Aren't you assuming that immortality has an effect on his fertility?" she asked Carina. "He should get some tests done to be sure."

Edwin leaned his head back on the overstuffed tweed sofa and stared at the rafters in the lofty ceiling. "I can't believe we're discussing this."

"This isn't so bad," Rob pointed out. "She was going to pump Gilgamesh about his reproductive history."

Everyone laughed at that but Carina, who said, "It was a perfectly reasonable research question!"

When he recovered, Edwin said, "The fact is, I'm in possession of some pretty conclusive before-and-after data.

When I was at MIT I was a sperm donor. They loved to tap us science majors for that. Obviously, all systems were good to go then. And these past few years—well, the physicals at NASA are very thorough. Now I'm back, I really should do some research on my condition. There must be lots of other little side effects like this. If I culture some of my own cells and calculate their Hayflick limit . . ."

Carina was not to be diverted. "If you don't want the immortality yourself," she said to Rob, "just park it somewhere. Put the pearl in a jar on the mantelpiece or something."

Julianne had offered a bite of apple to Rob, and he had to chew and swallow. "I don't think I ought to remove the pearl from Ed's custody," he said. "I hate to bring it up, Ed. But your undisputed immortality is the only thing between you and a murder rap."

Edwin winced. "I never thought of that."

"In fact, if it ever even gets out that you can pick it up and put it down, you may be in trouble. How would you prove then that you didn't become deathless *after* killing your colleagues?"

Julianne said, "Cut it out, Rob. You make my blood run cold."

Carina said to Julianne, "It's so useful, having a truly sick mind around the house."

Edwin sighed. "Adoption. Another thing to look into. I should start a list."

Julianne balanced her apple core on the hearth and frowned at it. "Wait a second," she said. "Why don't you just go back up to Boston and make a withdrawal from that sperm bank?"

Edwin stared at her. Carina exclaimed, "I should have thought of that!"

Julianne leaned over and hugged her, and abruptly the party fissioned, the women vanishing into the kitchen to discuss their fallopian tubes and brew herbal tea. "I must be getting stupid," Edwin told Rob.

"They have an edge because they read women's magazines." Rob punched him lightly on the arm. "I think you've been brooding too long about it."

"You're right. In fact, that first afternoon in Georgia— you remember? I didn't mean it. I apologize for dumping it on you. All that poisonous adultery stuff, it was things I was trying not to think about. And I'd been congratulating myself on how sensible and forgiving I was being, too. It's depressing how thin the veneer of civility really is."

"You have no veneer, Ed. You're solid all the way through to the core. Like these apples." Rob chose one and bit it.

"Have you heard this before, Rob? Listen: 'You have heard that it was said, An eye for an eye and a tooth for a tooth. But I say to you, do not resist one who is evil. But if any one strikes you on the right cheek turn to him the other also.' I've tried to live by that."

Rob goggled at him. It seemed a preposterous philosophy, utterly untenable in real life. "Do not resist one who is evil"? What would have happened to Julianne in front of the Willard Hotel if he hadn't resisted? But I didn't have to kill them— he jerked away from the thought.

Edwin was staring meditatively at the empty fireplace. "We've all got a hot button inside. Remember the monster inside you? Mine is nearly as primitive and primal. A stupid, sexist fellow who thinks of his wife as personal chattel. And somehow, while I was in the clinic, he got off the chain."

"There was no 'somehow' about it, Ed. Can you even remember how they were treating you? Maybe it's time to show you this." Rob went to the bedroom and fetched the envelope of photocopies.

Edwin opened it. "My hat!" Delighted, he pulled the baseball cap on. "I thought it was gone for good, along with my wedding ring!"

"You may yet get the ring back, too. It must be down at the Space Center, and these photocopies should make a dandy lever."

As Edwin turned over the pages his smile vanished. "Rob,

what the devil were they doing? This drug regimen should have killed me."

"My guess is that they wanted to keep you under control no matter what. And with your system, they had to use a lot of different drugs in overdose. You hang on to that package and decide what to do about it. Myself, I'd be inclined to sue their pants off."

Edwin stuffed the papers back into the envelope. "Some other day." He looked up. "Rob, I'm never going to be able to repay you for everything. You saved my life and sanity, pulling me out of there."

Rob blushed uncomfortably. " 'S okay. You've done the same for me."

"So I have—I forgot." Edwin grinned at him. "Next time it's my turn again."

It was high time to start redecking the boat dock, so Rob drove to the lumberyard in Covington the next day. Julianne came along to buy some groceries. "It'll do you good to prac-tice on Colin," she told Edwin at breakfast, and plumped the baby down into his lap.

"Right—nothing like an integrated sim." Still, Edwin's transparent countenance betrayed his unease. Seeing this, the twins instantly piled on.

"He always has a poop after breakfast," Annie remarked helpfully. "A runny one."

"Wait until he gags on his baby cereal, Uncle Eddie— that's the grossest." Davey's gray-blue eyes widened with mock horror. "It drips right down to his knees!" Well aware that he was the center of attention for the moment, Colin grinned and clapped his hands.

"Maybe we should rethink this parenthood agenda, Carina," Edwin said, laughing. "Rob, do you dare to leave this precious trio with a pair of greenhorns like us?"

Rob was laughing so hard he hurt. "You're on your own, Ed. Come on, Jul, quick!"

Julianne breezed by in denim shorts and a T-shirt. "Free at last, free at last! See you soon, dears!"

It was almost thirty miles over the mountains to town. Rob dropped Julianne at a Food Lion and went to the lumberyard for a truckload of pressure-treated two-by-sixes. When he came back she was sitting on the bench in the grocery loading area, her lap full of newspapers and magazines. "Rob, look at this!" She pushed the armload of publications through the window onto the seat.

Rob picked up *Time* magazine. On the cover was Edwin's smiling face under the red baseball cap, the dimples well in evidence. A vivid diagonal label read, MURDERER? AN ASTRONAUT VANISHES!

"Oh my god," Rob said faintly. "We'd better show Ed right away. It's great you bought this."

"I scarfed up every major paper and magazine they had." Quickly they loaded the groceries up and drove back. Rob found himself checking the rearview mirror for suspicious cars. There was no phone at the cabin, no computer or fax machine. Even if he had wanted to, Edwin couldn't contact anyone. He should be safely hidden there. Still, Rob couldn't relax until he had driven around the lake and saw Edwin on the gravel drive giving Annie a piggyback ride.

Annie squeezed his neck and squealed, "Giddyap!"

"No more trotting, Annie," Edwin panted. He plodded over to lean heavily against the side of the truck, sweat dripping off his chin. "Old Paint needs a breather. You want a hand with that lumber, bud?"

"I'd appreciate it, Ed. But I think you have other concerns." Rob held out a copy of the *Richmond Times-Dispatch*. The headline on the front page read, LOCAL PSYCHOLOGIST ATTACKS BARBAROSSA MURDER THEORY.

Edwin turned white under his olive tan. "Jesus," he whispered prayerfully.

Sensing the change in atmosphere, Annie slid off his back to the ground. "Can I read it too?"

"Later, sweetie," Rob said. "Come help me carry groceries now."

The others spent the afternoon going through all the

papers, but after one pass through *U.S. News & World Report*, Rob was too depressed to read more. Instead he took the twins down to the water and worked on the dock while they swam.

Everything had come out last week: Edwin's mysterious escape, the questions about his sanity, the suggestions of murder, the mystery of his current whereabouts. NASA had apparently been forced to give up the idea of a cover-up, and a white-hot flume of excitement had engulfed the nation. It was August, just the right time of year for a media manhunt. Edwin had already been sighted in Atlanta, San Diego, and France, as if he were Elvis. There was no way to ever turn this thing around.

The sun was low and orange behind the trees when Edwin came down to the shore. "Let me help you with the rest of the boards," he said.

"Thanks, that'd be great." Alone, Rob had been able to manage a couple at a time—the lumber was only six feet long. Between the two of them, they shifted the entire load in a few trips. "I figure I better wind this dock up fast," Rob said. "You're in pretty deep, pal. I don't know what even I can do for you."

"Never a dull moment." Edwin shook his head dolefully. "After the kids go to bed, Carina wants to discuss strategy. She and Jul are pulling together the biggest dinner you ever saw—steaks and potato salad."

"You should never brainstorm on an empty stomach," Rob agreed. "I better go fire up the grill."

It was a large but sober meal. The older children wolfed down their steaks and scurried off. After some time Annie came back into the dining room. She stared at Edwin with lofty reproach in her brown eyes. "Why didn't you tell us you're a spaceman?"

"But I'm on vacation." Edwin pushed his plate away. "Besides, I didn't think you were interested."

"I like to know stuff," Annie said.

"We're going to be in fourth grade," Davey came in to

say. "We do Current Events—we're not babies. Besides, I want to hear about killing the other guys."

Edwin shot a startled glance at Rob, who shook his head and shrugged. There was no way to keep the twins in the dark, now they could read the paper. Their questions were only the first Edwin would have to face. "I can tell you about going to outer space, and living on the Moon," Edwin offered. "But really and truly, I didn't kill anybody. My friends died, but it was an accident."

"Really?" If anything, Davey seemed disappointed. "But it said so in the *Post*."

"Bloodthirsty brat," Julianne remarked.

"All the papers are wrong about that," Edwin said gently. "Think about it. Your dad wouldn't let his kids swim with someone who killed three people, would he?"

Caught off-guard, Rob lurched to his feet. He hurried out onto the deck as his stomach revolted. For a second he thought he'd lose his meal right over the deck rail. Morris, Timms, Ellison. If only he could ask them to forgive him, the way he had been able to apologize to Edwin—but it was impossible.

Alarmed, Julianne followed him. "Rob, are you all right?"

The sweat prickled cold on Rob's forehead. His sworn promise to Julianne seemed to twist in his gut like a needle. But the door was stuck, the secret held too near to the bone. He forced a smile. "Just my nervous stomach. Let me do the dishes, that'll settle it."

Back inside, Edwin had the situation well in hand. He sat on the sofa with all three kids and talked about Independence Moonbase and low-grav life.

"I think he really misses the base," Carina said, drying plates. "Heaven knows why. He was stressed enough while he was there."

"Men like to suffer," Julianne said.

"Is that why we get married?" Rob asked, and Julianne snapped the dishtowel at the seat of his shorts.

When the kids were settled for the night, the adults gathered by the cold fireplace. Rob mulled some cider, and Carina brought pencils and a notebook. Edwin lounged on the braided rug with his head beside her bare knee, and said, "I need help. Boy, do I ever! Advise me."

Everyone looked at Rob, on the sofa. Embarrassed, he said, "Well, if it was me . . . I guess I'd run fast and far. There's plenty of rural places left on earth where nobody would recognize you, and you could live a quiet life."

"Like Kazakhstan," Carina said.

Julianne raised an eyebrow. "Live on what?"

"Um . . . well, wasn't your dig in Peru in a pretty primitive area, Carina? What if you two hid there? What do folks do?"

"Subsistence farming," Carina said. "And anchovy fishing."

"I don't think I'm called to fish for anchovies," Edwin said, shaking his head. "But that's a very characteristic solution, bud. For you, a peaceful life seems to be essential."

"That privacy fetish," Carina said.

"Then what's essential for you, Edwin?" Julianne asked. "What do you want most to salvage from this?"

Edwin sipped his cider, thinking. "Research. I have to get back to my research on cell structure. It's been on the shelf too long. It would be a shame not to delve into this immortality thing, too—a whole new angle on human physiology waiting to be found there. And the Moon colony is only a stepping stone: to Mars. I've been waiting for years to look for microscopic Martian life."

Appalled, Rob said, "Talk about impossible! Ed, you're too ambitious!"

Edwin smiled. "I have time on my side, bud."

"But you can't do any of that in Central Asia," Julianne said. "Or coastal Peru, either."

"Okay, I've done my share," Rob said. "Someone else kick in an idea."

Carina fixed him in that brilliant searchlight stare. "You

could do something, Rob. Like make everybody forget about this." She poked the stack of papers and magazines with her sandaled toe.

"Everyone who researched and wrote and read the articles," Edwin said. "And everyone who watches TV or listens to the radio. Say, at a guess, every person on earth except for a couple hermits in Tibetan monasteries. I'm not ambitious, she's ambitious."

"And it'd be a waste of time," Rob said. "So people forget. So what? The newspapers themselves still exist for anybody to read. I'd have to find and destroy every copy of every newspaper and magazine printed, too. It's a hopeless endeavor."

"You wouldn't have to destroy them yourself," Julianne suggested. "Make other people destroy them for you."

Rob hesitated. Edwin said smiling, "Maybe now's the time to mention Severneth, monarch of Mu."

Carina dug her fingers into Edwin's shaggy pate and pulled his head gently back to look into his face. "Is that a joke?"

Rob laughed. "Actually, it is—a private joke. While he was on the Moon, Ed and I pretended to be writing a schlock fantasy novel called *Severneth, Monarch of Mu.* It was a pretext, so we could discuss our weird stuff without other people knowing."

Carina covered her eyes. "Oh, Edwin—it was your idea, I just know it."

Edwin laughed too. "You got it. The point, though, is that we've been discussing for years whether it's right for Rob to make people do stuff. And under what circumstances. Minor fiddles are probably harmless, but major meddling . . ."

Julianne pushed her hand into Rob's, and he squeezed it gratefully. "I'm not smart enough," he said. "Not wise enough. I try to interfere as little as possible. Only when the chips are down, like in Florida."

"I'm so glad you did." Carina's smile was so incandescent it made Rob blink. Thank goodness Edwin was back, to exert his moderating influence on her.

Julianne looked up from their clasped hands. "You know what the problem is, Edwin? The central problem is that people don't know you're immortal."

"It *is* hard to believe," Carina said.

"But I told them," Edwin protested.

"You told the stuffed shirts at NASA," Julianne corrected him. "You didn't tell these guys." She pointed at the heap of papers. "And NASA didn't, either. They just said you were a raving psychotic. We read all these articles, and not one of them discussed your immortality. Nobody knows about it now. But what if everybody knew, without a shadow of a doubt, that you didn't need to kill to survive the lunar transfer vehicle fire?"

Carina frowned. "What you're saying is that Edwin didn't go far enough."

"He doesn't have a *legal* problem," Julianne said, with mounting excitement. "He has a *public relations* problem."

"There's the marketing lady talking," Rob said, smiling. "To a hammer, every problem looks like a nail."

"She has something, Rob, don't you see?" Edwin sat up on the rug and leaned forward like a greyhound straining at its leash. "If I could get the entire story out, the murder rap and the insanity thing would dry up and blow away. I could even call them on keeping me doped up in KSC."

"That's a mighty big 'if'!"

"But it could be done." Julianne held up the *Time* magazine cover. "You already have a huge boost, Edwin. All you need is spin. Your Q must be stratospheric. Everybody on earth must know about you. I know couturiers who'd sell their grandmothers for this level of coverage."

Carina looked at Rob. "You don't like it. Why?"

"The privacy fetish, I guess," Rob admitted. "Ed, you know that from this step there'd be no going back. Once you display your ability to the entire planet, your life will change in a million ways. You— well, they'll take you into labs and stick you with needles."

"He did want to do research on the immortality," Julianne reminded him.

Edwin rubbed his hands together in anticipation. "Yes, it'd be *my* lab."

Rob struggled to articulate a thought that refused to jell. "What I'd worry about is . . . envy, I guess. It's already so easy to hate people with all the luck. Coming out about the immortality will make it worse for you, Ed—a thousand times worse than Mozart had it . . ." Edwin stared blankly at him, uncomprehending, and Rob let the concept trail away. Such worldly, cynical notions had little resonance for Edwin, and it was probably a pointless concern anyway. How could anyone hate such a nice guy?

Edwin ran a hand through his hair. "You know, Jul, the more I look at this, the better I like it. I'm already half-unmasked. It'd be safer to be completely open, completely free. On the *Franklin*—I tried to tell Anna I wasn't going to die, and she didn't believe me. I'll always wonder if that knowledge might have made a difference. And I've never been quite comfortable with your secrecy, Rob. You waste a lot of energy on unnecessary paranoia."

Rob smiled at him. "What if they're really out to get you, though? I never met a bigger optimist than you, Ed."

"It's a part of his charm," Carina said stoutly.

Suddenly Edwin held both hands out, beckoning. "Rob— why don't you come too? Keep me company in this brave new world. Drop all the fanatic seclusion, tear off the shirt, and show the big red *S* underneath. Fling wide the portals of your life."

For a single moment Rob found himself considering it. He respected Edwin's opinion tremendously. His friend was so often right. But then he grinned and said, "And what do I do, when the President of the United States asks me to—oh, change the thinking of the government of France, say. What do I tell him?"

Edwin grinned too, because this was the old debate. "You lend him a copy of *Severneth, Monarch of Mu.*"

Rob laughed, but grew serious again right away. "Your bit is defensive, Ed. It affects mainly you. Mine goes outwards. It could change the world."

"Why not? Maybe for the better."

"I'm not wise enough to guarantee that, Ed. And I'm not foolish enough to hand the responsibility over to someone else. Besides, you just want to experiment on me."

Edwin didn't even blush. "Only a little bit. Just around the edges!"

"No way," Rob said. "Fling your portals alone!"

"What do you think, Jul?" Edwin said persuasively. "You're the PR expert. If you're in favor of his coming out, Rob can't oppose us both."

Julianne frowned. "It would be a terrible marketing move. Never subdivide your market share with two similar products."

Edwin and Carina both burst out laughing, and Rob gave her a loud kiss on the cheek. "Thank you, Jul!"

$\mathcal{T}$he Labor Day holiday had come and gone, and by Wednesday, all the vacationing staffers were back at work at the CBS offices in New York City. The secretary handed senior TV newsman Ed Bradley his mail as he passed by on the way to his private office. The urgent letters were flagged with color-coded Post-It Notes, and underneath was a wad of newspaper clippings photocopied for easy handling onto 8½- by 11-inch sheets: possible story ideas for *60 Minutes*. White-haired but still vigorous, the eminent journalist strode quickly into his office and dropped the stack on his overflowing desk so he could take off his jacket.

The office door swung shut with a click. Not until that moment did Bradley notice the three people standing at the farther end of the large room. How could he have not seen them till now? TV personalities always have to worry about stalkers, crazies, and overzealous fans. Bradley seized the phone to buzz for security. "You have no business here, folks."

One of the two men stepped forward. "Do you recognize me, Mr. Bradley?"

"No, I . . ." Bradley didn't need to see the red baseball cap—the face alone was enough. "Dr. Edwin Barbarossa! Holy god, man! Where have you been? What's been going on with you?"

"I thought I'd tell the public all about it," Edwin said with confidence. "Would *60 Minutes* like the exclusive?"

The veteran newsman clutched at his phone again. "Let me call Don Hewitt, okay? Don't go away! Have a seat!"

Edwin sat down, shooting a smile over his shoulder at Rob. No need to get weird at all, except for a little touch of the old tarnhelm. There were some major hurdles ahead, but Julianne—amazing woman!—had predicted that getting this far would be a breeze if he used the word "exclusive." Carina came over and sat down too, but Rob remained standing at the back to demonstrate he wasn't a part of the media maelstrom. "I'm only your backstop," he had warned Edwin in the truck on the drive to New York.

And Edwin had joked, "I'll drag you in yet, Rob!"

In a very short time the large room was crowded with producers and executives. Edwin brushed aside their eager questions, saying, "I have one big thing to demonstrate, and then I'll answer as many questions as you like, on camera or off."

"I think we're all here, Dr. Barbarossa," Bradley said. "Speak your piece—we're all ears."

"Call me Edwin. Everybody does. Oh, and this is my wife Carina—will you hold my cap, dear?—and over there in back is Rob Lewis, a friend. Wave for the nice newspeople, Rob, so they'll know you . . . Now! The question, ladies and gentlemen, is: How did I survive the *Franklin* fire? One theory is that I murdered my shipmates to do it. I'm here to offer you the real skinny. Mr. Bradley, do you have a wastebasket under your desk? Does it have a plastic-bag liner?"

Rob watched with admiration as Edwin got a CBS vice president to extract the clear plastic bag and blow it up to show it was airtight. His charm and confidence were so persuasive that she didn't object to slipping the bag over his head at first. Someone else had to exclaim, "But wait! He'll suffocate!"

"This is the crux of the explanation," Edwin said. "So let me do it my way just this once, please. Carina, you have the stopwatch? Ms. Portofino, twist it tight around my neck. I want an airtight seal. Mr. Bradley, as an astronaut I have a very high tolerance for boredom. I want you to stop this experiment yourself, when *you* want to. I will not act in the matter. Okay, Ms. Portofino, let's do it. Hang on until Mr. Bradley says to let go."

The poor woman didn't look happy at all, but she obeyed. Edwin exhaled hard, blowing the clear bag out to show it was still airtight. Carina started the clock and set it on the desk. A minute. Two minutes. Four. Five. People were beginning to mutter. "A Zen Buddhist trick, right?" "A circus stunt." "But he's moving, you know—not in a trance."

Ten minutes. Fifteen. Some of the executives were getting more restless than popcorn in a hot skillet. Rob surveyed their thinking with interest. He had warned Edwin he wouldn't warp their credulity or anything, but just looking was neutral. They had suspected trickery at first, but now the tide was turning. "What do they call those air-pressure-chamber things?" one executive whispered. "A hyperbaric chamber, that's it. They use them in hospitals. That would make a better visual than a garbage bag."

At the thirty-minute mark, Bradley took off his glasses and said, "Enough already! Edwin, you've got to explain how you do that!"

Edwin emerged from the bag completely healthy. "The short answer is, I don't know. All I know is, I'm unusually hard to kill. I can hold my breath for hours. I had a few problems on the *Franklin* only because I needed to breathe to talk to Capcom."

Everyone began talking at once. The names of doctors, scientists, and fraud-exposers were put forward. Edwin vanished behind a crowd of excited questioners. Carina stood up and came back to Rob. "You think there's any hope for a cup of tea?"

"I doubt it, Carina. I bet New York TV people mainline coffee. How are your high heels? I warned you to wear sneakers."

"You can't wear sneakers with a skirt and pantyhose. Didn't Julianne teach you anything? My feet are killing me. I wish she hadn't insisted we look respectable."

Rob loosened his necktie and agreed. But image was Jul's department. If she said that men in navy-blue sports coats and gray trousers conveyed a trustworthy appearance, he had to believe her. Certainly Carina looked conventional, though not much like herself, in a turquoise-blue coatdress and matching shoes.

Edwin waved for silence. "I'm willing to do another demo. Interested?"

Of course the answer was yes. Edwin took out his wallet and extracted two twenties. "Someone take this, and go to Bloomingdale's and buy a knife. A big carving knife or a hunting knife. It should be good and sharp and pointy, maybe about a foot long."

The most junior executive was sent on this errand. Bradley asked, "Why Bloomingdale's?"

"Oh, it doesn't matter," Edwin said, smiling. "Macy's would do. The point is that it be a brand-new ordinary knife—not a trick blade or anything."

While they waited for the knife, coffee appeared. Carina wrinkled her nose, but drank it. Producer Don Hewitt asked, "Edwin, how did you leave Kennedy Space Center? All sorts of loony ideas have been posited, but even NASA can't say."

"Or won't say," Steve Croft suggested.

"That question," Edwin said, "is the only question I will not answer. And I'm sure all of you are intelligent enough to see why."

"To protect the people who helped you, of course," Bradley said. "But those people aren't going to be able to hide their roles forever, Edwin."

Edwin smiled broadly, careful to not look at Rob. "You go right ahead and find them, Mr. Bradley. If anyone can do it, it's the American news media. Do the detective work, dig them out, persuade them to open up and tell you the whole story, and I promise to add my confirmation. It would be a pure pleasure, to express my gratitude in public." Rob could have punched him.

When the knife came, Edwin had another executive unwrap it while he took off his sports jacket. Underneath he wore a short-sleeved white shirt and a green bow tie. "Can I use your desk here? Maybe I'll pad it with this newspaper."

"Edwin," Bradley said, "is this going to be, uh, graphic?"

"You may not want to put it on prime-time TV," Edwin admitted. "But you'll see—it's way cool. I'd like somebody to hold my hand. No, not what you think, I mean down on the desk. And I'll hold my own elbow. This is why I had to bring Rob, Mr. Bradley. Carina absolutely refused to participate."

"I threatened to faint," Carina said robustly.

"Stay sitting, then. And do the timer. Okay, everybody ready?"

People gathered three-deep around Bradley's desk. Rob accepted the knife. He ran his thumb lightly along the edge and grimaced—not very sharp, and he had no sharpening steel. He and Edwin had discussed this stunt at the lake, but never tried it out. It was important to think correctly about this now, because if he didn't, even knowing what would happen, he would flinch and make a botch of it. Rob visualized a wood chisel in his hand, an innocuous work situation, and stabbed the knife as hard as he could into Edwin's right wrist, about two inches above his hand.

Several people screamed. Bradley, who had been holding the hand down, jerked back with a curse. Edwin turned a little green, but his voice was steady. "Rob, you're too strong. I think you've nailed me to the desk. Pull it out, will you?"

Feeling more than a little green himself, Rob gingerly rocked the blade free. It scraped gruesomely between the radius and ulna. He laid the dripping knife on the newspaper. Scarlet blood streamed from the punctures on the back and front of Edwin's forearm, smearing his shirt and pooling on the desk blotter. From her handbag Carina pulled out a dishtowel.

"You are out of your mind," someone exclaimed.

Edwin's eyes flashed, but he said, "No—watch this arm carefully. I give it five minutes. Carina, did you do the clock?"

Already the pain lines were relaxing out of his face. The arterial gush of blood slowed and then stopped. Carina passed the dishtowel over, and Edwin wiped the clotting gore off. The two-inch puncture wound was still visible, but shrinking fast. Edwin turned in his chair so people could cluster around and get a closer look. Behind him Rob said, "It's a pity it has to hurt, though. Otherwise it'd be the perfect demo."

"Aspirin wouldn't work on me, you think?"

"What you should learn is Lamaze," Rob suggested. "When Carina does the childbirth classes, pay real close attention."

In four minutes by the clock all that remained of the injury was a thin red line. "That should be gone by lunchtime," Edwin said. "Your desk is not very pretty, though, Mr. Bradley—sorry about that. And my shirt is ruined."

"It's a miracle!" somebody said.

"That's what Dan said when they opened up the *Franklin*!"

"Hot damn, we have the biggest story of the century!"

The noise of their excitement made Rob stagger. The office seemed far too crowded. Hard to believe this was only the beginning. If Edwin pulled this off, he'd be the most notorious man in America. Rob made his way through the jostling pandemonium to Carina. "Do you know Ed's shirt size?"

"Sixteen and a half, thirty-four. Are you going to get him a new one?"

"Yeah, it's getting to be too much for me in here."

"I wish I could come. But one of us should stay with Edwin."

"You can have the next turn." Rob made his escape into the fresher air of the outer office.

When he came back an hour later the atmosphere was still electric but much more purposeful. The entire floor buzzed like a beehive. A tight security had been set up, and he had to show an ID and sign in to enter.

Vast numbers of researchers had been brought on board. Edwin was being interviewed in relays. He was cheerful, though, and very glad to have a clean shirt. "They're going to take us to lunch, so I have to look decent," he said. "You ever been to Le Cirque? No? Then you'll enjoy it. This should be a blast, Rob. They're going to expose Pisspeep for the exploitative little bloodsuckers they are. With any luck, we can tidy up NASA and go to Mars with a clean slate. Those xeroxes are going to put some folks in jail." He retied his bow tie deftly, without needing a mirror.

For Rob, the only hurdle now was his own grilling. They had discussed and selected what would be told, and rehearsed it at leisure at the cabin under Julianne's exacting eye. When a pretty brunette researcher took charge of Rob, he knew he sounded perfectly natural. "Barbarossa just appeared at the cabin in West Virginia one afternoon last month. I think it was August fifth. He had no car, no vehicle. His wife Carina was vacationing with us. I think that's why he chose us over anyone else he knows." He told her about Ike, and the girlfriend, and the father, and the lake—all the easy, harmless stuff.

"And where did you first meet Dr. Barbarossa?"

More watchfully, Rob said, "We've been friends a good

few years now, since the nineties." In fact, he had first met Edwin only a couple blocks from here, in Central Park. But on principle, Rob had insisted they be vague about the date and location. He was thankful when the researcher lost interest in their history, and asked a question about the date of Edwin's arrival in West Virginia instead.

The TV network put them up in a palatial suite at the Plaza Hotel, but they didn't get to sleep until nearly midnight. Rob was worn out by the unaccustomed hustle of the news business and the mere hubbub of the city. He had spent an entire empty summer here once, as a homeless criminal. Now, clean and well-dressed, he felt impelled to dole out quarters to every panhandler on the street. He even quashed a crime, forcing a purse-snatcher to trip over the curbstone as he was pursued across Fifth Avenue by a cop. It was as if, here in Batman's Gotham City, hometown of the Fantastic Four, his old superhero ambitions stirred in their shallow grave.

But Edwin was in his element. He burst into Rob's room early the next morning, dressed in shorts and a tank top. "Would you rather visit the hotel gym, Rob? Or is a jog in Central Park more in your line?"

"I want to sleep," Rob moaned. He pulled the covers up over his head, and Edwin withdrew reproachfully.

By the time Rob was able to face the day, Edwin had returned, streaming with sweat. Carina asked, "Did anyone recognize you, dear?"

"The sunglasses still work fine. I jogged right around the reservoir—it was great! I love running in Central Park. Oh boy, breakfast! I ordered room service before I left." He sat down at the laden breakfast table and began lifting covers off plates.

Rob leaned blearily over his coffee, and groaned at the injustice of it. If *he* had run around the reservoir, Rob knew he wouldn't have been able to stomach a meal until noon. "Ed, in thirty years I'll be an old man, and you wouldn't dream of raking me up to exercise. But already now, I'm falling behind. Cut me some slack, okay?"

Edwin grinned. "Carina—am I *exhausting*?"

"Oh, I don't think so, dear," she said, her face sunny behind the big silver coffeepot as she poured. "You just have a high energy level. See if they can tell you your cholesterol count, okay? Steak and eggs is not a low-fat breakfast."

"What a terrifying pair you make!" Rob said. "Is that the agenda today? Fun with doctors?"

"Yep." Edwin buttered his toast lavishly. "Oh, and you remember how Jul told us never to use the word 'immortality,' ever again? I told Ed Bradley to name my condition, and they were going for 'Barbarossa Syndrome.' But I think I'll make it the 'Franklin Syndrome' instead—sort of as a memorial. It should be very interesting. I'm looking forward to getting really scientifically rigorous."

Rob shuddered. "Better you than me, Ed. You seem to have the tiger nicely by the tail. I think I'll push on home. I have a business to run."

"Oh, too bad—I was hoping you'd do your knife bit again for the cameras."

"Good gosh, can't the network find someone else to do it? New York City is full of violent cases."

"I believe your panache, the refinement of your stroke, was greatly admired. Maybe they can fly you back. There's no one else I'd rather have stab me."

His glance was so mischievous Rob had to laugh. "Oh, wait, one more thing. I picked up a souvenir for Jul yesterday, and I thought Carina would like one too." He passed a paper bag across the table to her.

She pulled out a pink T-shirt. "'My NEXT husband will be *normal*!' How perfect! Thank you!"

Edwin sputtered with laughter through a mouthful of steak. "Wear it today—I want to see what the producers will do."

.   .   .

For the season premiere of *60 Minutes* the Lewises threw a small family party. Rob's younger sister Angie flew in from Chicago, and Ike brought Tiffany, and Julianne's father Ralph Bogard drove up from Richmond. Rob had never met Tiffany before, and was a little startled to find she was half Ike's age. And should a pretty teenager dye her hair such a fake red? Even old Ralph rolled his eyes. "Jailbait," he whispered to Rob. "My son, the cradle-robber."

The small, shabby living room was crowded to the gills. Rob sat on the carpet with the kids, keeping them quiet with popcorn and juice. Already he could see that he was only going to get intermittent glimpses of the program. But he could look at the tape later. The network had kept a tight lid on their exclusive. But rumors had been running rampant, and it was common knowledge now that the entire show was about Edwin. "When are *you* on, Daddy?" Davey asked, one minute after the program began.

Rob shushed him. "Uncle Eddie's going first." Edwin was describing the *Franklin* disaster. Old news footage was flashing on the screen—the LLS, the *Franklin* itself, Pontipp and Li and Mahomet.

"She's not so cute, with that reddish hair," Tiffany said. "Edwin's like hunkalicious, though. Not just a stud—a star."

"I don't see it," Ike said. He gave the TV screen the lip-curling scowl which was supposed to make him look like Elvis.

"It's the dimples," Angie said, and all three women giggled.

"Girls are another species," Ike told Rob, who had to agree.

"Will you keep it down?" Ralph barked. "Gimme the remote, Rob. I'll turn the sound up."

When they moved on to the Franklin Syndrome, everyone was riveted. The producers had borrowed the hyperbaric chamber at the Rockfeller Medical Center. It was a massive metal vault large enough to roll a gurney into, and fitted with thick glass windows. Inside, Edwin sat comfortably with the Sunday crossword, a bobbing bunch of red and blue party balloons, and a cage containing a white mouse. As the air was pumped out and the pressure dropped, the balloons expanded. "The air inside them is pushing outwards," Ralph explained to the kids. "Watch, in a minute they'll pop. And that mouse, without anything to breathe, it's history." Edwin didn't look up at the balloon explosions, seemingly perplexed by his puzzle.

"And he's doing it in *pen*," Julianne noticed.

"I hate people like that," Ike said.

A number of important but dull scientists and doctors explained to Leslie Stahl exactly why what Edwin was doing was impossible. Julianne passed chips and salsa around, and Tiffany rejected beer in favor of vodka.

"Oh, look, Grandpa! There's Daddy," Annie cried. "About time!"

"A knife, coo-ull!" Davey said. "Can I have one for Christmas, Dad?"

"No. Remember this is just one of Uncle Eddie's tricks," Rob told the twins once more. "Daddy isn't really hurting his arm."

The producers had supplied a butcher-block table for the demonstration. Rob had demanded and gotten a decent carbon-steel knife, which he had whetted himself, off camera. There were many more towels, but otherwise everything was the same. The camera got a continuous shot of the wound's steady closure.

"That is weird," Ralph pronounced.

"Absolutely bizarro," Ike agreed. "Wonder what happens if you pump some assault fire into him."

Cold rage surged up abruptly in Rob's chest, but he was able to keep still and say nothing. With the contempt of an older sister, Julianne said, "Ike, you are such a bozo."

Tiffany clapped a hand to each cheek. "Eeeew, I've never seen anything so gross! Like, I can't believe you did that, Rob! It would make me, like, just *toss*!"

"My moment of fame," Rob said, with only a slight effort. After some commercials, Steve Croft went to Kennedy

Space Center and embarrassed many NASA and PSPIP offi-
cials on camera in the best TV newsmagazine style, grabbing
them in parking lots, tracking them into offices, bearding
them in lobbies. Dr. Nakamura was forced to look at Rob's
xeroxes and try to justify his course of treatment. The seg-
ment concluded with a short interview of Burton S. Rovilatt.
With 15 percent of PSPIP's shares, he was a majority stock-
holder and the logical spokesman.

The children got bored and went upstairs to play video
games. Freed from distractions, Rob paid close attention as
Rovilatt made his case. The billionaire was a good speaker,
with a flat Western twang and a sunburn under thick gray
hair. "In the 1980s, NASA was bloated," he said with
twinkly authority. "Everyone knows that. Technological
achievement went down and the price tag went up. Then,
when the crash came in '97 and the gravy train quit running,
why, we all still wanted a space program, but the country
couldn't afford it—you get me, Steve? You had this over-
weight porker of an agency with empty pockets.

"That's when PSPIP came in. We pumped nine billion private-sector dollars into the space effort, and reorganized the
agency to slim her down. And we did a damn good job. We
had to table the Mars mission, but we got us Independence
Moonbase, the first human settlement in space. How can you
beat that?"

Steve Croft cut in. "But Dr. Barbarossa's shocking expe-
riences don't sound like good managerial practice to me. It
appears that NASA found itself in a dicey situation with
Dr. Barbarossa's survival, and they leaped to the worst possible explanation. And then they tried to sweep the entire
mess under the rug. Dr. Barbarossa argues that the bottom
line and the image of the agency took precedence, not only
over a major scientific breakthrough, but over all human
decency."

The tycoon's dark eyes shone with steely sincerity. Rob
would have liked to peek into Rovilatt's mind. But working
his stunts on a TV image was impossible—the interview had

probably been taped days ago. "Steve, nothing shocked me more than hearing about Barbarossa's treatment. Those clinic doctors are loose cannons. I urge the Florida State Medical Board to pull their licenses to practice. And if Dr. Barbarossa wants to prosecute them for malpractice, I'll be rooting for him all the way."

"He can't say better than that," Julianne said.

"He couldn't say much else," Ralph noted.

"I don't know, Jul," Tiffany said critically. "D'you think that gray hair is, like, a toupee? It's so thick on top, like it's unreal."

"I'd dye it, myself," Angie said. "And I'd use sunscreen."

In the final third of the program, Edwin talked with Ed Bradley. Ike and Tiffany lost interest and went out into the backyard to neck on the swing. Edwin wore a blue sweater that Rob recognized immediately as Carina's handiwork. The studio stylists had trimmed his hair and combed gel through it, but Edwin must have absentmindedly run his fingers through it in his habitual gesture, since the effect was entirely rumpled and casual. His voice was intelligent and reflective, and his well-fleshed face glowed with health. The easy, boyish handsomeness, allied with an adult assurance, was irresistibly magnetic. Rob realized that Tiffany, of all people, had been right on the money: Edwin was going to take the country by storm.

"There's so much to be discovered, Mr. Bradley," Edwin was saying. "The *Franklin* Syndrome isn't magic, it can't really be defying physical laws as it appears to. If we—I speak as a scientist here—if we could get a handle on how the Syndrome works, the benefits to humanity could be beyond price."

"Surgeons sure wouldn't mind having your wound-closing trick on tap," Bradley agreed. "Or the Army."

"And how is it that the cells in my body don't keep on growing until I die of galloping cancer? A tremendous amount of research needs to be done."

"And you're willing to be—well, a guinea pig."

Edwin raised an eyebrow. "Doesn't that sound unattractive? I was thinking more of a partnership. I can't possibly do all the research myself. For one thing, I'm trained as a microbiologist, not as a research M.D. I'd be willing to participate in tests and so on, but I can't give one hundred percent of my time. I have my own work to do."

"So you envision a split: fifty-fifty, sixty-forty, something like that. A part-time guinea-pig position."

Edwin laughed. "And then there's Mars."

"You still want to go on the Mars mission?"

"At some point, I absolutely do. I'm the one who's supposed to find Martian nannobacteria, you know. That's how I got into the astronaut corps in the first place."

Bradley exhaled a long breath. "You're confident, I'll give you that! But tell me, Edwin—this research will cost a fortune. You're talking doctors, facilities, labs, equipment. Granted, the possibility of a fantastic return is there. Do you look for government funding?"

"Nobody looks for government funding these days, Mr. Bradley—don't you read the papers?"

Both men laughed. "So you'd be willing to participate in another private-sector investment program again."

Edwin ran a hand through his hair. "I think yes, given the proper safeguards. The concept is perfectly sound. It's just that the NASA-PSPIP partnership had problems in execution. But you learn from your mistakes, and go on."

Ralph sniffed. "He can't be so smart, if he's willing to stick his neck back in the noose again."

Rob didn't much care for the idea himself, but presumably, Ed knew what he was doing. Certainly there would be no lack of investors for research into immortality—or rather, the Franklin Syndrome. Watching the media vultures circle on TV brought home to Rob how lucky they'd been to have Julianne's PR-savvy counsel. Gilgamesh's immortality shimmered now with peril, a third rail that neither he nor Ed would dare refer to by its true name. "Ed's not going to have a dull time," Rob said. He felt rather than saw Julianne's curious gaze. "No, I don't regret a thing."

"Mind-reader!" She gave him a peck on the cheek as she got up. "Those two are too quiet up there. I'm going to put them to bed. You want another beer, Dad?"

"I'll get it for you, Ralph," Rob said.

Ike was already in the kitchen, raiding the refrigerator. "Oh, Rob," he said casually. "You know how they showed pictures of the lake cabin?"

Knowing what was coming, Rob smiled. "Yeah, didn't the dock show up great? I think two-by-sixes was the right choice."

A look of profound embarrassment spread over Ike's handsome weak face. "They had to get permission from Tiff's dad to film it, you know? And he found out, well, that you've been doing all these keen repairs."

"I discussed them with you, Ike," Rob reminded him. He wasn't going to help Ike with the confession at all.

"Well—the old man thought all this time that *I'd* been fixing the place up. A silly misunderstanding, huh? So if he calls you, will you tell him that, uh, that I helped you?" He gave Rob his best oily smile.

"I kind of suspected that was the way of it," Rob said, enjoying the situation. "What a parasite you are, Ike!" Ike ducked his head into the refrigerator and muttered something about Tiff liking him for himself. Rob leaned on the door and said, "I won't lie to the old guy for you, but if he calls, I won't do a separate deal and cut you out, how about that? You can still play the middleman—if he'll put up with you."

"The dock is fixed," Ike grumbled. "Why should he care who did it?" He made his escape, leaving the refrigerator door ajar. Rob took two beers out and elbowed it shut. With his hand-to-mouth existence and total amorality, Ike had always been the ideal candidate for blatant mental renovation. Rob could almost hear the case Edwin could make for intervention: the girls ungroped, the space freed up in drug-rehab programs, the petty scams not perpetrated, the minor rip-offs aborted. A judicious application of weirdness, and Ike might actually become a decent human being! Well, with any luck, the two men would never meet—Rob certainly intended never to make the introduction.

*T*heir schedules prevented the two men from meeting that autumn. Rob kept up with Edwin's affairs through e-mail and the odd phone call, and of course on the news. Edwin spent more than three weeks testifying before various House and Senate committees on space, science, and medicine. He was interviewed incessantly on TV, and profiled in every magazine from *People* to the *Journal of the American Medical Association.* He was nearly mobbed by excited scientists when he returned to his old office at NIH. A tidal wave of fascination with the Franklin syndrome and its implications roared through the world, and Edwin rode it with characteristic aplomb.

During the same season, Rob rebuilt nine wheelchair-access ramps for a garden-apartment complex in Burke, Virginia. He also erected two decks, surrounded a cottage with an arched gate and a picket fence, and fenced three acres of horse pasture out near Leesburg with post and rail. Julianne flew to Milan for a week to discuss Italian-designer fashion marketing, the twins started fourth grade, and Colin, having mastered sitting and crawling, was trying to stand up.

Edwin's fame even affected the home-improvement business. Rob was surprised—if anything, he would have thought homeowners would be less willing to hire a carpenter who had stabbed Dr. Edwin Barbarossa with a Sabatier carving knife on nationwide TV. But people were strange. The increased volume of his work proved it. The picket-fence woman, for example, had specifically demanded the guy with the knife.

Even Annie and Davey got some fallout. Rob looked out the front window one October afternoon after school and was jolted to see the twins holding court for a TV crew on the front lawn. He hurried out, Colin under his arm. "Kids, what about not talking to strangers, huh?"

"They're not molesters," Davey reasoned. "Molesters don't have sound trucks and minicams."

Rob herded them away from the cameras. "Gentlemen, if you pester these children again, I'll see you in court. . . . No, they are not news. They're minors. I specifically deny you permission to use their words or their images."

The news crew retreated, grumbling. Incorrigible, Annie called after them, "And my full name is Angela. A-N-G-E-L-A—spell it right!"

"They asked how Uncle Eddie got to the cabin," Davey told Rob. "I told them he had a Pocket Rocket, and they got all excited."

Rob had to laugh at that. Edwin had given that name to his new car, a butter-yellow Porsche Turbo convertible. He had mailed Davey a glossy poster of it, which Davey had pinned to the wall above his bed. In e-mail Rob had written,

Of all the impractical vehicles! Ed, you idiot—how will you ever install an infant seat into a two-passenger sports car?

Edwin had written in return:

Cross that bridge when we come to it. Did I tell you that
the sperm bank is making a fortune off of my old dona-
tions? Lord knows what nonsense they're telling the
mothers! I had to twist arms to get Carina onto their
waiting list. As for the car, I just couldn't resist it, Rob.
You know I'm a sucker for muscle metal. It has a 6-speed
manual transmission and a power convertible top—up or
down with the push of a button. And four-wheel drive!
You know how RARE a 4-w.d. sports car is? And, oh
man, when the dealer began cutting the price especially for
me! Occasionally there are real advantages to notoriety!

Just before the Thanksgiving recess Congress passed legislation to partially fund the Franklin Syndrome Research Institute. Political and economic realities also dictated another
PSPIP partnership. The new organization threw a huge party
in December to announce its arrival.

"I didn't know you could rent the Air and Space Museum
for a party," Julianne marveled as they walked up the steps.
"Do you suppose it was Edwin's idea?"

"I doubt if any of this is his idea. He'd rather spend the
money on test tubes." Rob's tuxedo had not become any
roomier under the arms in the last six months, and the dis-
comfort made him morose. "That's the problem with renting
out your soul like this. You have to accommodate other people. I think I have to get this jacket let out. I've gained too
much weight." He paused to look in through the soaring
glass wall. From the high ceiling hung historical airplanes:
the *Spirit of St. Louis*, the Wright brothers' biplane. The
enormous lobby below thronged with people in evening
clothes. Rob knew nobody except Edwin and Carina. "And
there's noplace to sit down," he observed.

"What an old misery you are!" Julianne tucked her hand

under his arm. "Come on, let's try and find the guest of honor. That'll help you break the ice."

They pushed through the revolving doors. Expertly, Julianne dove through the crush, collecting glasses of champagne for them on the way. Her new party dress was delightfully foolish, a flufffy short green thing from Milan that looked like a demented nylon pot-scrubber. Rob soon lost sight of her sparkly skirt in the crowd.

"Hey, hey! I recognize you!" A short man in glasses grabbed Rob's arm and nearly jerked the champagne down his starched shirtfront. "You're the friend with the knife!"

"Umm . . ." Even if he didn't know people, they all knew Rob. Why had he ever consented to the stabbing bit in the first place?

"Beth, you remember this guy!"

An equally short Asian woman in red sequins materialized before him and held out a heavily-ringed hand. "Mr. Lewis, is that right? I'm Dr. Beth Chang, one of the people who's going to find out what makes Edwin tick."

Rob stared at her, trying to hide his dismay. "Are you going to dissect him?"

She laughed. "Oh no! Edwin's a friend—I taught him in grad school. And he's a priceless resource. We'll treat him like a prince!"

"Except for the odd CAT scan here and blood sample there," the short man added, with ghoulish glee.

Rob relaxed. If Edwin's friends—a class of people that numbered in the thousands—were in on the research, he had nothing to fear. Another very young woman in a recycled pink bridesmaid's gown said, "Mr. Lewis, I'm a science historian, and plan to write Dr. Barbarossa's biography. Will you come to the university and tell me about the first manifestation of the Syndrome? I understand you were a witness at the climbing accident."

Rob chose his words with care. "Maybe someday, when I have time."

"Let me give you my card!"

Rob stuck it in his pocket, resolving to lose it as soon as he could. The crowd suddenly thinned around him, and it was possible to flex his elbows and draw a deep breath. Then he realized that people were letting someone through to meet him, a man who moved like a lion. His tuxedo fitted him perfectly. Under the thick gray hair his face was like a side of beef. "Burt Rovilatt," he introduced himself. "And I saw you on TV. Robertson Lewis, is it?"

"How do you do." Awkwardly Rob shook hands. He had not thought that a tycoon would have such an iron grip. Could he actually be testing Rob's strength? Carefully, Rob didn't smile. With his years of hammering and hefting power tools, his hands were easily the stronger. He squeezed, and Rovilatt's eyebrows rose a fraction.

"Will you have lunch with me one of these days, Mr. Lewis? I operate out of Chicago mostly, but I'm here a lot."

"What, are you having a *60 Minutes* reunion?"

Rovilatt chuckled. "That was fun, wasn't it? The expression on that doctor's face when the camera chased him into the john! I won't beat around the bush—I'm deeply interested in Dr. Barbarossa and his Syndrome, and I want to know more about him. This thing is the most exciting scientific phenomenon since the atom bomb."

Everyone listening nodded at this. Very rich men probably never heard a word of dissent, Rob decided. How did they ever learn anything new? Out of pure mischief he said, "Edwin's full of the most profound mysteries, that I've never fathomed."

"Like what?" The biographer groped in her handbag for a notebook, and Rovilatt's dark eyes gleamed with excitement.

"Oh, his venture into rock music, for instance," Rob said blithely. "I've only seen his green electric guitar once, and I've yet to hear the full story."

"Green electric guitar," the biographer muttered, writing it down.

Rovilatt said, "You've known him a long time, then. Since when?"

Fortunately, at that moment Carina pushed through the press with her usual uncanny speed. She wore creamy velvet, very short and sexy. "Rob, I've been looking all over for you. Come on! Excuse us, folks—Rob has to see the cake before it's cut."

She grabbed his hand and towed him away. "What cake?" Rob demanded.

"The only thing Edwin said he wanted for this wingding was dessert. You know how he is about food. And the caterers made him this thing—you won't believe it!"

Rob laughed out loud at the sight. The cake, a huge flat one, had the entire Moonbase sculpted on it in hard sugar. The craters were piped in white frosting, silvery candies outlined the solar arrays, and the badger was modeled in gumdrop candy. Matchbox Moon rovers and a toy landing shuttle were parked artistically here and there.

Edwin came forward to greet him, in a jazzy blue satin cummerbund and tie. He was glowing with conviviality, and held a triangular silver cake knife. "Have you ever seen anything more ridiculous? The lunar surface isn't white, for one thing."

"But light-gray icing would look terrible," Rob said.

"Listen, Rob, we must get together for a long talk. I have some ideas. Would lunch do you?"

"This is my second or third lunch invite already! Sure, I'm in."

A photographer with a camera on a tripod interrupted them. "Dr. Barbarossa, would you turn a little this way?"

"I want Julianne and Carina in this shot, too," Edwin said, beckoning.

Julianne came up and linked her arm through Rob's. "You mind being in a picture, Rob?" Carina asked him, with her old dazzling smile.

"On one condition, Ed," Rob said, grinning. "That you put away the knife. Never again am I appearing together with you and a naked blade." Laughing, Edwin stuck the cake knife into his tuxedo pocket.

. . .

By the new year Edwin's life had shaken down into shape, and it was possible to set up the lunch date. Rob drove to meet Edwin at his new office in the NIH complex in Bethesda, Maryland. The Franklin Syndrome Research Institute had been installed in its own building, one of the older brick ones that dated back to the 1970s. Security was tremendously tight, and no wonder. When Rob signed in and displayed a photo ID, a group of oddball demonstrators surged into the lobby and demanded to see "the Antichrist." Rob looked at the security guard. "Do they mean Dr. Barbarossa?"

The guard nodded, resigned. "All the loonies need an outlet, now that the millennium's gone by and the world didn't end. Let me just phone up, and then I'll escort you to the elevator."

Rob shoved his wallet into the back pocket of his jeans. A millennialist held a leaflet out to him, saying, "Barbarossa is the Great Beast, sent by Satan. Read Revelations 13:3 and you'll see that he has to die!"

Rob didn't take the leaflet. "I think you're mistaken. Dr. Barbarossa is one of the most Christian men I know."

The security guard gestured towards the elevator. "If you'll come this way, Mr. Lewis?"

The millennialist shouted after him, "You're one of *his* servants, a pawn of the Devil!"

"Does this happen often?" Rob asked, fascinated.

The guard punched the elevator button. "Oh, every week or so. It's not so bad now. We used to get a different gang morning and evening: animal rights, nuclear proliferation, religions, world peace, Pakistan reunification, groupies who wanted to have his baby—you name it."

"It must drive him nuts!"

"Actually, the ones who think he's Satan don't faze him so much. It's the ones who hail him as Jesus Christ returned, that really get his goat."

The lethargic elevator arrived at last, and Rob rode up to

the third floor. There was a pretty receptionist in the hall, and then a secretary keeping vigil over the inner door. Wealth and fame can alter the best of men, Rob reflected uneasily.

Then Edwin emerged, saying, "Rob! You came!"—and nothing had changed at all. Edwin's white lab coat still had too many pens in the breast pocket, and he had sat on or leaned against something that had left a vivid purple stain on the seat. His thick dark curls needed a trim again, and his eyes danced with humor. "Come on in. I'm just unpacking a little. Will you mind a cafeteria lunch?"

Edwin's office had big corner windows and an untidy desk. From a bookcase CD player came the mellow jazz trumpet of Wynton Marsalis. File boxes stood in the corners, and a framed poster from the Santa Fe Opera Company leaned against the wall, waiting to be hung. Edwin went through into a smaller connecting room crowded with the usual NIH research paraphernalia: refrigerators, microscopes, shelves of jars and bottles, file cabinets, slide carousels stacked high. Edwin began squeezing more three-ring binders onto the already crowded shelves. "If I could just get this organizational stuff over with, I could pick up my research again."

"Discontent, Ed? From the look of it, you have everything you asked for and more."

"Oh, I do—I've really lucked out. It's only a little hectic now that the funding's come through."

Unable to just stand and watch, Rob helped hand up notebooks. "And this is your own lab?"

"At the moment, it's all I need. Dr. Chang has the entire second floor of the building. Only one flight of steps down, and I'm a research subject instead of a researcher. All very convenient." With a clatter of glass Edwin shoved a row of dark brown jars aside. "And that brings me, Rob, to the favor I wanted to ask you."

Rob lifted the flaps of another moving box, revealing yet more notebooks. "Am I going to like it?"

"Just hear me out, bud. I was laying out in my head all the things I have to pursue, here at NIH and at NASA. Mars, the mitochondrial research, the Syndrome. And I realized a real important bet was being missed—you."

Rob covered his face with his hand. "Oh, no, Ed."

"I think I'm going to have to move these jars over by the sink. You know your weirdness is at least as unique as the Syndrome, Rob. And you're mortal. Once you die there'll be nothing of it left. What I want is to just accumulate data: bloodwork, tissue samples, MRIs, that kind of thing. And I'll file everything away, right here in this room, for fifty or sixty years, until you're sitting safely on a cloud in Heaven. All your notoriety will be posthumous, cross my heart."

"You're going to stick me with needles," Rob said, handing over jars.

Edwin climbed up on a chair to stack the jars on top of a cabinet. "What is it with you and needles? It won't take a lot out of your schedule, Rob. Maybe a couple mornings a year. We could take our time. In the interests of human knowledge—please?"

"As if you haven't got enough to keep you busy," Rob grumbled. "Okay, okay. I'm in."

Edwin grinned down at him, happy as a boy. "You don't know how important this is, bud. I'm really grateful. Oh—you haven't signed an organ-donor card, have you?"

"I should have, but now I guess I better not," Rob said with resignation. "And—wait, don't tell me—I should leave my body to you, you grave-robber. Maybe you know how I should word the clause in my will."

"Actually, they're medical forms. My secretary will send you the paperwork." Edwin hefted a jar in each hand. "Tell me you were reading my mind."

"Didn't have to. I could see your lust for my corpse in your face. Oh my gosh, but I do have a confession in that line to make. At that party in December—I told a bunch of people about your green electric guitar."

"My—what?" Edwin sat down on the lab counter and

stared into space. "Good grief, I haven't thought about that guitar in years! How'd you get hold of that factoid?"

"You should never ask me 'how,' Ed," Rob said, grinning. "The answer's always a weird one, you know that. I realized afterwards that you might not want your brief career as a rock musician to be known."

"A rock musician," Edwin hooted. "The piano's my instrument! But for my bit role in our high-school production of *Bye, Bye, Birdie*, I picked up a couple bass chords—they drafted every boy who could sing on-key. Gosh, that takes me back! Come on—this unpacking is endless, and I didn't bring you here to work. Let's go eat lunch, and then maybe I'll take you for a ride in the Pocket Rocket."

"Where to?" Rob asked, instantly suspicious.

"Well, over to the Blood Institute," Edwin admitted. "As long as you're down here—oh, don't look at me like that, Rob. Taking a blood sample doesn't really hurt!"

Edwin shucked off his lab coat, revealing a blue-and-green-striped rugby shirt and corduroys underneath. "Kendra, we're going to lunch," he told the secretary in passing. "Here's something you'll get a kick out of, Rob. I got a letter from a science-fiction publisher in New York City the other day. They've offered to publish *Severneth, Monarch of Mu*."

Rob guffawed. "Ed! You're joking! How'd they hear about it?"

Edwin pushed the elevator button and began to laugh too. "Every word I've ever written is of surpassing interest these days. The archives of the Moonbase bulletin board and e-mail have been in circulation for weeks. That must be how Betsy Wollheim got wind of the novel."

"There *is* no novel!" Rob protested, laughing. "It's nothing but a bunch of character ruminations."

"Ha ha! They're anxious to see the manuscript anyway, God help them!" Edwin spoke with difficulty. "I don't have the time to sit down and figure out how to keep Mu from sinking beneath the waves. Do you want to?"

"No way!" Both men were roaring with laughter now so hard they could barely stand up. The receptionist giggled too, and people on the other hallway looked out their doors and smiled. The sound of Edwin's mirth was always infectious.

"Oh, I can't stand waiting for this elevator anymore," Edwin gasped at last.

"Let's take the stairs," Rob agreed.

As he followed Rob down the stairs, Edwin said, "So I'll tell Kendra to tell 'em we're both too busy, okay?"

"You bet—I'm no writer!" Still chortling, Rob pushed open the door on the ground floor. As he stepped through, a thunderbolt exploded, filling the stairwell with noise and smoke.

A sledgehammer hit Edwin several times in the chest. Hot salty blood filled his mouth, and he tumbled down the last few steps to sprawl facedown on something warm and lumpy and wet. Through the shrill ringing in his ears, he could hear people screaming and running. And he could feel his system kicking into overdrive—severed arteries sealing over, smashed bones surging back together again. His chest seemed to be boiling. It hurt so much, it almost didn't hurt at all. The strain was tremendous, worse than he'd ever experienced before. But the Syndrome was saving his life.

Then Edwin saw what he had fallen onto. Rob lay facedown beneath him in a spreading crimson pool. Big blots of dark red widened and joined on the back of his plaid flannel shirt. "Rob!" Edwin shouted hoarsely. "Rob, quick, before you die! Take it back—you need it!" He seized Rob's shoulder and turned him over. But already he was too late. Rob's eyes were open, but blank. Blood poured from his nose and mouth, dripping from the short fair beard.

There were other people all around now, doctors and paramedics crowding the stairwell. Sirens howled steadily in the driveway outside. Edwin wrenched away from the grasping hands and shouting voices and found himself face-to-face with Dr. Beth Chang. She grabbed his arm. "Eddie, leave him! These are trained people. They'll save his life if it's possible!"

"I couldn't save him!" Edwin's shout of anguish was swallowed up in the cacophony.

"You have other things to do, Ed." Inexplicably, Burt Rovilatt was beside him, shepherding him back up the stair. "Do you know you took a bullet in the heart?"

"This is an opportunity we can't miss, Eddie. Don't you see?" Beth spread open the bloody rags of his rugby shirt. "You can't do anything here. But up in the lab—to get you within a couple minutes of a major trauma—oh, come, please come!"

Dazed, Edwin looked down at his blood-smeared chest. A sticky red hole the size of a teacup was punched in his breast-bone, but no blood flowed from it. "I'll keep on top of Lewis's condition for you," Rovilatt promised. "An update every fifteen minutes, whatever you want. But get a move on, man! A golden opportunity's slipping by!"

"Jesus," Edwin groaned. As they guided him up to the second floor he looked back from the turn of the stair. Rob was invisible behind the clustering paramedics. "Oh Jesus, have mercy."

It was past midnight before Edwin could get away. Carina was waiting for him. "I knew you'd want to go to the hospital ASAP," she said. "But you're in no shape to drive."

Edwin hugged her fiercely, burying his face in her hair. He would have denied it, but he was trembling with misery and exhaustion. "Oh, Carina, if it weren't for me—if I hadn't—"

"Hush, dear! It was *not* your fault. The police have the gunman in custody. He's a lunatic named Ferdinand Bowyer, one of those guys who thought you were the Antichrist. Put this on, it's cold outside." She held out his brown loden coat.

The night was achingly cold and crystal-clear. Edwin slumped into the passenger seat of the Porsche and stared unseeing through the sleek raked windshield, his hands deep in his coat pockets. "They have him at Georgetown University Hospital," Carina said as she drove. "Julianne has been there all afternoon. She left the kids with some friends. I made her eat some dinner before I came to get you. He was in the critical unit for a while, but then he began to hemorrhage and they had to rush him back to surgery again. It's—it's real bad, dear."

"I know." A man born lucky, Edwin knew about despair mainly from books. In novels, particularly the classics, the characters cursed God when their lives collapsed. Now he faced the reality himself, and it was crushing. He wanted to run down Wisconsin Avenue screaming that God wasn't being fair to Rob. Even the *Franklin* hadn't been like this. At least then he'd been able to help, to do things to try and save his friends. Here there was nothing, no action to take, no plans to make. The world lay empty and cold and dark all around.

In the small waiting room, Julianne sat hunched over a torn hanky. A towering and funereal flower arrangement on the Formica coffee table filled the air with sickening sweetness. She looked up as they came in, her tear-blotched face as bewildered and woebegone as a child's. Edwin sat on the sofa beside her and hugged her. "Jul, I am so terribly, terribly sorry."

"The doctors don't know what will happen, Edwin." Julianne's voice trembled. "He took five bullets through the stomach and left lung."

Edwin had heard this already, from Rovilatt's conscientious updates, but he let Julianne tell him again. She was crying now, in gulping sobs that tore at his heart. "Oh, Edwin! Isn't there anything you can *do*? He's dying!"

Carina sat down on her other side and held her hand. "Don't you think he would if he could?"

Edwin slid to one knee so he could look up into Julianne's bowed face. His entire heart was in his words. "I know what you're asking me, Jul. And the answer is, I'm helpless. Rob is the center of all this weird stuff. I'm just a passenger, holding the Syndrome for him. In the stairwell—I begged him to take it back again. To save himself. But it was too late. He was already in shock. Oh God . . ."

He was crying himself now, sobbing into her lap like a character in a Victorian novel. Her tears fell into his hair, or maybe they were Carina's, because they were all three breaking down, huddled together on the sofa.

Carina recovered first. She blew her nose and said, "But it's not hopeless, right? All you have to do is wait, Edwin—until he's conscious. Even partly conscious. As soon as he's able to do it, he takes the Syndrome back from you, and then he's safe."

"Oh, do you think so? Can it work that way?" Julianne asked, gulping.

"That's how it worked for me, Jul." He squeezed her hand. "He won't die. I swear it."

Carina stood up. "You've got to get some sleep, Julianne. We all do. Suppose I drive you back to Fairfax, and we'll come in again first thing in the morning."

She consulted Edwin with a glance. "I have to be at the lab bright and early tomorrow," he sighed.

"Well, you can take the Porsche home, and I'll drive Julianne in the van." She bent and pulled the card off the elaborate flower arrangement. " 'From Burt, with deepest sympathy.' If you want, I'll write all the thank-you notes for you—no reason you should have to cope with this."

"Thanks, Carina." Julianne looked utterly drained, like a slim blonde ghost.

Edwin helped her to her feet. "Everything will be fine," he promised her. With all his soul he willed the words to be true.

A week ago, if asked, Edwin would have named four or five people as his closest friends. Rob would have been among them, of course, but Edwin had the gift for friendship. Where Rob's affections ran deep and narrow, Edwin's were broad. He could enumerate a galaxy of friends: family, NASA, sports, NIH, college, church, school. Every sphere in his life had its dear ones.

Yet the threat of losing Rob was like a blow over the heart—as if the *Franklin* deaths had sensitized Edwin's emotional immune system so that now, in a similar crisis, the allergic reaction was overwhelming. How loathsome the idea was, of losing a friend—redolent of agony, acrid with despair! His own pain gave Edwin a queer new insight into Rob's value system. Living with Gilgamesh's legacy had fixed in Rob, marrow-deep and inarguable, the tenet that all change was painful and for the worse. Thus his instinctive conservatism, the death-grip devotion to the remaining foun-

dations of his life—and his helpless horror when those foundations were shaken, as when Julianne had suggested
divorce. He really was just like Mark Twain's cat. His feet
once set on rock, Rob was immovable. Which made it imper-
ative, Edwin mused, for Rob to choose his rocks wisely—and
for a friend to help him in that choice. Later, perhaps, when
all this was over.

In the meantime, Edwin did what he could to help. He
and Carina took charge of the twins for the long Martin
Luther King holiday weekend. They hauled the kids on a grueling round of zoos, game arcades, museums, and other juvenile amusements. It was all a dismal failure, and nobody
enjoyed it. "We're ten years old," Davey said with polite
contempt. "You can't lie to us." Annie merely swung wildly
between tears and obnoxiousness.

At the lab on Tuesday, everyone was still extremely
jumpy. The building security detail had been trebled, and
there was talk of erecting concrete anti-terrorist barriers in the
driveway. Edwin couldn't bear to scamper up and down the
stairs the way he used to. Ominous brown stains still lingered
on the linoleum stair treads, and the wallboard was cratered
and gashed where the police scientists had dug out the bullets. Edwin wasted what felt like hours waiting for the elevator.

He swung by the hospital after work. Rob was still in the
intensive-care unit, with a tube stuck down his throat into his
lungs. It was idle to ask if he had regained consciousness. It
wasn't strictly kosher for the doctors to talk to him about the
case, but Edwin's notoriety and charm persuaded the physi-
cian in charge to unbend a little.

"No, no, you won't see him coherent for some days yet,"
Dr. McCauley said, nodding his bald head so that his glasses
glittered. "He was a strong and healthy man before the incident. There's every hope that he'll bounce back."

Edwin went softly into the outer room and stared
through the glass into the ICU. Rob lay flat and still under a
sheet. IVs dripped into his arms, three or four on each side,

and in addition to the big mouth tube, another line was taped
to his nose. The little of his face that could be seen was gray-
white, like virgin newspaper. Monitors at the foot of the bed
showed his vital signs in trailing blips of green light.

"You're far away, Rob," Edwin said softly. He could
guess where Rob was. The doctor's optimism was unfounded.
Seven years ago, when the weirdness first descended on him,
Rob had fought a long battle to tame it. With raw will and
courage he had forged iron bonds to control a power suffi-
cient to dominate every brain on the planet. And he had suc-
ceeded so well he had achieved his dearest goal: an ordinary
suburban life with his family.

The bullets had done more than tear up Rob's body. They
had undermined a delicate yet steely mental fortification.
Rob must be deep within himself now, sleeplessly guarding
that inner furnace. He would have no energy to spare for his
battered physical self, and that augured a long and painful
recovery.

Sadly Edwin wondered what would happen if Rob died.
It was only an assumption that the weirdness would die with
him. Nobody knew what would actually happen. What if it
didn't? In his gloom, Edwin imagined the parcel of titanic
power wandering around loose. Would everyone in the
greater Washington area go mad? Or would the nearest doctor or nurse suddenly get the entire lump of weirdness
dumped on them? Seven years ago Rob had come within a
whisker of losing his sanity. "Come back soon, bud," Edwin
begged, suddenly frightened.

When Edwin came in on Wednesday morning, Kendra
had a message for him. "Mr. Rovilatt wants to drop by
sometime today. Maybe after lunch. He said he'd call back."

"I'm going to be busy," Edwin said absently. "Today's
the first day since—since Friday, to get any work done." He
forgot all about it. Two candidates for the lab-assistant job
arrived to be interviewed, and he needed several uninter-
rupted hours to set up a series of bacterial cultures.

As a result, when Rovilatt turned up around four,

Edwin's surprise was genuine. "What are you doing here, Burt? You seem to have taken up residence."

"Just keeping an eye on my investments, Ed, like a prudent man. You got a couple minutes?"

"Sure. Come sit down in the office, it's more comfortable. I'll make us some coffee." The stereo was set up to play whenever anyone was in the room, so as they came in Gershwin's piano rendition of *Rhapsody in Blue* flowed like drops from a diamond waterfall. Rovilatt took an armchair. Edwin ran water into his electric kettle and scooped fresh-ground coffee into the press's glass cylinder. "What's on your mind, Burt?"

"D'you read your own news, Ed? All the stories and articles they do about you and the Franklin Syndrome?"

"Hardly ever," Edwin confessed. "I just don't have time. Carina tells me if there's anything I really ought to see."

Rovilatt's black eyebrows knitted in a brief frown of disappointment. "Then you might not have seen the op-ed piece of mine that appeared in the *Chicago Tribune* last fall, when the funding legislation was going through."

"Can't say I did."

"I wrote that this Franklin Syndrome was the most significant thing to hit the human race since the nuke."

The kettle gave a preliminary toot and mutter. "I've heard of it," Edwin said. "Do you like French press coffee?" He poured the boiling water over the grounds in the press.

"I'll try a cup. That's why I bought in, Ed. I want a piece of the most important thing since nukes."

Edwin stood by the table with his hands in the pockets of his lab coat, waiting for the coffee to infuse. "I don't like to think of it as a 'piece,' " he said. This conversation didn't seem very important. "That attitude was really cramping on Moonbase."

"It's a fact," Rovilatt said flatly. "Live with it. God knows you live on it right enough."

Edwin raised an eyebrow. "Is that what you came to say, Burt?"

"No. What I want, Ed, is for you to play straight with me. I hold the maximum allowable percentage of the Institute's PSPIP. I think I deserve the inside dope."

"I don't understand you." Edwin pushed the plunger steadily down through the glass cylinder, forcing the coffee grounds to the bottom. He poured two mugs, set one by Rovilatt's elbow, and returned to his own chair. "What exactly are you trying to ask me?"

"You're a slippery one, Barbarossa. But I think I got you this time. Listen to this."

He took out a pocket tape recorder and pressed the play button, laying the small machine on the desk. With mounting alarm Edwin listened to his own voice, tinny and small: *". . . I'm helpless. Rob is the center of all this weird stuff. I'm just a passenger, holding the Syndrome for him. In the stairwell—I begged him to take it back again. To save himself. But it was too late. He was already in shock. Oh God . . ."* His sob sounded like a flaw in the tape.

Rovilatt pushed STOP. "Okay," he said. "Tell me about it."

Edwin stared at him over his steaming coffee mug. "The flowers. That monster sympathy bouquet. You had it wired for sound."

"You've never been stupid, Ed, I'll give you that." Rovilatt sipped his coffee. "Actually, it was what you said on the staircase that inspired me to eavesdrop. You yelling at Lewis to take it back."

Edwin set down his untasted coffee. "Of all the dirty, low-down tricks!"

Rovilatt's smile was like a slap across the face. "Is it as low-down as defrauding the U.S. Government, Ed? As dirty as obtaining PSPIP monies under false pretenses? You knew this guy Lewis was central to the Syndrome. And you didn't say damn-all."

Edwin could feel his face flushing red. "I kept quiet because Rob asked me to. But I can fix it. Nobody's calling me a fraud! Let's go downstairs right now, and I'll tell Dr. Chang all about it." He stood up, his fists clenched. Rob would just have to understand, when he got out of intensive care. The whole situation had broken wide open.

"No, Ed. Sit." Rovilatt pointed at the desk chair. "I mean it—sit down. Drink your coffee while it's hot. We're not done yet."

Edwin hesitated, and then sat. "What do you want?" he demanded through clenched teeth.

"I think I'm getting it." The dark eyes in the sunburned face measured him like calipers. "You and Lewis have a nice, tight little twosome going, shuffling these mysterious powers around like marked cards. Now you're a threesome. You deal me in."

Edwin was so horrified, he was glad he was sitting down. With a tremendous effort he kept his face bland, his tone casual. "No can do, Burt. You heard it on the tape—Rob's the dealer. And he's in critical condition. I can't do a thing for you."

Rovilatt swallowed coffee. "Either he'll live, or die. If he lives, we'll all three of us talk. If he dies—well, I still have you by the short hairs. You haven't told me everything yet, have you, Ed? But you will."

"I think I'd rather deal with Dr. Chang."

"Tell her you can pop the Syndrome on and off like a pair of cheap sunglasses? That could make the whole *Franklin* thing look pretty ugly. You strangle three astronauts with your bare hands, and then your magical buddy Rob fits you up with immortality as an alibi."

Edwin could hardly think coherently anymore, but that one word penetrated. "What did you call it?"

"Immortality. That's what *you* called it, Ed. When you spilled your guts down at KSC last summer."

"That's right! You were there!"

"And I believed you, Ed. I told you that."

"And it was the NASA PSPIP who stuck me in that clinic," Edwin said, his mind racing. "You knew I wasn't insane. You knew I was telling the exact truth. You were behind it. What the hell were you at?"

Rovilatt smiled at him. "You were pretty smart to start calling it the 'Franklin Syndrome.' People hear the word 'immortality,' they get excited. I did. That's what I want, Ed—it's perfectly simple. I want to live forever. A prize like that is worth playing hardball for. The clinic was my idea. I would've kept you on ice in Florida until my tame lab figured you out. But you wiggled out and went public. So I cut the clinic boys loose, hung on, stuck close to you, bought in again. And it's paid off. You give me a piece now, and I'll keep quiet and be your best buddy. Forever."

"Forever." Transfixed, Edwin stared across the desk at him. He still had the occasional nightmare about that clinic. And Rovilatt had deliberately put him there on the off chance of living forever. None better, Edwin knew the decades of research the Institute would have to do. You didn't unravel a major biomedical puzzle all in a minute. How long would he have been a prisoner in Florida? "You evil bastard!"

"Talk nice, Ed. You're in no position to get snippy." He set his empty cup on the desk and stood up, dusting the knees of his pants. "Now, I have only one thing for you to do, until Lewis gets on the ball again. I don't want you two getting together, maybe cooking up another slick scheme. So you stay away from that hospital until we can make a nice sick visit together."

"No way!" Edwin said hotly. "You are not telling me what to do!"

"I can enforce it, Ed." The flat Western twang was faintly menacing. "I sit on the Georgetown Hospital board, and I've passed the word. The doctors won't let you in."

"I don't believe this!"

"Live with it, Ed. What I say, goes. Now you be good, and I'll be in touch. Thanks for the coffee." He strolled out like a well-fed leopard, not looking back.

Edwin sat numbly at his desk for a minute, his hands curved around his cooling coffee mug. A fly newly caught in the spider's subtle web must feel like this—stunned. He could scarcely imagine the work, the forethought, the serpentine cunning necessary to entrap a person like this. Rob could, but Rob had that sort of mind. Edwin could only marvel, helpless.

But this was close to self-pity, an emotion Edwin had no truck with. "Entirely contrary to PSPIP policy," he said aloud. He jumped to his feet and thrust his arms into his coat. Obviously the thing to do was to defy Rovilatt immediately and go see Rob at the hospital. And if Rob had regained consciousness, then everything would be all right. The one indisputable bright spot in this mess was that Rovilatt didn't know the extent of Rob's power. He hadn't the vaguest inkling he was pulling a tiger's tail.

It was great to climb into the yellow Porsche and zoom down Wisconsin Avenue into the District. The rich leather atmosphere of the interior and the sleek businesslike cockpit could only boost his confidence. Rush hour was at its peak. The winter night had already descended, and the streets were treacherous with new-fallen sleet. But Edwin pushed it, slipping from lane to lane and powering effortlessly past slower cars. What was the point of having six cylinders, and 270 horses under the hood, and four-wheel drive, if you didn't use them?

At the hospital he hurried to the ICU, brushing by the nurses' station. "Dr. Barbarossa?" the nurse called as he passed.

"Just dropping in on Rob Lewis," he said.

"I'm sorry, sir—no visitors."

Edwin held on to his temper. "I visited him only yesterday. What's changed?"

"Let me call the doctor, all right?"

Dr. McCauley arrived looking flustered. "I'll be blunt with you, Dr. Barbarossa. It's as much as my job's worth to let you in."

"But why?" Edwin almost shouted.

"There's been a suggestion that the Lewis family plans to file suit against you, for reckless endangerment. If that's so, then you can meet Lewis at your own place and time, but not here. The hospital can't get drawn into a legal imbroglio, you understand."

"The Lewis family? You mean Julianne Lewis? This is nonsense. We're friends!"

Dr. McCauley took off his glasses and polished them on a crumpled hanky. "It won't be an issue much longer anyway."

Edwin's heart seemed to jerk to a stop in his chest. "What do you mean?"

"His respiratory distress has taken a turn for the worse in the last few hours. We've just phoned his wife."

"Then you *have* to let me in! Before it's too late!"

Belatedly Edwin heard his own voice rising in a shout. The doctor recoiled, but his voice was stern. "Dr. Barbarossa, if you don't settle down, I'm calling security. You aren't a member of the family. The hospital is fully within its rights."

Sick with frustration, Edwin flung himself down in a vinyl armchair in the TV area and covered his eyes with his hands. He had no idea Rovilatt's power extended so far. Was this going to be the end—Rob dying down the hall, while he sat out here holding the pearl of immortality? Was there any other course of action open to him? He clutched his forehead, forcing his reeling mind to think calmly, rationally. There had to be something. All of his training, his entire professional experience, said so. Always, there is a solution.

Only one possibility came to him—a long shot. Rob was a private man, and he meticulously respected other people's privacy. He didn't often trawl around in other heads. But he could easily do so. If Edwin called to him, mentally, it was possible that Rob could hear the call. In theory. If he wasn't too deep in coma. If he wasn't already dead.

There was no time to dredge up any other ideas. Edwin shifted his seat to the sofa, so he could face towards the ICU ward, and closed his eyes. He had never done this before. He had no idea how to go about it. Even in close contact, touching Rob, perhaps—he remembered how the power was linked to touch—it would be a questionable exercise. Did the inverse-square law apply to the weirdness? Two rooms away might well be an insuperable distance. He visualized it as e-mail, a message squirting from one computer to another: Rob! Rob, talk to me!

It was like shouting into a void. Or like launching a space shuttle, a prodigal expenditure of fuel to claw free of gravity. He didn't know whether anything was getting through, whether Rob was listening, or even able to hear. After ten minutes of concentrated voiceless calling Edwin gave it up, defeated. He could have wept. He slumped in despair on the clammy vinyl sofa, staring at the evening news reeling by on the TV without seeing it.

"Excuse me." A teenager in a hospital volunteer uniform bent to speak to him. "Are you Dr. Edwin Barbarossa?"

"Yes, I am," Edwin said warily. A groupie—just the way to top off a disastrous day!

She had dark red hair, a rather horsey long face, and a fearless brown-eyed gaze. "You probably don't remember me. But I remember you from before you were famous. I'm Janey Phillipson."

"Pastor Phillipson's daughter! Gosh, I'm glad to see you!" He shook her hand, his heart already lifting. Any friendly face was a comfort. "How's your family? And everyone at the old church?"

"Same as ever. I'm real sorry about your friend in the ICU. I saw you were praying for him. Would you like some help?"

Edwin drew in a deep grateful breath. "More than anything in the world. You're a godsend, Janey. Have a sit—let's do it."

She sat in the armchair and shyly joined hands with him. Edwin closed his eyes again. Prayer was not like space shuttles. There was no struggle to shove the words out and up into space. Prayer was like a helium balloon. You let it go, and the message went up of itself. Janey murmured something inaudible about healing the sick. Edwin prayed aloud, but softly: "Lord God, have mercy on Rob. Rally his body's strength. Call him back from death. Lord, we've run through every hope but you. Show your power, save him, please . . ."

It was an inexpressible relief to hand the burden off to God. The tight knot in his middle loosened. He relaxed into a sense of being supported and enfolded, like lying back in a hammock. Everything was under control, whatever happened to Rob, whatever craziness came down with Rovilatt. That confidence and security was part of the furniture of his life. Edwin had moved in it for as long as he could remember, the way a fish swims in the river, its home.

He hung for a long moment, balanced in peace, and then something small and foreign and entirely mundane intruded—like a baseball falling into his hammock. With a start Edwin recognized it. It was Rob's voice, very small but clear: "Oh my gosh, Ed—don't say I'm so bad off I have to be prayed for . . ."

"Rob! Rob!" A frantic mental shout. "Rob, take the pearl, now! You have to have it! You're going into respiratory arrest!"

There was no reply. Stunned, Edwin opened his eyes and met Janey's awed brown stare. "Did you hear that?" she said.

"Hear what?" Oh, great, he thought. The poor girl got Rob's mental message.

"It was Jesus," she said with complete confidence. "He said your friend was going to get well."

Edwin's mouth opened in surprise. "But that's not what I—" Oblivion surged up and over him from behind, toppling him like a cut tree. As he bounced off the coffee table and hit the floor, he dimly heard Janey's shriek. Then nothing.

He came to himself and looked up at a circle of awestruck and frightened faces. Dr. McCauley knelt beside him, gaping like a hooked trout and holding a bloodstained gauze pad. "You fainted," he said breathlessly. "You hit your head on the corner of the coffee table. And the cut closed up. Right under my hand."

A watching doctor said, "That was so creepy. The creepiest thing I've seen in my entire life."

Edwin knew he couldn't have been unconscious long, a couple minutes at the most—Peter Jennings was still doing the evening news. He sat up. Janey said, "We were saying a prayer. He wasn't doing anything." Her face was the color of skim milk, pinched with terror.

"Nothing to do with you," Edwin said, dizzy. "Don't know why it happened."

"Don't try to stand yet," Dr. McCauley warned. "Maybe a glass of water—"

But Edwin brushed his hand aside. A familiar ash-blonde head was passing the nurses' station. "Julianne!" he yelled.

"Edwin?" She wore a smart blue plaid business suit, and must have come straight from work. "Oh, I might have known you'd come. I'm so glad!"

"Jul, they said you don't want me in the ICU!"

"What?" The misery evaporated from Julianne's face, replaced by anger. "What is this? He's been visiting all week!"

Edwin stepped back, very glad to let her take the ball. It was funny how Rob, the gentlest guy in the world, had married this Valkyrie. Edwin would never have dared to cross Julianne himself. He watched appreciatively as the miserable Dr. McCauley was blasted out of his lawsuit position and forced to retreat behind the shelter of nameless hospital regulations. "It's as much as my job is worth," he pleaded again.

"I don't give a tinker's damn about your job," Julianne raged. "You won't have it long if I have anything to do with it! My husband's dying, and you're wasting time on petty hospital regulations instead of saving his life! Edwin, where are you?"

"Right here." Hastily he stepped forward.

She linked her arm tightly through his. "I'm prostrate with grief," she announced in a voice of ringing steel. "I need the moral support of a family friend. Who's going to stop me?" The onlookers had long since beaten a strategic retreat.

Dr. McCauley only mopped his damp bald forehead. "Right." Julianne surveyed the field of battle. "Let's go in, Edwin."

"You are a delight, Jul." Edwin patted her hand. "Rob is a lucky man."

Her face crumpled a little. "Oh, if only that were true, Edwin! He was so sure he'd never get hurt . . ."

Edwin couldn't help grinning like a fool. In a flash of pure inspiration, he knew what that mysterious faint of his meant. Rob must have borrowed the pearl during that time! "I'm certain he's okay, Jul. Absolutely certain."

They went in through the outer room with its glass window and past the double doors, right to Rob's bedside. The nurses had cranked the bed up so he lay in a half-sitting position. His eyes were closed and his face was still obscured by tubes and tape. But his color was better, and when Julianne held his hand, the fingers moved in her grasp. Edwin surveyed the monitors. Everything looked stable enough, certainly not so bad as to call for notifying relatives. He pushed the call button, and when the ICU nurse came in he said, "Tell me more about his respiratory distress. His breathing looks okay to me."

The nurse took one look at the monitors. "Let me call the doctor!"

After an examination, the unhappy Dr. McCauley said to Julianne, "Sometimes these rallies will occur. Medicine is an art, you know, not a science. If he can build on this advance . . ."

Edwin didn't listen to these platitudes any more. He didn't dare mention the pearl to Julianne. Even here in intensive care, Rovilatt might have bugged the room. His tentacles extended everywhere. And Edwin couldn't talk to Rob while he was still so sick. But now the corner was turned, it was only a matter of time. He could have waltzed around the room, he was so happy.

He patted Rob's motionless arm, careful of the shunts. No mental contact, but it wasn't necessary now. Loudly, for the listening bug, he said, "You're going to be okay, bud. Guaranteed. We got the word from Jesus Himself, that you'll recover fine." And let Rovilatt try to get a corner on Him, Edwin thought with triumph.

*T*he following day, Carina left for a long-scheduled archaeological conference in Mexico. It was still dark when Edwin drove her to the gleaming new terminal at Reagan National Airport to catch her six A.M. flight. He had arrived home last night too late to do more than collapse into bed, and now it seemed unkind to burden her with the whole Rovilatt crisis. She'd be gone for two weeks, and in that time a lot of things—please, God!—might change.

He helped her drag her bags out of the Porsche's vestigial front trunk. "Have a wonderful time, darling." He kissed her, and kissed her again more urgently, sliding his hands around her warm waist inside her leather coat. Wiser than he, his body was suddenly famished for the security of her love. He wanted to drag her behind the curbside baggage check and possess her, right now.

She laughed up at him. "Why didn't you do this last

night? Now you'll have to save it for a couple weeks until Boston."

"There's something to look forward to," he said. The words were hoarse with desire. He could have kissed her forever. He lifted her mouth to his own again, but a shrill wolf-whistle came from a taxi driver, and the shuttle bus behind the Porsche tooted its horn. "Damn it. I love you."

"And I love you. Oh, you better get going. That guy's going to burst a blood vessel."

He drove straight to NIH to get an early start on the day. At this hour there was little in-town traffic, and it was worthwhile to cut through northwest D.C. Until Rob was well enough to intervene, there was nothing to be done about Burt Rovilatt. Edwin's strategy now was to lie low, avoid the man, and wait.

At eight A.M. his phone rang. Kendra didn't come in until eight-thirty, and Edwin was busy with his centrifuge. But it seemed silly to let the voice-mail system handle the call. He picked up the lab extension. "Barbarossa here."

"Ed? 'S me, Burt."

Edwin's first impulse was to drop the receiver into the sink. "I have nothing to say to you, Burt."

"Well, I got things to say to you. I was thinking lunch, that's my meal."

"No thanks, Burt." He wouldn't stoop to lie about a previous lunch date.

"Now don't be that way, Ed. You want me to point out I'm not asking you, I'm telling you? I have us a reservation at this restaurant, Red Sage, all the way downtown. A car'll pick you up at noon sharp. See you then."

Deprived of speech, Edwin held the receiver as Rovilatt hung up. What was the point of this charade? Surely Burt had other important people he could lunch with. Edwin couldn't imagine sitting across a table from the man for an hour or two. What on earth would they talk about: blackmail? murder?

Still, Edwin was downstairs at noon. If the car was even

five minutes late he planned to cry off, but right on time a gleaming black limousine pulled up in front. Reluctantly he got in and was whisked downtown to 14th and F Streets. Red Sage had been the height of culinary fashion ten years ago and was now slightly gone by. It was now a place to see and be seen, rather than to eat decent Tex-Mex cooking.

Edwin gazed around at the over-the-top Southwestern decor with distaste. The maître d' recognized him immediately, and ushered him down the rustic stairs. Rovilatt smiled broadly at him as Edwin came into the main dining room, and waved a lean hand. He sat at the best and most visible table, in a curving central nook of fake adobe surmounted by pseudo lodgepoles. His dark gray hair was impeccably combed, and he wore a custom-made gray wool suit with a red-striped tie. Edwin realized he was underdressed in the cords and turtleneck he usually favored for winter wear. At least he'd thought to change his lab coat for a tweed jacket. He looked like what he was—a scientist.

"Have a margarita, Ed," Rovilatt greeted him. "They do them good here." He licked the salt off a green plastic swizzle stick shaped like a rattlesnake.

"Sorry, no alcohol for me today. They're running some blood-sugar tests on me later. In fact, I have to be back by two-thirty." Edwin had gone to some trouble to set that test up. He did not want to be trapped here all afternoon.

"No problem—order what you like."

Edwin busied himself with the menu, feeling very ill at ease. It was bizarre sitting here in a plush restaurant, sharing a meal with Burt. This was not how you were supposed to interact with someone who had held you prisoner and dosed you with drugs. Aping friendship like this was horribly jarring. He ordered his lunch at random, the first item on the lunch menu: a roasted red chile–pecan quail stuffed with barley. What could he possibly say or do, once the waiter finished consulting with Burt over the fat leatherbound volume that was the wine list?

". . . a saddlebag undertone you'll find attractive," the waiter was saying, and Burt nodded his approval.

For a dreadful plunging moment Edwin faced Burt across the empty pink tablecloth. "What do you want, Burt?"

"I want you to relax," Rovilatt said genially. "You look like a cat on a hot stove."

"How can I—" Edwin broke it off as a woman approached the table. She looked vaguely familiar, a dark, middle-aged lawyerish type in a red skirt suit and big pearl earrings.

"Hello, Burt, how are you? Is this Dr. Edwin Barbarossa? I had to come over and introduce myself, Doctor. I'm Congresswoman Connie Morella, and I believe you've just moved into my district."

"You know, I think so!" Edwin tried to keep the relief and delight out of his voice. "My wife and I bought a condo over near Glen Echo last month."

"Then you're a constituent—I'm thrilled! Would you care to attend a Republican Party fund-raiser? I'll have my people send you tickets . . ."

Edwin didn't often remember he was famous. Now his notoriety became a refuge of sorts. Every mover and shaker dining here today came over to say a word—people he'd testified for on the Hill, Cabinet members who'd seen him on TV, a *Post* columnist angling for an interview. Usually a little of this stroking went a long way for Edwin, but today he was effusive, more talkative than ever. With any luck he wouldn't have to say a word to Rovilatt until dessert.

The meal service was so slow, and so much time was taken up with networking, that Edwin didn't even get to dessert. "Gosh, look at the time," he said cheerfully to his host. "I have to run. Thank you so much for the hospitality. I love Tex-Mex food." *Real* Tex-Mex, he silently amended.

"We'll do it again sometime soon," Rovilatt said. He took a bite of his entrée—steak tartare formed into a cactus shape on the plate. His cordial tone didn't alter as he added, "I heard you went and visited Lewis anyway, Ed. You'll pay for that little defiance." Still the square red face kept its pleasant public countenance. In the grating dissonance between words and look, Edwin felt the enmeshing spider silk again. He muttered something incoherent and made his escape, running up the curving staircase to 14th Street.

When Carina was out of town there was no reason to keep a schedule. Edwin kept busy all day at the lab on Saturday, and spent a convivial evening at a potluck supper at Pastor Phillipson's church.

He didn't dare rock the boat by trying to visit Rob again. There was no point, until Rob could actually talk and think. Instead, Edwin kept up on his condition through Julianne, phoning her once a day. "He's out of intensive care, but not really himself yet," she reported on Sunday after lunch. "I mean, to talk to, because he's so weak. But they've upgraded his condition to fair, did I tell you? So he's making progress. And he's off the ventilator, and I'm bringing the kids out to visit him this afternoon for the first time."

"There's no better medicine for him," Edwin said. He wondered if his line was bugged. He was getting as paranoid as Rob. "Give him my regards and tell him I want to talk as soon as he's up to it. Do you have an idea when that might be?"

"I don't know, Edwin. This coming week, maybe. He's better every day now."

"Thank God for that!" The weather seemed to be closing in, so after hanging up, Edwin climbed into a warm-up suit and went out for a run. Glen Echo was one of the most pleasant suburbs in Maryland, right on the Potomac River. On the C & O canal path he could jog for miles on a smooth level trail, with the turbulent river on one side and the quiet dark canal on the other. He had just come through the condo lobby onto the sidewalk when someone called, "Hey, Ed!"

With a sinking heart, Edwin recognized the long black limo pulled up at the curb. Burt Rovilatt powered the rear window all the way down. "I gave you a call this morning, but you were out."

"At church," Edwin muttered.

"I thought we might play some tennis. I got a membership at a club with indoor courts in Chevy Chase. Go up and
get your racket, and a change of clothes."

"I don't play."

"Now, I'm warning you, Ed," Rovilatt said pleasantly.
"Your slippery stuff doesn't work with me. I know you play
tennis. I've seen the photograph of you in the school paper,
when you played for MIT in 1980."

Goaded beyond endurance, Edwin snapped, "What the
hell are you at, checking up on me?"

Burt's square sunburned face split in a smile. "I have a file
on you a foot thick, Ed. Now I know where to dig, I'm going
to know you inside and out before I'm done, and Rob Lewis,
too. Knowledge is power, you know that. Now, you're
dressed for exercise, so let's exercise. Go up and get your
racket."

Defiant words boiled up in Edwin's chest. But he clenched
his teeth on them. Defiance meant exposure, not for himself,
but for Rob. There was still hope of saving the situation, if he
could just keep Rovilatt placated for a couple more days.
Surely Rob would recover enough to intervene, soon! But in
the meantime, Burt had him in his power and was going to
rub his nose in it. There was no help for that. And it's nothing but a tennis game, Edwin told himself. He drew in a deep
breath, and went upstairs to get his racket.

The exclusive sports club near Chevy Chase Circle was so
quietly and discreetly luxurious, Burt's membership must
have cost a mint. Its two dozen indoor courts were separated
by canvas-and-net curtains, and furnished with bottled water
from Europe. Rovilatt was a hotshot with a racket. Though
he was at least fifty, he was in great condition, wiry-slim and
limitlessly enduring. Edwin had an edge on strength and
speed, but he was rusty, not having played tennis since his
return from space. He lost two sets, 2–6 and 4–6, before getting it together and wringing victory out of the last three,
6–4, 7–5, and 6–4.

Edwin's initial tension vanished in the pleasure of long

rallies and powerhouse strokes. Rovilatt was exactly the type of tennis partner he enjoyed playing with—energetic and physical, expert enough so that each set was a challenge. For Edwin, sports were more than mere opportunities for exercise. They were an instinctive arena for relationships. Friendship, to Edwin, meant doing things together, the excitement of activity and achievement flowing naturally into bonding and companionship. It seemed entirely normal afterwards in the plush locker room to grin at Burt and say, "Good game!"

"And you call yourself rusty." Rovilatt wiped the sweat off his lean neck and arms. "Next time you'll trash me. We should play doubles instead. Probably we'd steamroller the opposition."

Showered and changed, when he got back in the limo, Edwin was a little disconcerted to see they were driving into town. "Thought we'd swing by my place," Rovilatt said. "Maybe have a drink."

"I'd rather not—I'm not much of a drinker."

Rovilatt's smile was suddenly edged with cynicism. "I happen to know you don't hew to the Baptist upbringing any more, Ed. Wasn't that place you went to this morning a Lutheran church?"

"I'm not picky about denominations, and Pastor Phillipson is an old friend. And alcohol has no effect on me, so I don't waste it." Edwin spoke lightly, but the reminder that he was closely watched was disturbing. The limo halted at a light, and for a moment the impulse seized him to just open the door and escape, dash away down the street. But the social conventions made him hesitate—it would be a downright impolite exit after such a pleasant afternoon of tennis— and the limo glided into motion again. He had to resolve the situation, seize the bull by the horns. "What exactly do you want, Burt?"

"You're my ticket to eternal life, Ed," Rovilatt said reasonably. "I thought we could talk about it. How did your pal Lewis get ahold of the immortality in the first place?"

Edwin spoke with care. "You ask Rob, when he's up to it."

Rovilatt's eyes glinted under his thick black eyebrows. "You don't know? Or you won't say?"

"I don't know." It is true, Edwin argued to himself. An inarticulate man, Rob never could describe Gilgamesh's defeat clearly. He would begin with cryptic phrases about pearls and jewels—and zippers!—and finally subside into frustrated silence. But Rovilatt's gaze made Edwin nervous.

"Where'd you meet up with him?"

Again Edwin had to think fast. What would be safe to admit—Central Park? The time when Rob walked into his office at NIH? The homeless shelter? He was being too silent. Better to say anything. "You know, I can't quite recall. It's been a good few years."

"But not before 1994."

Edwin gulped. "I couldn't say."

"The way I see it," Rovilatt said thoughtfully, "anyone'd give their eyeteeth to live forever. How come Lewis gave it to you? If he had the Franklin Syndrome himself, he wouldn't be in the hospital today. The only reasonable explanation is that he's got something even bigger for himself. You know anything about that?"

If only he were James Bond, Edwin reflected bitterly. Or Han Solo. Then he'd be able to make up a convincing story about his own ignorance, maybe insist that Rob had kept him completely in the dark. He'd be able to lie with conviction. As it was, he could only say, "You'd better ask Rob."

The limo stopped on a quiet Georgetown street lined with ostentatious Federal houses crowded onto the very small lots. The heavy February overcast had brought the streetlights on though it was scarcely four in the afternoon. The first dry, tentative flakes of snow had begun to fall. A steep brick staircase pierced a brick retaining wall and ascended to the portico of a large brick house. Winter-weary box hedges topped the wall and flanked the stair, so that getting to the front door was like climbing a green tunnel. Rovilatt unlocked the door. "My wife and kids prefer the big house in Chicago, but this one's convenient when I have to be in D.C."

Edwin said nothing as he followed Burt inside. Silence didn't come naturally to him, but he didn't dare open up even slightly. The only ace they had was the true extent and nature of Rob's weirdness. To keep that secret was vital.

The front hall was furnished with a dark red Oriental rug, and the sitting room beyond was gloomy with antiques and brownish oil paintings. No daylight came through the windows from the frowning sky outside. Rovilatt flicked all the lights on. "What'll you have, Ed?"

"Club soda, if you have it. Or tonic." Edwin perched on the edge of the sofa. It was hard not to watch out of the corner of his eye as Burt cracked open a bottle and poured. Edwin could no longer recall how they'd first doped him in Florida. He reminded himself that Burt didn't need to resort to Mickey Finns any more.

From a basket under the grand piano came a dog, a chocolate-and-white springer spaniel. Edwin held out a hand. "Hey, fella, what's your name?" The dog came forward, head low, and sniffed Edwin cautiously. "Good boy," he said, reaching to pat the smooth head. The white teeth sparkled as the animal suddenly snapped at him. Edwin jerked his hand away just in time.

"Sparky, come!" Rovilatt snapped his fingers. The dog slunk to its master and coiled up behind his heels. "Stupid mutt. Some of them are just neurotic. He used to be my first wife's, until the divorce."

"He seems obedient, though," Edwin said. If a man was liked by his dog, he wasn't a complete loss—wasn't that how it worked in the old movies?

Rovilatt handed him his glass and sat down at the other end of the sofa. "All those newspapers you don't read? They call you lucky, Ed. But you know and I know, it's hard work that does it—lays the ground, so that when the lucky break breaks your way, you're ready to run with it."

"Everybody knows that," Edwin said. What was Burt working up to?

"So you've worked hard for years, cultivating Lewis."

"It's not work—we're friends!"

Rovilatt was watching him, gauging the effect of his words. "That innocent look is perfect, Ed. You could win an Oscar for it. But it doesn't fool me. You have nothing in common with Lewis. What does a blue-collar working stiff have to say to a science nerd? You probably don't even like him. You're in it for something, working your tail off, stroking him and jollying him along. That sci-fi novel, for instance. It was a joke, right? You weren't ever going to actually write it with him."

That at least was true, but Edwin didn't dare to admit it. He centered his drink carefully on a coaster on the coffee table and tried to dodge the question. "DAW Books in New York City is all hot to publish it."

"Yeah, right. Ed, I can see your point of view—you get what I'm saying? You're on to something really sweet. Why should you let the Johnny-come-lately in by the fire?"

The smart thing to do would be to allow Burt to continue building his cloud-castles. But Edwin was unable to tolerate the crass and selfish portrait of him Burt was painting. "That's not it," he had to say. "That's not it at all."

"Then what is, Ed? You tell me. Lewis is holding some cards up his sleeve. I know it. I just don't know what they are. I don't have enough data. That's where you come in. You must've picked up some hint, a tiny clue . . ."

Rovilatt was facing him now, his eyes bright and sharp. Edwin felt like a specimen under his own microscope, pinned down and focused under a strong light. He tried to smile, to think of a joke or something to distract Burt. But it was already too late. With a little snort of satisfaction, Rovilatt leaned back, picking up his scotch and downing half the tumblerful in a swallow. "Right," he said. "You aren't stupid. Even if Lewis is a clam, you've used your eyes and your head over the years. So give, Ed. What's the story?"

Somehow his damnably transparent countenance had betrayed him. Dissembling was so alien to Edwin—he knew he was no good at it, the worst liar in the world. He resorted to the only possible refuge: the truth. "I can't tell you, Burt. Truly, I can't."

Rovilatt flushed brick red. But his voice gave no hint of the angry frustration he must have felt. "You've been pretty pushy with your Franklin Syndrome, Ed. But Lewis has done damn-all, as far as I can discover. He has no paper trail—except for building permits, easements for decks, all that crap. If he really has something, how come he's working construction?"

It's what he wants to do, Edwin nearly said, but he held the words back. Burt would find no clues in the day-to-day operations of Lewis Home Improvement. Thank Heaven Rob had always maintained that fanatic discretion! Edwin vowed never to razz him about it again. Rovilatt could build a terrifying structure on even the tiniest data point. What if he began to probe into precisely why Rob became a carpenter?

"It's so wasteful, Ed!" Rovilatt stood up, displacing the dog's chin from his foot, and crossed over to refresh his glass. "Look at all the good you're going to do with that Syndrome of yours. Once the white-coat brigade figures it out, you'll be a bigger benefactor than Jennings or Salk. And Lewis, sitting on another piece of the same pie, he's playing around with decks! It's nowhere in the same league, Ed, don't you see it?"

Edwin did see. A very similar argument had scrolled past on the glowing gray screen in the comm dome on Moonbase. His own casual arguments about Severneth, monarch of Mu, came bouncing back to him like a tennis ball, from Burt: "It's wrong to be so wasteful, Ed. And you can't tell me you don't know that."

Edwin had to admit it. "Yes—I've discussed this with Rob."

"I knew it." Rovilatt slapped the Glenlivet bottle back down on the bar. "It was in that damned novel of yours! And you haven't been able to convince him."

So Burt had never deciphered *Severneth*'s elementary code! But the knowledge gave Edwin no pleasure. He leaned his head on his hands. "If only I could be sure what was right! Let me tell you a story, Burt."

Rovilatt sat down on the sofa again. "Sure, Ed. I'm all ears."

His alacrity made Edwin smile for a moment. "Once upon a time, a rich man had to go on travel for a year. He entrusted his cash assets to his three employees, according to each's ability—five grand to one, two to the next, and one thousand dollars to the third. Then the rich man left. The first clerk went into business with the five grand, and doubled the money. The second guy invested wisely, and also made good. But the man with a thousand dollars went and hid the cash in his mattress. When the boss came back, he looked over the accounts—"

"And handed the third guy his head?" Rovilatt interrupted. "Too right! Just what he deserved, the turkey! That's a damned smart story."

"It's in the Bible."

"You're kidding. 'Cause it's exactly what I'm saying, Ed. You look at your buddy Rob, and you're looking at a criminal mismanagement of resources."

And that was precisely it—Burt was right. Edwin didn't think of Rob's attitude as all that big a problem, and would never summarize it in such harsh and uncharitable terms. But he was too honest not to acknowledge that Burt essentially had the right pig by the ear. Edwin had the dizzying sense now of standing at the edge of a cliff. He wanted to hold back, mulishly dig in his heels, but all he could do was pick up his glass of club soda and stare into it. There was no guidance in its frosty depths, nor out in the blank black void of the windows where snowflakes flung themselves against the glass. He spoke slowly: "If . . . if that were so . . . what could be done?"

Rovilatt relaxed, leaning back and crossing one leg over his knee. "My daddy saw to it that I got a classical education, Ed. D'you ever study the history of ancient Rome?"

"Rome? I've read some books, but never really delved into it. That's more Carina's line."

"What do you know about the Triumvirate?"

"Mmmm . . . They were the three co-rulers of Rome, after Julius Caesar was assassinated. Mark Antony, Octavius, and Marcus Lepidus, wasn't it? It was in Shakespeare, in *Julius Caesar*."

"You are a smart one," Rovilatt said, smiling. The dog crowded close to his legs, and he stroked its ears without looking at it. "What I learned in school was, a triumvirate is inherently unstable."

"Well, in ancient Rome, sure," Edwin said uneasily. "They were a quarrelsome bunch. Antony and Octavius put Lepidus out of the way, and then they fought a war over the Empire until Octavius won."

"A triumvirate is unstable," Rovilatt repeated. "What if this one is unstable?"

"You mean . . . Oh, but we're not a trio yet! We haven't consulted Rob."

"He's got you well-trained, hasn't he? Sparky here isn't half so loyal. We could handle Lewis's tricks much better, Ed. You and me, we're the can-do type. None of this hiding the dough in the mattress, like the stupid clerk—we could invest it wisely, do good things with it. Whatever talents Lewis has, they're totally wasted on him."

"You think you could do better."

"I could." He smiled. "Don't you doubt it."

Edwin had not noticed before how much Rovilatt's smile resembled a shark's toothy grin. "And you want me to help you," he said, suddenly enlightened. "We play Antony and Octavius to Rob's Lepidus."

"What do you think?"

Edwin set his untouched glass down on the glossy coffee table and stood up, white with rage. "I think you're so full of shit your eyes are brown!"

"What is it between you two?" Rovilatt's temper snapped too, and he was on his feet and shouting. "He keeps you on a short leash. He hogs the gravy but doesn't use it himself. What kind of hold does he have on you, that you put up with it?"

"One you'll never have or understand, Burt!" Edwin blazed. "Not in a thousand years!"

"Were you lovers, is that it? You're that tight, I'd believe it! He must screw you—you don't have the *cojones* to stick it to him!"

Edwin snorted in contempt. "How can you stand to shave every morning, Burt? Looking at that sleazy face of yours in the mirror would make me gag!"

Rovilatt scooped up the glass from the coffee table and dashed the club soda into Edwin's eyes. Quickly Edwin shook the stinging wetness away. But in that second of blindness Burt was on him, seizing his arm and twisting it up behind his back until the left hand touched his shirt collar. Pain knifed through Edwin's shoulder. "I owe you one already, Ed," Rovilatt snarled into his ear. "Talk to me. Start answering questions. Otherwise it's payday."

"How about this?" Edwin panted. He stamped his heel hard onto Burt's instep and wrenched away. Burt's grip on his arm was like a vise. He could feel the rotator-cuff tendons ripping in his left shoulder, the joint itself creaking out of the socket. But he was free—reeling with pain, but free. He struck out blindly with his right and connected with Burt's head. Burt staggered back, caught his feet on the hearth, and fell, knocking the wrought-iron fireplace tools over onto himself with a tremendous clangor. The cringing springer spaniel barked and whined, but didn't dare close in to bite.

"There's a limit to how far manhandling will carry you, Burt," Edwin said, breathing hard, "when you try it on someone who doesn't care if his arm's torn off." Burt sat up, a hand clapped to his eye. Edwin wiped his wet face with his right arm. His sweatshirt cut into his left armpit. The arm itself was grotesquely swollen from neck to elbow, too sore to move. But already it was improving. "Good night. Thanks for the game." As Edwin strode past, the dog growled at him.

.   .   .

On Wednesday afternoon, Edwin pushed the door open into Rob's hospital room. Rob looked up and smiled. He wore a light-blue hospital gown, and held a library biography of Beethoven unopened on his lap. Before he could speak, Edwin held a finger to his lips and said, "Well, Mr. Lewis, and how are we today?" He took the remote from the rolling table and turned on the wall TV, cycling through the channels until an obnoxious children's cartoon appeared. He hiked the volume up until the room resounded with karate yells and explosion effects. "How do you feel, bud?"

"Ed, you comedian," Rob said feebly.

"You like my disguise, huh?" Edwin sat down next to the head of the bed, keeping his voice low. "Isn't it cool? Ingenuity as a substitute for the tarnhelm! I realized that a white coat is generic. These ID tags are my condo pool pass and my NIH parking permit—nobody ever looks closely at these things. A stethoscope from Dr. Chang, some hair cream, a pair of dime-store reading glasses, and nobody would know me."

Rob grinned. "What for?"

"I can't prove it, but this room may or may not be bugged, Rob. And they won't let me in to see you. We are in big, big trouble. We're being blackmailed."

"Tell me."

Edwin could hardly hear Rob over the TV tumult. "First things first, bud. How are you doing?"

"It hurts when I speak up," Rob complained, in a pale phantom of his old baritone. "And when I laugh. And it's a stone bitch when I cough. Otherwise I'm okay."

"And you can't eat." Edwin glanced at the barely-touched lunch tray on the bedside table. "And you've lost twenty pounds." He stared doubtfully down at Rob's haggard and wasted face. "Maybe I should come back later."

Rob shook his head. "Tell me."

"Would it be easier for you to hear me tell it? Or would you feel less exhausted doing a weird data dump?"

Rob smiled. "Your trust amazes me, Ed." He laid his right hand on top of the covers.

"Lord, Rob, it is so *good* to talk to you." Edwin put his hand over Rob's. The work calluses were thick on the palms, and Rob's knuckles were still enlarged with heavy labor. But the hand itself felt as hollow and light as a fistful of soda straws. New silvery streaks dulled the dark blond of Rob's hair and short beard. With a prickle of terror, Edwin realized a day would come, not very far from now, when Rob would be old. Rob and Julianne and Carina, everyone in existence was being swept away down a river of time. Only Edwin would be left behind, alone on the shore. Rob's weird powers had an up-front cost, a high one. But the cost of immortality was end-loaded—the pain of loss. The mortgage compounded every year, and Edwin had paid scarcely a cent on the debt yet. But year by year it would cost him more.

"Golly, you're depressing," Rob murmured.

Edwin laughed. "I'm better already, seeing you. Now, what about Burt Rovilatt? Did you get it all, so fast? What can be done?"

Rob drew his hand away and sighed, shallowly. "It's funny. I was wishing for someone like Rovilatt only last week."

"You *what*?" Edwin sat up in shock.

"Someone who'd be willing to take on these powers. I was dying, until you saved me. What would have happened to the weirdness if I'd died?"

"Rob, I had nothing to do with that. You saved yourself! And it would be madness to give Burt the time of day. The man's a controller, a foul-minded, grabby, insinuating blackmailer and kidnapper! The things he'd do, the things he's already done—anybody would be a better heir, Rob. Julianne, me, anyone!" Edwin found he was sputtering with the vehemence of his feelings.

"Ed," Rob said with soft surprise. "You're frightened of this guy. Unbelievable!"

Edwin gave a shaky laugh. "I guess you're right. I am. I wonder why? It's— maybe it's because he was acting like a friend, when he wasn't. Faking cordiality, forcing me to enjoy his hospitality—it's a travesty. It drives me buggy. I know it's irrational, but I'd sooner face the rack and thumb-screw. I have to trust people, even when it's the stupid thing to do. It was actually a relief, when he tried to twist my arm—he was out in the open then, and I could fight him."

"I can see that," Rob said, very quietly. "You aren't happy with covert battles . . . I'd like to talk to him."

"He's hot to talk to you. What will you do to him?"

"I don't know. It depends." Rob closed his eyes. "I wish I wasn't such a wreck . . ." His voice was almost inaudible.

Edwin saw he was exhausted. With sudden clarity he realized how stupid it was to come charging in to dump all his problems on an ailing man. Rob had always pulled him out of his difficulties—in New York, in Florida, too many past incidents to recall. Had it become a habit for Edwin to count on Rob to save the day? His own spinelessness appalled him. It was intolerable. This one dilemma he'd resolve by himself. "You're running out of steam, Rob," he said. "At least we know the enemy—that's important. We'll talk again later."

Rob's eyes glinted gray-blue for a second. "Jul's bringing a laptop," he whispered.

"Good idea. Typing'll be easier than talking. You sleep now, and e-mail me when you're ready to move." He hitched the counterpane up to Rob's chin and turned off the TV before he tiptoed out.

*E*dwin spent the next day or so mulling over the problem. The simplest and most elegant solution was for Rob to wipe Rovilatt's mind, forcing Burt to forget everything he ever knew or learned about them. But Edwin resolved not to advise Rob to do this. Severneth, monarch of Mu, wouldn't like it. If Edwin could find a solution to implement himself, Rob need not get involved at all.

But what would this notional solution involve? Edwin grimaced when he remembered the foot-thick dossier Burt had already amassed. All the papers would have to be recovered. Burt had to be quiet about Rob's role—not only today, but forever. And what about the Franklin Syndrome? Rovilatt was surely not going to give up on his fascination with that. He wanted to live forever. Edwin's spine crawled when he recalled how casually Burt had discussed getting rid of Rob. And I'm the one who has what Burt wants, he reminded

himself. If he ever gets the Syndrome away from me, my ass
is grass.

And if he got a piece of it, maybe duplicated the immortality somehow? Edwin realized that centuries of life, passed in
Burt's company, would be hell, pure and simple—an eternal
torment unsurpassed by anything in Dante. And what about
the PSPIP? Impossible to imagine simply maintaining a casual
business acquaintance with Burt anymore. How very pleasant
it would be never to see or deal with the man again . . .

Edwin was intelligent enough to draw the logical conclusion, and too honest not to admit it to himself. If Burton
Rovilatt died today, all their problems would evaporate. He
remembered quoting Scripture to Rob: do not resist, turn the
cheek, love your enemy. Easy enough, when you had no ene-
mies. His own glib shallowness disgusted him now. He had
no more Christianity in him than a cat. "There's got to be
another answer," he said out loud.

On Friday he was astonished to get an e-mail from Rob.
It read:

> Dear Mr. Rovilatt,
> I understand from Dr. Barbarossa that you wish to talk to
> me. I'm likely to be in Georgetown Hospital for some
> time yet, so perhaps you will not mind meeting me here. I
> suggest this Saturday at ten A.M. Please let me know if this
> is convenient.
> Robertson M. Lewis
> cc: Edwin A. Barbarossa

Edwin picked up the phone and pressed the number out
before he remembered Rob's difficulty with talking. Switch-
ing to e-mail, he typed,

> Rob, are you sure you're strong enough to do this? The
> MOST important thing is not to jeopardize your recov-
> ery. NOTHING should stand in the way of that.

He yearned to say more, but e-mail is not really private. Finally he added,

> Of course I'll be there. Did I tell you I'm meeting Carina in Boston on Sunday? We plan to rob a bank on Monday. E.

Edwin meant to arrive at the hospital on Saturday early enough to get a private word with Rob. But he worked late on Friday and then overslept. The limousine was pulling away from the snowy hospital driveway as he approached. Triumvirates are unstable, he remembered. What was Burt telling Rob?

But when he dashed up to Rob's room there was nothing to worry about. The nurses had barricaded the door to do some procedure or other, and Rovilatt sat cooling his heels in the TV lounge. The bruise from Edwin's punch still showed dark around Burt's right eye. Suppressing a grin of delight, Edwin ducked into the vending room and bought himself a cup of coffee. The last thing he wanted was another tête-à-tête with Burt.

Both visitors came into the room together, but Edwin got in the first word. "You look better, bud."

This was not an entirely true statement. The bony structure of Rob's skull was comely, but entirely too visible under the pallid skin. Above the neckline of the blue hospital gown, his collarbones stuck out in stark relief. "I'm getting mighty tired of hospitals," Rob said in his new thin voice. "I won't revolt you by telling what those nurses were doing just now." He pressed the button to raise his hospital bed to a sitting position.

Edwin pushed a chair up and sat at Rob's elbow, to make his allegiance plain. Rovilatt took the armchair on the other side, near the foot. He wore a three-piece navy suit with a maroon tie, as if this were a pivotal business meeting. He folded his arms and looked at Rob intently for at least a minute. "They say you should never judge a book by its cover," he remarked at last.

"I'm not at my best," Rob agreed softly. "I can't talk much, Rovilatt. Suppose you take the floor, and I'll listen."

"Right." Rovilatt opened a leatherbound notebook on his knee but scarcely referred to it. Instead he watched Rob as he spoke. "I know it all, Lewis. I know how Ed here didn't just spontaneously develop the Franklin Syndrome. You gave it to him like a present, probably during that rock-climbing vacation in the nineties. And from what Ed has said, I gather you have even more tricks in your bag. The center of this thing isn't with Ed. It's with you. That's the big secret. I have no objection to you two keeping the goodies private. But I want in."

The unfairness, the blatant shading of the truth in this statement, drove Edwin to speak. After last Sunday he wasn't going to give Burt a single inch. "You eavesdrop on stairwells. You bugged a sympathy bouquet and sent it to Julianne. You've had spies digging through our pasts, looking for dirt. You didn't mention all that."

Rovilatt shot a look at him. "Next time, Ed, it'll be a lot more than twisting your arm. When I feed a dog I expect it to heel."

"I'm not that pathetic spaniel of yours, Burt," Edwin said, furious. "Lincoln freed the slaves, remember?"

"Ed," Rob said. "Let him speak his piece."

"His master's voice." Rovilatt's silken tone cut like a razor. "Okay. Why should you deal me in? I can contribute. I've got money enough to finance any scheme you can name."

"You've always thought you could buy anything," Edwin said.

"Don't knock it. You chubby ungrateful geek, you're wearing and eating and driving and tinkering in that damn lab with my money."

"Point-oh-three percent of it is your money," Edwin corrected him. "And I don't recall signing away my soul for it. What the PSPIP gets is in the contract."

Rovilatt swiveled to face Rob again. "Here's a more practical point. I don't know if you've taken a gander at the bills you've racked up here in the hospital . . . No? Well, your wife's health insurance covers eighty percent of it, but that remaining twenty percent runs well into five figures so far. You'll never see those bills, Lewis. I've paid them all, and I'll continue to pick up the tab."

Edwin tensed with alarm. This was how Burt got his foot in the door: by buying his way in. Rob raised his eyebrows in mild surprise. "Thank you."

"You should be grateful," Rovilatt agreed. "And here's another thing. You can't possibly be getting everything you can out of these powers. Otherwise you wouldn't be in this fix. Bring me up to speed on them, and I guarantee to find you a more productive direction."

"You're not offering anything we're interested in, Burt," Edwin said with contempt.

"Fine, Ed. You want to play hardball? We'll play." Suddenly Rovilatt's sunburned face was flinty. "You strike me as a man who values his peace, Lewis. What do you think'll be left of it, if I go pour my heart out to the *New York Times*? Ed's not the only one who can play the media game. I have tapes, I have documents, and I'll get more. Now that I know you're the key man holding the cards, there's no way to keep me out of the game. Why not deal me in gracefully?"

Rob seemed unmoved. His thin face was perfectly still, and the gray-blue eyes didn't flicker. When it was clear he wasn't going to respond, Rovilatt went on. "I've mentioned to Ed that there's no length I won't go to for a shot at eternal life. Both of you are vulnerable as hell. You're fond of that pretty little wife of yours, aren't you, Ed? And they say, Lewis, that a man with children has given hostages to Fortune."

At the mention of Carina, it became crystal-clear to Edwin that here was a man entirely deserving of death. He didn't remember jumping up and diving across the hospital room. But suddenly he had Rovilatt's hand-tailored shirt collar twisted in both hands. It felt wonderful to shake him like a rat, to watch the red face turn purple.

But the dark eyes were still needle-sharp. "So you have got murder in you," Rovilatt wheezed.

With a gasp, Edwin jerked his hands away. Free, Rovilatt whipped a fist around in a backhand blow, the lightning-reflex swing of a tennis player. It caught Edwin in the mouth and sent him sprawling backwards onto the linoleum. "You little prick!" Rovilatt panted. He slammed his black wingtip shoe hard into Edwin's stomach. Red and yellow stars of pain blurred Edwin's vision, and his breath hissed in agony. "I know exactly how to manage you when you bite." There was an ugly twist to Rovilatt's mouth. "I could make that immortality of yours a burden from hell, Ed. Put you through the coarse blade of a mincer every day, and every night you'd be recovered and ready for more."

"Like Prometheus," Rob said.

Rovilatt turned, surprised. "That's right. Prometheus. You aren't as dumb as you pretend to be, Lewis. You're the one who calls the shots. What do you say? Are you going to be a reasonable man?"

"Come closer," Rob said quietly.

Edwin rolled to his hands and knees as Rovilatt stepped past him and up to the bed. Blood spurted from his split lip, but already it was stopping. A box of tissues dropped to the floor beside him, and he looked up. But Rob's gaze was fixed on Rovilatt, and his eyes had an icicle-blue glint. "Tell me about the papers," he said. "And the tapes. Where are they?"

"The investigators 've been mailing their reports to my Chicago headquarters," Rovilatt said readily. "I get copies by fax. The tapes are in my office safe."

"That doesn't sound very secure," Rob remarked.

Behind a handful of tissues, Edwin relaxed. Rob was fidgeting with Burt's head, increasing his openness to suggestion. A minor muscling, but enough—Burt's own distrustful nature would carry him the rest of the way. Rovilatt stared at Rob in horror. "My god, I'll say it isn't! The only safe place for everything is right under my hand!"

"At home," Rob suggested.

"You betcha, at home! I got a security system, a safe, the works! Who knows what my private secretary is getting up to back in Chicago?"

"Good," Rob said. "You deal with that. Gather everything together and keep it safe under lock and key, and we'll look at it when I get out of here."

Rovilatt held out a lean hand. "It's a pleasure to do business with you, Lewis. You have horse sense."

Rob shook his hand. "Oh, and I think you should stop bullying Edwin. He doesn't like it."

"Aah, he's easy meat. Now you get better, you hear?" He went out with a final jaunty wave.

The door swung shut behind him, and Edwin scrambled to his feet.

"You hurt?" Rob asked.

"Not to speak of—you know me. Holy Mike, Rob, I'm glad you muscled him! I tried to come up with some way to cope myself, but I couldn't. Except murder," he added. The vivid memory of Burt's neck under his hands was a sudden and bitter shock. It was as if he'd never seen himself before. He sat down again and folded his hands under his armpits, shivering. "Oh Jesus. I would have killed him just now, Rob. I could taste it. What monsters are inside me? What kind of a person am I?"

Rob's voice was quiet. "I can answer that, Ed. You're the kind of person who's so bighearted, you'd let a frightener lean on you for days, rather than sell out a friend."

Edwin was so astonished he looked up. "You're joking."

Rob's gaze was focused on nothing, but it seemed from his expression to be a bleak vista. "You wanted to kill him, Ed. But when he called you on it, you didn't do it. There was thought, but no action. 'Do not resist one who is evil,' they taught you. And you didn't."

There was some undercurrent in Rob's words, a spice of bitter memory, that Edwin would have probed at any other time. Right now, though, Rob's basic misapprehension was so appalling he had to protest. "But that's just the point, Rob. The whole idea is to be good from the thought outwards. You shouldn't even want to kill somebody."

Rob smiled. "Don't you have more important things to fret about, Ed? Is this bank in Boston you mentioned what I think it is?"

Distracted, Edwin blushed. "Carina said she'd need moral support."

"I'll just bet!" Rob began to laugh, and then winced.

Edwin seized the opening. "Look, Rob, there's no need for you to put up with this agonizing recovery. You borrowed the pearl once, right? Borrow it again, right now, and get well—today."

"What happened, by the way, when I did that?"

"I passed out. I don't know why it works like that. It didn't seem to hit old Gil that way. But it doesn't bother me at all. I'll just sit here in the chair and be unconscious."

"Can't do it, Ed. The doctors check up on me every day. It would look too strange. They know how my recovery's progressing, and if I suddenly leap ahead, they'll smell a rat."

"Then as soon as they release you, okay? It can't be much longer. Promise me, please!"

Rob closed his eyes. "All right, Ed. If it'll get you off my back, I promise."

"I'll hold you to it," Edwin said, with satisfaction. "I'm going to be in Boston for most of February, but I'll leave my number with Julianne. You call me, night or day, if you need help with Burt. Or e-mail. What do you have in mind for him?"

"I haven't decided," Rob said. "But I've bought us some time to think it over. Leave it to me, Ed."

Edwin sighed with relief. "You got it, bud."

$\mathcal{R}$esilient as ever, Edwin had no difficulty in putting Rovilatt out of his mind and enjoying his stay in Boston. Both he and Carina favored working vacations. She conducted a seminar on Moche burial cerements at Tufts University, while Edwin gave a series of guest lectures about space colonies at MIT. He ate lobster and clams with all his academic and professional friends in the area, and enthusiastically supported Carina before and after the artificial-insemination procedure.

In bed afterwards, it came naturally to tell her all about the Rovilatt complications. "But I don't understand," Carina said. "He seemed like such a nice man. How could he be such a skunk?"

"I don't understand it myself," Edwin confessed. "But I wish I could've managed without dragging Rob into it."

"It was Rob who caught Burt's interest," Carina pointed out. "You were ancillary . . . Do I mean 'ancillary'?"

"Beats me—there's never a dictionary in a hotel room

when you need one. You are the only woman I know who'd want a dictionary in bed . . . When are we going to find out if science has triumphed this cycle?"

"I think these days you can do a pee-in-a-jar pregnancy test in a week."

Edwin laughed into the dark, pulling her nearer. "It wouldn't hurt, you think, to keep up the pressure on the home front until then?"

He could feel her smiling into his bare shoulder as she said, "Oh, I'm sure it wouldn't hurt!"

It wasn't until midmonth that Edwin got a message from Julianne that Rob was coming home. Edwin cancelled appointments and caught an air shuttle back to D.C. When he pulled the sports car up to the main hospital door, the aides were just rolling Rob in a wheelchair out to the curb. Julianne greeted Edwin with a scowl. "He can't drive for a couple months," she announced. "His breastbone has to knit back together. I want him to come home and go straight to bed."

"Excellent idea," Edwin said. "He gave me a promise I want him to keep."

"You can talk to *me*, you know," Rob said in a small grumpy voice. He was wearing a topcoat over a blue sweat-suit loose enough to accommodate the dressings and drainage tubes. "And I made us an appointment in George-town, Ed."

"Oh no, you don't!" Julianne said.

"Some other day'll do for that," Edwin said. He was in no rush to see Burt again. Besides, Rob looked so fragile, skeleton-thin, his face still lined with pain. Out in the day-light, it was plain how much ground he had lost. Edwin had to bite his lip when he remembered Rob effortlessly wielding the chain saw last summer. If he had to go up against Burt, at least he could be restored to full health.

"I don't think we should postpone it," Rob said.

"Not your first afternoon out of the hospital! What's the rush? What could possibly be so important?" Julianne

hauled open the minivan's sliding center door, allowing two
french fries, the plastic case to a Nintendo game cassette, and
a Dalmatian dog Beanie Baby to fall out onto the icy pavement. "Oh, for dumb. This is the last time we do Happy
Meals in the car!"

Rob drew in a sharp breath. The look of ancient pain that
shadowed his face was so alarming that Edwin reached for
his wrist, feeling for the pulse. "What is it, bud? Where does
it hurt, what can I do?"

Rob pulled away. "It's nothing."

"Bull. The iron-man attitude doesn't fool—"

"Later, Ed." He was watching Julianne, who had slung
the game case and the Beanie into the front seat and was now
excavating more desiccated french fries from the van's floor.

There was no question of muscle, of Rob deftly using his
powers to get his own way. But somehow, by mere gentle
strength of character, he prevailed. Edwin helped him into
the front seat of the Porsche instead of Julianne's minivan,
while Julianne took the suitcase. "Bring him straight home
afterwards, Edwin," Julianne begged. "And Rob, I want to
know what's going on!"

"When we get back," Rob said. "Promise. We won't be
long."

"I'll make it as quick as we can," Edwin told her. The
Porsche's engine rolled over with a smooth powerful purr,
underlining his words. "What do you plan to do?" he asked
as they pulled away. "Flush Burt's brain like a toilet?"

Rob smiled. "Now, Ed. Would Severneth, monarch of
Mu, approve? Talk to me about the Pocket Rocket here. I
never did get to ride in it that day. It must devour gasoline."

Edwin looked around. Rob wasn't usually evasive with
him. But accepting the change of subject, he said, "Gas? Like
a ramjet sucks air!" They talked cars until they arrived at
Rovilatt's Georgetown mansion. Lingering snowdrifts ate
into the street parking, and he had to cruise around until they
lucked into a slot half a block down the street. Not until then
did something occur to Edwin. "Rob, can you hike up those

steps? Maybe I should drive around back, see if there's a service entrance."

"What, and lose a legal parking space? I can manage fine. The nurses made me walk every day in the hospital."

Dubious, Edwin helped him out of the car and gave him his arm. Rob made slow but steady progress down the icy sidewalk and up the steep brick stairs. Only towards the top did he begin to flag. In the portico he leaned on a white column while Edwin buzzed the doorbell. "You say he's expecting us?"

Rob nodded, voiceless. Inside, the springer spaniel set up a monotonous bark, suddenly cut off. Rovilatt unlocked the door and opened it wide. "Ed, Rob! Come on in! Let me take your coats!"

Edwin had to force himself to step over the threshold. He could now recognize his previous adventure here as a species of seduction—an overt invitation to betrayal, novel and utterly repellent. Burt's proximity affected him now like the smell of greasy cooking after a stomach flu. He swallowed and breathed deep and slow, trying to calm himself down. "You better have a seat, Rob."

Rob pointed past the sitting room. "How about out there?" he suggested breathlessly.

"You'll appreciate what I'm having done out back," Rovilatt said in hearty tones. "The sunroom's new, for instance. As soon as the cold weather lets up, they're going to pour the concrete for the lily pond outside."

He ushered them into a luxurious sunroom roofed and walled with glass. Pale February sunshine poured in. Fig trees and jungly monstera plants rioted in the corners, and white wicker sofas with flowery cushions faced each other across a towering stone fireplace. The fire, a gas-fed one, flickered low between the fake logs. Rob sank slowly, carefully, into the deep down cushions, and leaned his head back. "You look like you could do with a brewski, Rob," Rovilatt said. "How 'bout you, Ed?"

"Love one," Edwin forced himself to say, as enthusiastically as he could. Burt was right. Rob's face had a chalky, wan look. Maybe a beer would help.

"Come lend a hand, then!"

Reluctantly Edwin followed him into a palatial kitchen. "I got Sam Adams, Chicago's Finest, Heineken," Rovilatt said, with a silly smile. Chilly air poured from the mammoth refrigerator as he held the door open. "There's a tray here. Or no, let's use this tea-trolley thing . . ."

Edwin felt a sudden rush of pity for the man. His unnatural cordiality was all Rob's doing, of course—completely uncharacteristic of Burt's usual muscular hospitality. He was a puppet on a string now, his personality utterly overshadowed. Rob had described this process for Edwin, mainly in fictional guise. Now, faced with the actuality, Edwin discovered that King Severneth of Mu had not really been splitting hairs or exercising finicky scruples. Edwin had talked too blithely about flushing Burt's brain. This was a terrible thing to do, to anybody.

When they came back with the beer, Rob asked, "Did you remember the shredder?"

"Sure did," Rovilatt said. "Borrowed it from my Hill office. You want it set up? Where?"

Rob stared thoughtfully out through the greenhouse glass into the small back garden. This was enclosed by tall brick walls, to block out neighboring houses. Directly outside the French doors was a brick terrace. To the right was a gas grill, a stack of patio chairs, and a bar, all veiled for the winter in heavy plastic covers. The snow had been swept away, and a square of bricks in the center had been pried up for the future lily pond. "I think we can shred right here," Rob said. "If Ed won't mind carting the trash out back, we can burn it in the lily pond. You shouldn't ignite gasoline indoors, even in a fireplace."

"What gasoline?" Edwin was startled.

"The gasoline Burt is going to go buy, after he brings out the documents," Rob said simply.

Increasingly uncomfortable, Edwin helped Rovilatt carry

out a dozen big cardboard file boxes. The springer spaniel trotted back and forth with them, getting underfoot until Burt shouted at it. "Stupid mutt," he said again. "Don't know how Josie put up with him."

He kept the dog after the divorce, Edwin remembered. "How long did she own him?"

"From a puppy. Maybe six years. But he's mine now." The tone was that of ownership, not affection. How does one suborn the loyalty of a dog—or a man? Feed the creature, dominate it? Sickened, Edwin realized he'd experienced only the beginning of some long deforming process. How far would Burt have gone? What would he have forced Edwin to submit to? Mere physical punishment, the coarse blade of the mincer Burt had promised him, was nothing. It was the psychological intimidation that Edwin couldn't comprehend or fight. He hurried with the last box back to Rob.

Rovilatt set up the shredder near the fireplace and positioned its bin underneath. "You all comfy now with that? Good! I think I'll pop out for that gas."

"Go to a station where they know you," Rob suggested softly.

"It's cold, but nice," Rovilatt said. "I think I'll take the dog and walk down to the Mobil station on M Street. I won't be a jiffy."

"We'll be here," Rob said.

As soon as he was gone Edwin turned to Rob. "What's happening, bud? You're not going to torch his house!"

"Of course not." Rob opened a folder and turned the pages over. "Just the papers. Shred and burn, that's the safest way. Start skimming, Ed. This is our last chance to inspect the evidence and make sure of what he's got on us."

"You've poked around in his head."

Rob gave him an "of course" look. Edwin dumped out a boxful of bulging manila envelopes and began skimming. There were newspaper clippings, hundreds of them, about the *Franklin* disaster and the murder insinuations and then the Syndrome; thick PSPIP financial reports and sheaves of

statements all the way back to 1998 and the NASA reorga-
nization; and older things, feasibility studies on Moonbase
and Marsbase, reports that dated back to the dawn of the
Space Age. "He's got the makings here of a dynamite Ph.D.
thesis," Edwin said after half an hour. He turned the shredder on, and shoved an armload into the hopper. The engine
whined like a power tool, dropping in pitch as the blades bit
into paper, and the cutting blades munched and crunched
hungrily. A spaghetti of shreds slowly extruded and fell into
the bin.

"You must have got the boring files." Behind the short
blond beard Rob's mouth was set in a grim line. "Look at
this."

Edwin glanced at the file Rob passed him, and his gorge
rose. On top was a large glossy full-color photograph of a
man's left forearm, scientifically and deeply slashed right
open. The bloody red meat and white gleam of bone looked
like something in a butcher shop. Beyond the point of the
shoulder the subject's lolling head could just be glimpsed. It
had his own curly dark hair. "What is this?" Edwin gasped.
"I don't remember that!" Like an idiot he pushed up his
striped turtleneck's sleeve. But of course there was nothing to
be seen on his arm.

"I do," Rob said. "The day I found you in Florida, it was
down to a thin red line."

"Oh boy." Edwin swallowed down the queasiness. "Did I
ever thank you for pulling me out of there?"

"It was nothing, pal. The two of us, together, handled it.
Shove it into the shredder—it's history. Should you maybe
empty that bin?"

Edwin was glad to step out into the cold clean air and
dump the shreddings into the future lily pond. By the time
Rovilatt came back, the mound of shreddings was a yard
high. "Better set that outside," Rob said, nodding at the one-
gallon gasoline can. "It'd be safer."

"What else can I do to help?" Rovilatt asked when he
came in again.

"Suppose you do these tapes," Rob said. "Unwind them all and dump them on the pile."

Edwin watched as Rovilatt eagerly gathered up an armload of cassettes. Smiling broadly, the tycoon broke one open and began disemboweling it, pulling out yard upon yard of shiny brown magnetic tape. How huge Rob's strength was, if he could force the man not only to destroy his own work like this, but to enjoy it! "This is eerie," Edwin couldn't help saying. "Totally unreal."

"I'm sorry," Rob said quietly.

The chilly February afternoon faded into dusk as they worked. Rovilatt turned on the halogen lamps and the downlights, and used a remote to power up the flames in the fireplace. "Rob," Edwin said. "Look at this." It was a photocopy of both sides of a cancelled check. The check, for $3,000, was made out to "CASH," but the back was endorsed by a Ferdinand Bowyer. "Isn't he the one who . . ."

Rob nodded, unsurprised. "I knew, from sorting through his brain. Burt, would you like to talk about this?"

Rovilatt looked at the photocopy with a dopey smile. "Oh, that was my own little contribution to the Franklin Syndrome research effort. They showed me the list of experiments planned out for your first year, Ed. Such a bunch of wussy, tentative probes I never saw—thallium imaging, brain scans, stuff like that. I figured a real vigorous attempt on your life might be more productive of results. And it was, too—Dr. Chang got some real hot data that afternoon."

"So you paid this lunatic to take a shot at me with an automatic rifle?" Edwin's voice shook with anger. "And what about Rob here? Or any of the other people in the lobby that day. Suppose they'd caught a bullet?"

"It was a real worthwhile investment," Rovilatt said, as if he were being perfectly reasonable. "How else would I ever have got a line on Rob?"

"You, you—" But Edwin's righteous anger deflated at the sight of Burt's vacant expression. Retribution was very near.

Inexorable and pitiless as winter, Rob would see to that. Edwin looked away from the square red face, shuddering.

At last the final armload slid through the shredder. "Do you have some matches, Burt?" Rob asked.

"Let me get 'em."

"Shall we?" Rob said. Edwin helped him to his feet and held the French door. Outdoors, it was bitterly cold and dark now. The chill nipped the inside of Edwin's nose and cut through the fabric of his red-and-blue turtleneck. The mound of fluffy shreddings looked like snow, a pile of dirty snow six feet high. Edwin bent to pick up the gas can, but Rob said sharply, "No, Ed. Let Burt do it."

"Fingerprints, you mean? What about the beer bottles and stuff, then?"

"There's a perfectly legitimate reason for your marks to be on a beer bottle. But not a gas can." Rovilatt came out, and Rob said, "Will you do the honors, Burt?"

Rovilatt drenched the fluffy pile of shreddings with gasoline, emptying the can and then tossing it on top of the pile. With a barbecue fork, he pulled a long tangle of reeking shreds out onto the brick pavement. Then he took the matchbook out of his pocket.

"Give it here," Rob said softly.

"Fingerprints?" Edwin asked.

"No, Ed. This is one thing it's important that I do myself." After the long day Rob's hands, particularly the left one, were clumsy with the matchbook. Edwin itched to help out. But at last a match was lit. Rob dropped it onto the protruding strands. With a soft puffing sound, the entire heap was aflame. The sudden heat and glare struck Edwin in the face, and he held a hand up. Rob tossed the matchbook into a roaring inferno that jumped higher than the garden walls. "Burt, will you walk with us out to the car?"

Edwin helped Rob with his coat and scrambled into his own. Burt pulled on a leather jacket. The three men descended the dark front stairs to the street and walked to the Porsche. The fire was just visible behind them in the night sky, as a reddish glow above the rooftops. Edwin used his keychain remote to unlock the car doors and turn on the courtesy lights. He helped Rob lower himself into the passenger seat, and then shut the door.

Rob powered the window down. "All right," he said very softly. "You're free, Burt."

"What?" Edwin stared aghast at Rovilatt. By the yellow light of the streetlamps he could see the sunburned face suddenly hardening, focusing, becoming itself again. "Rob, are you crazy?"

"I mean it," Rob said. "We've destroyed all the evidence, Burt. You have zero on us now. Let it drop. Go and live your life. And I'll never lift a hand against you again. That's a promise."

"Rob, no!" In shock, Edwin leaned against the taut black canvas roof of the car.

"You—you've been messing with me somehow," Rovilatt said hoarsely. He dug his fingers into the sheaf of iron-gray hair. "With my brain. Making me do stuff!"

"That's right," Rob said. "It's a hard lesson, one that's taken me years to learn. But I know now that I have to be honest, completely scrupulous with everyone close to me. I have to keep my doors open. You've come sufficiently close to me yourself to come under that rule. If you want, we can start fresh. You give up the blackmail and intimidation, and I'll put aside the mind games. And we'll see how it goes. I had to force you to light that fire, Burt. But it's over now. You're completely free to make your choice."

"Rob, you're asking the impossible!" Edwin warned.

"Like hell it's over!" Rovilatt's eyes bulged with fury. "You stinking bastard, you slippery scarecrow, I'll—" He raised a clenched fist.

Edwin stepped in. "You'd sock a sick man, Burt. I expect no less of you. But think about whether you enjoyed being mindless that much."

Rovilatt snarled in his face. "I'll get you for this, Ed. You'll pay for this on your hands and knees, begging for

242

242

242

242

242

242

242

242

mercy! And you, Lewis—no way this is over, do you hear me? No way! By god, I'll be on your case for the rest of my life!"

"I know it," Rob said, almost inaudibly.

Suddenly Rovilatt looked up the street. "Shit—the fire! Those tapes!" He turned and dashed away into the night, back to his stairway.

Edwin ran around to the driver's side and got in. "Rob, are you *nuts*? Letting him go scot-free is asking for mega-trouble—you heard him! At the very minimum, you ought to induce some selective amnesia. It isn't too late. Nail him now!"

"You're wrong there, Ed," Rob said tiredly. "It is too late. Let's wait and see what happens, okay?"

"He's got enough money to collect new clippings and reports," Edwin pointed out. "He'll tap our phone lines and bug our homes until doomsday. Our lives won't be our own. He'll—"

"Ed," Rob cut in. "You said yourself that you're not entirely rational about Rovilatt. And how is it that I come to be quoting your Bible to you? 'Do not resist one who is evil.' Are you going to talk the talk, or walk the walk?"

Edwin opened his mouth, but nothing came out except an abortive preliminary click. Everything he thought of to say, he could think of a rejoinder to. Useless to claim this instance as an exception to the rule; if you made an exception every time things got tough, the rules were pointless. Nor could he argue that Jesus had propounded general principles and not specific instruction—

A ball of fire suddenly ballooned up from behind the brick house. Immediately the explosion followed like a clap of thunder. Black smoke began to plume up from the roof, and through Rob's open window the hungry crackle of flame could be heard.

"Holy Mike, the fire! It blew up somehow!" Edwin flung open the car door. "Rob, use the car phone and call 911! I'll try and get Burt out!" He galloped through the cold firelit dark and up the brick stairs three at a time. Hot ash fell from the sky, and the haze of smoke made him cough. Already he could hear sirens. Some watchful neighbor must have phoned right away. He flung himself against the front door, but it was locked. "Burt!" he shouted. "Burt!"

The fire engines came howling up the street. Edwin stood out of the way on the icy lawn as the firemen broke down the door and dragged their hoses up. Rovilatt didn't emerge. Only the spaniel bolted out yelping, dodging past the firemen and scrabbling frantically over the hoses. It halted, vibrating with terror, by the hedge.

By stepping warily over the ice, Edwin was able to edge close enough to make a grab for its collar. The dog twisted in his grip, snapping and whining and dribbling urine, but Edwin hung on. If he let Burt's dog escape, it would be run over in a New York minute. He fended off Sparky's teeth with his shoe, all the while pulling the belt out through the loops of his jeans with his free hand. Noticing the commotion a fireman yelled, "Out mister. Rubberneck from across the street, unless you want to get brained by falling debris."

Edwin threaded the belt through the dog's collar. "Sorry, I'm going." But he didn't move for another moment, because they were hustling a stretcher out the front door. It must be Rovilatt. There had been nobody else in the house. The stretcher was covered with a sheet. Chilled to the core, Edwin turned and cut across the crunchy frozen grass towards the car. The dog growled and fought every inch of the way.

In the car, Rob had closed his window and seemed to be asleep. But when Edwin pulled open the driver-side door he opened his eyes. "What on earth, Ed?"

"Burt's dead or hurt bad," Edwin said, dragging the dog up. "And I couldn't just let this guy run loose, could I? Ow!" Sparky had finally gotten a solid nip into his bare hand. Edwin flicked the blood away, biting back a florid comment. At least he didn't have to worry about tetanus or rabies. "I think I better hand him over to the Fire Department boys. I can't drive with a hysterical dog loose in the car. And if they euth you, Sparky, I'm sorry," he added grimly.

"Is that his name?" Rob beckoned, gently but with absolute authority. "Come, Sparky."

The dog had been straining backwards against Edwin's tug, back arched, head low, the collar dragged up around the base of his ears. When he abruptly reversed direction, Edwin lost balance and almost pitched over into the slush. Sparky put his wet muddy front paws onto the driver's seat and panted hoarsely into Rob's face. "Oh Lord, my leather upholstery," Edwin muttered. He reached past the suddenly wagging tail to snag the roll of paper towels in back.

Rob patted the brown-and-white neck. "You've been one messed-up puppy," he said softly. "Dry off his paws, Ed. He'll be good now."

Dubious but obedient, Edwin gave the dog a tentative swipe, prepared to dodge teeth. Sparky only wagged. "He's soaked, Rob. I have an old bath mat in the trunk—do you think he'd lie down in back?"

"Sure. We'll take him back to Fairfax, until Rovilatt's situation resolves."

The space behind the two bucket seats was merely a trough. The convertible-roof machinery took up too much space for any passenger seating. At Rob's word, Sparky bounded obediently into the slot, and curled up as if he'd traveled in Porsches every day of his life. Of course for Rob, rearranging a dog's thinking was no challenge at all. The thought sobered Edwin immediately. He sat down, stuck the key into the ignition, and turned the dashboard light on to see Rob's face more clearly. "Rob. You knew that was going to happen, didn't you?"

Rob seemed to be examining the worn hands folded in his lap. "Yes, Ed."

"You made it happen."

"In the sense that I set up the situation? Yes." Rob's voice was very low. "I hear what you're saying, Ed. With my knowledge of Burt's character, to set up a scenario where he'd dash into mortal peril wasn't hard. Call it murder if you like. Because he's dead. I know it."

Edwin saw, but hardly noticed, Rob's hands squeezing each other into a pallid knot. His mind was racing. He had added up the numbers himself and gotten Burt's death as the solution. Rob was no fool. He had made the same grim calculation, and coldly acted on it. "To kill him, to preserve a secret . . . Rob, wouldn't it have been less drastic to just trim his memory a little?"

Rob stared straight ahead. "Which is worse, Ed—to take a man's life, or his personality?"

Edwin realized that when the moral dilemma had no reality, when it just involved cardboard characters in a novel that was a joke, his answers came pat. But here, now? He didn't know. He had never known. He had manipulated the playing pieces lightheartedly, not without thought, but without wisdom. And Rob had listened to him, had truly taken to heart every careless word. What had Edwin's breezy advice wrought today? In silence he flicked off the dashboard light and started the engine.

But there was another ingredient in the roiling stew of emotions in his chest. With surprise Edwin identified it as sorrow—not for Burt, but for Rob. The Porsche could go zero to sixty in five and a half seconds. He drove very fast up 66 to Fairfax, fast enough so that his shoulders pressed against the reinforced side bolsters in the seat, and glancing over at the passenger side would be folly.

Why was he so upset? He had long known that, in certain situations, Rob could be merciless. Edwin had faced down Rob's killer rage himself once. He still counted it as one of the most reckless and brave stunts of his life. But this was different. To cold-bloodedly set up a man's death—it was the sort of thing Burt Rovilatt himself would have done. It came to Edwin that things could never be quite the same between them now, and that was why he was grieving. Something irrevocable had been done today.

It was almost eleven when Edwin pulled the Porsche up at

the Lewis house. The headlights glittered off the old snow congealed into ice on the hood of Rob's light-blue pickup truck, parked and forlorn at the top of the driveway. Julianne must have been on watch for them, because the porch light came on and she ran out in a purple terrycloth bathrobe and slippers. She jerked open the passenger door, but her glare was for Edwin. "It's the middle of the night!" she said in a subdued scream. "You're wearing him out!"

From behind Rob's seat, Sparky's head poked out. The dog panted good-naturedly at her, tongue lolling. Julianne squeaked in shock, and Edwin quickly said, "We brought a houseguest back, Jul."

"You went gallivanting off all night to get a *dog*?" For a second Julianne seemed deprived of speech. "Rob hasn't the strength for this!"

"Not his fault," Rob said, coughing in the sudden icy air.

"Let's get him indoors, quick," Edwin said in alarm. He remembered how Rob had complained that coughing hurt. They helped him into the light and warmth of the front hall, Sparky following behind. Rob coughed and coughed, seemingly unable to stop, racked until he was ashen with pain and clutching his side. Edwin held him up, or he would have fallen. "Can he sleep down here, so he won't have to do the stairs?"

"Not with kids in the house," Julianne said, and Rob shook his head.

"Okay, then, bud. One more push and you're done."

Edwin had to almost carry him up the stairs, which were too narrow for three. He looped Rob's right arm over his own broad shoulders and took as much of his weight as he could. Julianne hovered behind, pouring out a mixture of advice and admonition: "I'll bet you didn't feed him either, did you? You two don't have any common sense! Oh, Rob, you're skin and bone. Be careful, Edwin, that's his bad side! The least you could have done is phone me. I've been out of my mind with worry!"

In the overfurnished bedroom, the king-size bed was

turned down and ready. Julianne hurried to arrange pillows and the electric blanket. Edwin lowered Rob onto the bed and knelt to untie his sneakers, remembering with a pang how Rob had done the same service for him last August. Rob collapsed onto his pillows and lay with his eyes closed as Julianne tucked the covers tenderly around him. "You sleep, darling. I can see you're exhausted."

"Wait." Rob's voice was barely more than a breath. "Ed. Tell her about it."

"You mean, about Burt?"

"Oh Rob, it's not important!" Julianne said.

A glint from between the sunken waxy eyelids. "Promised you."

"Sure, bud," Edwin said willingly. "I'll bring her up to speed tonight. Anything to make you comfortable."

"And Jul. You tell him. About the Willard."

"The Willard? What about it? We haven't been there in ages. I don't want to hear you talking anymore, Rob Lewis. Whatever it is, it can wait until morning. Edwin, if you stay here, he'll chatter at you. Come down and I'll cook you some dinner." She clicked off the bedside lamp.

"I'm starving," Edwin admitted, as he followed her down to the kitchen.

Sparky had made himself at home on the kitchen linoleum. "I can't believe you two could do this to me," Julianne muttered, at the sight of him. "A dog—as if three kids weren't enough work! You think he'll drink water out of an old margarine tub, Edwin? And it'll only be microwave pizza, I'm afraid. Since Rob got hurt, we haven't had proper meals."

"There's no such thing as bad pizza . . . Did he mean the Willard Hotel? Down on Pennsylvania Avenue?"

"I guess. I— oh!" Julianne paused, the microwave door in hand. "Maybe he's talking about those guys who drowned. Let me start this—then I'll get you the clippings. I think they're still around somewhere." She punched the buttons to start the cooking.

A few minutes later, Edwin sat at the dining-room table and turned over the three clippings in the old yellow file folder. Julianne set a plate with mismatched cutlery balanced on it down beside him. "I thought they were muggers at first, because they grabbed my purse. But then they began to tear my dress, and I was so frightened. And then Rob came roaring up in the truck. And they went away."

"They went away." Edwin looked sharply at her. "Just that."

"Well, Rob put me in the truck, and then he talked to them for a minute . . . Edwin! Do you think he made them jump into the Potomac? With his weird powers?"

"I'm sure of it," Edwin said slowly. He closed the file folder and laid his strong square hands flat on it. "He commanded them to commit suicide. And, of course, they had to do it. I wonder why he wants us to know about it tonight."

The microwave beeped. Julianne brought out the pizza and set it on a hot pad made of mosaic tiles from a kid's craft kit. "He was so miserable," she said, remembering. "He wouldn't tell me anything about it—that was before he let me in on all the weird stuff. But I could tell, I always can. He even had this nightmare about it. With you."

"Me?" Edwin looked up so suddenly the limp wedge of pizza almost slipped off his knife and fork halfway to the plate.

"He was talking in his sleep, anyway. Saying, 'Ed won't like it.' "

"Oh yeah?" Edwin burst out. "Well, Ed doesn't like muggers or rapists, either!" With a sudden flash of insight he saw what Rob was trying to tell him with this story. It was a confession—and a plea for forgiveness. Rob could kill without pity, but not without remorse. He paid the price in mental anguish: guilt, in fact. And in this stern inner courtroom Edwin sat in judgment on him, to redeem or condemn. It was a strange honor, but an undeniable one. And a responsibility—to be one of the rocks under Rob's feet. Edwin had to lean his brow on his hand and swallow hard, he was so touched.

"You're not going to eat that, are you?" Julianne said, looking at the pizza.

Edwin took a deep shaky breath. "Let me tell you about Burt Rovilatt first."

It was a long, complicated story, and the pizza grew stone-cold while he recounted it. But in conjunction with these three clippings, the account clarified Edwin's mind tremendously. "The poor devil," he concluded. "Rovilatt was doomed. I understand that now, Jul. He told Rob—let me see if I can get this right—he said that children are hostages to Fortune. For Rob, that was absolutely unforgivable. From that moment on, the question wasn't whether, just when."

"He was *threatening* them?"

Edwin shrugged. "He threatened me, and Rob, and Carina, so why stop at you and the kids?"

Julianne's hazel eyes blazed. "Then you shouldn't have just tossed him on a gasoline fire. You should have beaten him bloody first. Of all the nerve, suggesting something so horrible! Rob did *exactly* right. I don't think either of you should worry one more minute about it!"

"You two really suit each other." Edwin got up. "I'll put this in for a few more trons." When he came back with the warmed pizza he sat down and said, "Rob is the strongest being on this planet, Jul. And the only time he'll let it all out is in defense of you and the kids. And me," he added, as a surprised afterthought. "It's really scary. Of his own choice, out of his own heart, he's given us power over him. Should we do anything? use it for good? Encourage a spirit of moderation or something?"

"What we should do," Julianne said in a practical tone, "is to keep ourselves very safe and sound. Then he won't have to defend us. I don't see what the problem is."

Edwin laughed, his mouth full. "It's a point of view . . . Listen, Jul, would it be all right if I crashed here tonight?"

"Well, sure, if you don't mind the sofabed."

"That'd be fine. My idea was, I can't stand how painful Rob's recovery is. So tomorrow morning first thing, I could lend him my Syndrome."

"And he'd be well? Just like that? Edwin, is that possible? It sounds too good to be true!"

"I don't know." Edwin took another big bite. "Rob promised to give it a try, and I don't want to wait."

"I should say not! Look, you finish eating. I'll get a blanket for you out of the cedar chest. You think the dog could sleep out in the tile passage?"

*E*dwin woke at first light the next morning on the sofabed, with the covers weighted down uncomfortably on either side of him, and something extremely warm overlaying his ankles. Inwardly he groaned—the twins! And all he had on were his jockey shorts. Perhaps if he lay very still, pretending to be asleep, they'd go away?

On his left Annie said happily, "That's what I like about Uncle Eddie. And Aunt Carina. They way they just turn up—surprise! And with the *best* presents, better than Christmas, even."

On the right Davey said, "What I like about Uncle Eddie is his car. It's *maximal*."

"A car, pooh! A doggy is better." The steady *thump-thump-thump* at the far corner of the bed must be Sparky wagging his tail.

"Do you think he'll drive us to school in it?"

"I get the front seat!"

"It was *my* idea! And you said 'pooh'—I want the front seat!"

Suddenly they were wrestling right on top of him. "Hey!" Edwin sat up. "Cut it out! Kids who fight can't ride in the Pocket Rocket!"

"But if we're good, can we?" Davey asked hopefully.

"I guess." He reached for his striped turtleneck and black denim jeans at the foot of the bed, and Sparky rose up from his sprawl to thoroughly lick his face.

Both kids began giggling like idiots, and Annie said, "I see Uncle Eddie's underpants!"

Edwin sighed. "Let's scout out some breakfast, shall we?"

When Julianne came down with Colin they were all peaceably eating toast, cereal, and milk, the dog included. At the sight of their mother, the twins set up an ear-splitting antiphonal clamor: "We love him, Mommy!" "Thank you!" "And thanks for bringing him, Uncle Eddie!" "He's ours, we can keep him!" "Right, Mom? Right?" "A doggy, we've *always* wanted a doggy!" "Look, he *loves* us!" "And I'll feed him—" "And I'll walk him—" "And he can sleep at the foot of my bed!" "No, *my* bed!"

Julianne shot a poisonous glance at Edwin. "I knew this would happen, I just knew it," she said between gritted teeth. "Darlings, this doggy belongs to dear Uncle Eddie. He's going to take it away again when he leaves. Right, Edwin?"

From observing Rob's dealings with his wife, Edwin knew it was essential now to adhere to the truth, the whole truth, and nothing but the truth. "Actually, Sparky is Mr. Rovilatt's dog. He got sick, so Rob and I brought the dog here. I'll phone his family ASAP, and see what they'd like us to do with him."

"You do that," Julianne said sternly.

"I can drive the kids to school," Edwin said, quickly changing the subject. "How's Rob doing?"

"Still asleep, and I didn't disturb him." She set Colin in the high chair and began spooning baby fruit into a plastic dish shaped like a hot-air balloon. "What are your plans,

Edwin? How long is your stunt going to take? I could take the day off."

"I don't think you have to." Edwin crunched sugary flakes, thinking. "I want to give him as long as he needs, all day if necessary. So I'll be here. Suppose I stay until you come back?"

"That would be such a help! I'll break away early, and be home by four. And Colin will go to Miss Linda, won't you, baby?"

Colin displayed his eight teeth in a grin and slammed his red airplane spoon hard into his dish. Strained bananas geysered up and out. Edwin shielded himself with an outspread hand, but took some hits anyway. "Maybe we should get going, kids. I'll pick up some dog chow on the way back." He cleaned fruit puree off his jeans with a napkin which he realized, too late, Annie had already used to blow her nose with.

"Can you French-braid my ponytail, Uncle Eddie?" Annie demanded.

"And I need the laces put into my shoes," Davey said.

The front-seat dilemma seemed insoluble to Edwin, but both twins crowded into the bucket seat with unexpected harmony. Edwin dismissed Davey's pleas to drive real fast, and poked the Porsche along at the speed limit to school. He was unable, however, to wiggle out of Annie's invitation to come to show-and-tell. "Someday, but not today," he said feebly. "And no, I will *not* do the knife trick."

Back at the house, Julianne and Colin were gone. Reveling in the quiet, Edwin brought in the paper, made coffee, and poured out some orange juice. The backyard was fenced with chain-link, so he set out some dog food on the patio and let the dog out. "Stay in the yard, fella," he warned him. "If you get lost, the kids will be heartbroken." Sparky padded out, wagging his tail as if he knew the routine perfectly.

When he went upstairs, mug and glass in hand, Rob was awake. Edwin drew the blinds up and helped to arrange the pillows so that Rob could sit propped up. "I'll bring you breakfast, bud, if you'll eat it."

Rob shook his head. "I'm not hungry."

Edwin decided not to insist. After today it should no longer be a problem. "At least get some fluid into you, okay? How do you feel? Better than last night?"

"A lot better," Rob insisted. But his voice was still a ghost of its old self, and his eyes were tormented, smudged with shadow. His fair hair had lost its summer burnish and straggled, the color of old hay, on the pillow. In the watery morning light, he looked like a scarecrow after a storm.

There was just room to pull the red plaid armchair up to the bedside. Edwin made himself comfortable in it with his coffee mug. "I have two things to get through with you, bud. The first is difficult but very important, and the second is easy. You let me know the moment you're tired, and we'll switch."

Rob sipped orange juice and smiled. "I slept ten hours straight. How can I be tired?"

Edwin smiled back with genuine affection. Rob could no more admit weakness than fly. "Julianne told me about the muggers, last May down at the Willard Hotel."

Rob looked away, leaning back on his pillows. "I meant to tell you about that, Ed. I wanted to. But somehow I couldn't."

"I understand, Rob. Truly I do."

"But you don't approve."

"Who am I, to approve or condemn? I'm not so hot myself as you seem to think, Rob. Someday I should tell you about my great-grandfather. You wouldn't let me help with the gas or the matches yesterday. You let me keep my hands clean."

"I . . . didn't want it to be suicide this time," Rob said. "Might as well call a spade a spade."

"Call it murder, you mean." The thin pale fingers tightened around the glass, but Rob, his head bowed, didn't speak. So Edwin went on. "You're not alone on that one, Rob. We're in this together. If you killed him, I killed him too. 'We teach bloody instructions, which, being taught, return to plague the inventor'—Macbeth, another notable killer."

Rob stared steadily down at the surface of his drink, and, following his gaze, Edwin noticed how Rob's nails were bitten down to the quick. Rob said, "Is this that 'intention equals doing it' reasoning again? I didn't want you to be burdened with this, Ed. I knew it would make you unhappy."

"And you—you're not unhappy?" Edwin watched him narrowly, waiting for Rob to look up, and at last he did. "Come on, bud, open up. Admit it."

One by one the words came. "I knew he wouldn't do it. I knew. But . . . oh god, I wish Burt had listened to me. It haunts me, Ed. I wish I could have made him listen."

"But then he would have been a different person entirely. You would have made him different."

Rob's smile was crooked. "I was asking him to do what I wouldn't do myself. Asking him to not resist an evil."

"Rob, pulling a Bible verse out of context can fool you. That bit is the toughest verse, and you know how it goes on? Jesus commands, 'You must be perfect, as your heavenly Father is perfect.' "

"Then it's impossible," Rob said thinly.

"Without help, it sure is," Edwin agreed. "And in this life it may not be achievable. But the point is, a standard needed to be set. And I think you acknowledge that standard, Rob. Because it hurts you so bitterly when you fail. You're trying to carry all the burdens of conscience alone. And it can't be done, Rob, not even by you. The awareness of sin is a load too heavy for mortal man."

Rob closed his eyes. "I'm going to dream about that explosion for the rest of my life. Did it make the *Post* this morning?"

"Yeah," Edwin said, accepting the digression. "The paper said Rovilatt was burning papers and trash out back, and then tried to control the fire with a garden hose."

Rob opened his eyes in shock. "He put water on a gasoline fire? The idiot!"

"The burning paper washed down to that barbecue grill—you remember it? That big bang we heard was when it blew. Burt caught the full impact." Edwin leaned forward and took the half-empty glass out of Rob's hand. He met Rob's troubled gaze squarely, and held it. It was obvious that Rob's tormented conscience had to be eased before he could hear any other message. And if Rob submitted to his judgment, then between justice and mercy, Edwin gave the decision he would want himself: mercy. "I wish there'd been some other way too, Rob. But he began it, and he wouldn't let go. You told him to let it drop. If he had, he'd be alive today. You gave him every chance to back out. I don't see what more you could have done. And the final outcome, the explosion, was an accident. No one could have foreseen that. Let God shoulder the responsibility this time, bud. You don't have to bear it."

Gradually the tension drained out of Rob's thin body. Very quietly he said, "Thanks, Ed. I . . . sort of needed to hear that. Your opinion means a lot to me. Yesterday I felt horrible."

"You should," Edwin said. "If you ever get cold-blooded and casual about killing, you'd be a menace, Rob. As long as it costs you something, you aren't lost."

Rob sighed, carefully. "If we ever write that book, you be sure to tell Severneth."

Edwin laughed. "Firrin is going to be more stingy and careful of his advice, don't you worry. Your mistake, Rob, is that you actually listen to and heed every word I say. I was shocked yesterday, when I realized. Even Carina doesn't do that!"

Rob smiled into his beard. "And how long have you been repeating to me, that you do not know it all? I'm afraid it's too late to change my habit of listening to you, Ed. Maybe it's a flaw in my character."

"Let's try to keep this simple, Rob. Living with the weirdness is tough. It's empowered you to do a lot of good deeds, and some really bad ones. No, we don't have to get legalistic, and debate the how and the why. The fact that they trouble you is enough. You've been groping for tools to handle this burden. And I'm one of them—am I right?"

"How do you *do* it, that perceptive bit?" Rob looked embarrassed. "Is it okay?"

"Sure—but it's not very efficient, Rob. You're hungry for forgiveness, you're starving for help to avoid sin, and I'm not the best tool for this kind of work. People in general aren't—we're sand, not rock. Ask for the help that's there, bud. Open the door of your heart, and let in the God waiting on the other side. It won't hurt, I promise. I bet it'll be a relief. You're nine-tenths of the way there already. Make the experiment, give it a try, and if it doesn't help, bail."

Rob shifted restlessly on his pillows, and Edwin sat waiting without impatience. His faith was so woven into the fabric of his life that Edwin rarely spoke of it. This was the first time he'd discussed the subject with Rob. And, knowing his man, Edwin was willing to bet any money that no decision would be made today. After all, Rob had stalled, and hesitated, and postponed for seven years before telling his own wife about the weirdness. Change was bad, to be avoided. And sure enough, his reply was, "Maybe later, Ed. Let me think about it."

"No problem, don't worry about it." Grinning at his own perspicuity, Edwin set his empty coffee cup down on the nightstand beside Rob's glass. "Okay, bud. On to the second item on the agenda: Let's juggle that pearl."

Rob said, "I don't much like the idea of you passing out for it."

"That's one hundred percent unimportant, Rob. It may not even happen. If I'm awake I'll go downstairs and wash up the breakfast dishes. If I'm unconscious, this is a comfortable chair." He leaned back and propped his feet up on the edge of the bed. "See?"

"You're too trusting, Ed. That's *your* major flaw."

"Get on with it, bud, or I'll tell Julianne on you . . ." He slipped into oblivion without noticing, and Rob closed his eyes, too.

It seemed to Rob that he stood in a low dark space, a rocky cave or a basement perhaps. He held a gem the size of a golf ball in each hand: the red-orange jewel of his power, and the pearl of eternal life that Gilgamesh had won from the ocean floor five thousand years ago. From close by came a pale, diffused light from a doorway or a cave mouth. He walked towards it.

It was no door, but rather a breach in a stone wall. Some explosion or impact had smashed a large gap. Weariness dragged at Rob's legs as he climbed up and over the loose broken blocks. He couldn't use his hands because of the gems he held. Since he was wearing the loose blue sweatsuit he'd gone to bed in, he had no pockets.

Once outside in the cold fresh air, he looked back, panting. He had emerged from under a large ruined building. It was the sort of structure that in downtown Washington, houses the Department of Agriculture or the Interstate Commerce Commission—a nondescript bureaucratic hive, all imitation Greek columns and Indiana limestone. Except that this one looked like it had been bombed. The windows were broken, some columns cracked and fallen, and one entire corner of the building slumped into rubble.

From long experience, Rob recognized not the building, nor the bleak dry landscape all around, but the symbol, the image. This boring ruin was himself. Five bullets from an automatic rifle had toppled the columns and smashed these stones. He sat down on the ground against a fallen column drum to rest and think about it.

It was obvious what he had to do. He ought to rebuild. Rob looked down at the big gems resting on his knees. There was power here to do that. The red jewel gave him dominion over other people, and the pearl could handle this building. But as he leaned against the broken column Rob realized he didn't want to do it. He was tired, so tired he couldn't sit up straight. The worst thing about being in the hospital was the medication. Under morphine and Percocet he couldn't think straight. Keeping the weirdness from leaking out, out of his control, had demanded utter vigilance.

And when he refused the Percocet, the pain ambushed him. With his good health and physically active life, Rob hadn't been ill in years. He'd had to learn to be sick. The tremendous mental powers didn't extend to his body in any way. Being weak, hurting all the time, keeping his voice down to keep his chest from tearing itself apart—he was fed up with it. When he looked at his jewels, he could see there was untapped potential here, just as Burt Rovilatt had insisted. He didn't have to sweat over repairs to this dilapidated and uninspired old structure. It would be much more fun, more interesting, to build something new.

With renewed enthusiasm, Rob jumped to his feet, the gems in hand. He would need both of them to start construction, and the work would take some time. For a moment he hesitated, thinking of Edwin unconscious in the red plaid armchair at home. But time ran oddly here. Perhaps it wouldn't take all that long, by the clock. And Edwin was so lucky anyway—every lemon life handed him spontaneously morphed into lemonade. Living without the pearl for a while might even work out to Edwin's benefit. Carina could take this opportunity to get their family started, for instance.

The old building perched on a ledge halfway down a shallow rocky valley. A creek must have flowed down there once, but now the land was desert-dry. Only the beige dust stirred in the wind, a wind strong enough to pluck at his blue sweatsuit. Rob surveyed the landscape critically. A lower site would be better, by a river maybe, where the ground was flat and fertile. He began to walk down and around the hill.

A high and glaring noon reigned endlessly in the cloudless sky, but the buffeting wind was icy. He wandered over the rough ground for a long time until he came across a narrow dusty footpath. Without debate he turned to follow it. It climbed up over the hill and then down. Rob halted at the top, astonished. Just below were five round felt yurts with their conical roofs, a corrugated iron shed, and a handsome drystone sheep pen. He was in Kazakhstan, at the shepherds' summer settlement.

From the shed came an older boy in a round wooly cap, holding a bucket—Zahni, Rob remembered. At the sight of Rob, the boy dropped the bucket and screamed shrilly. "It's all right," Rob called as he descended. "You recognize me." But the boy bolted like a rabbit for the yurt.

He came out dragging the old uncle along by the sleeve. "Look! Uncle, look!"

The old man's brown Asian face turned ashy pale. "Allah! The ghost! The old one is back from his grave!"

"I'm not a ghost," Rob said irritably. But as he glanced down at his own hands a terrible doubt assailed him. He had thought they were just very skinny hands, wasted from his long illness. But now he looked more closely and saw only scraps of leathery brown skin clinging to the knuckles. His hand and finger bones showed naked and dirty white clutched around each gem.

Weak with horror, Rob dragged the loose front of his sweatshirt up. The gauze dressings and the drainage tubes were gone. His bare rib bones curved over emptiness. All the way inside, the dry and decayed strands of viscera clung to his spine in rotten black strings. A faint roadkill whiff came to his nostrils and turned his stomach. Except he didn't have a stomach anymore.

The ruined building he'd climbed up out of—it had been Gilgamesh's grave. The old shepherd was right. He was Gilgamesh. How had that happened? "I am not Gilgamesh," Rob whispered, almost sobbing with terror. "I'm me. How did I lose myself?"

He ran stumbling down the windy path to the yurts, but Zahni and the old man fled screaming inside. In the brilliant desert sunshine, the gems clenched in his claws glowed like stars. The pearl! Rob thought frantically. Gilgamesh held both the pearl and the jewel for five thousand years. When I hold them both, I'm exactly like him. I have to put the pearl down.

Gasping, he halted between the curving felt walls and tried to throw the pearl away. The fingers of his left hand defied him. When he peered closely at the grisly limb he saw that the skinny whitish fingertips were tightly interlocked with the fleshless metacarpals. Even slamming his skeletal fist against the ground didn't jar the bones loose. He could not let the pearl go—it was impossible.

"No!" Rob screamed hoarsely. "No!" There had to be a way out. What if he chopped the bones through? He was dead now anyway. The shepherds would have a knife or hatchet. But with the red jewel clenched in his right hand he couldn't manage a blade. Could he persuade the old Kazakh to cut the hand off for him? Somewhere, somehow, there had to be someone who would hear him, and understand his plight. "Help me!" he shouted. "Save me! I can't save myself!"

His yell shattered the dream like glass. He sat up gasping in his own bed, in his own house in Fairfax. The afternoon sunshine slanted in through the windows. Edwin was still slumped in the armchair, his feet propped up on the edge of the bed and his curly dark head tipped back in an uncomfortable-looking attitude. Shuddering all over, Rob flung the covers back and quickly thrust the mental construct that was the pearl back into Edwin's care. In conjunction over any length of time, the two jewels were deadly. And had that ruined grave building mirrored his physical body, or his inner self, his soul? He had assumed the wreckage was external, inflicted by bullets. But what if a more fundamental flaw in the construction, right down in the footings and foundation, was responsible?

Edwin stirred. "Out like a light . . . Rob, what's wrong?"

Rob leaned his wet forehead on the knees of his sweat-pants. "Oh my god. I wanted to let the pearl go, but I couldn't. We can't ever do this again, Ed. The two things together, it's too much. No wonder Gilgamesh was crazy."

"But you're okay," Edwin said, bewildered. "You're better. Just listen to you. And you didn't have any trouble giving the pearl back to me again, right?"

"No . . ." Rob ran a trembling hand under his sweatshirt. The relief of actually touching his own familiar skin and flesh under there made him gasp. The incisions didn't hurt when he pressed the gauze dressings. There was no agonizing tightness when he drew a deep breath. "I guess—God, it was so real! I got away in time. Or maybe it was a warning, sort of a preview of coming attractions. As long as the two of us, together, share the jewels . . ."

Edwin put his feet down and sat up. "One of your patent incomprehensible explanations again. I love it."

But his own shouted words, shivery with raw terror, still rang in Rob's ears. He recognized them. They were Edwin's. "I can't save myself," he said again, quietly this time. "Yeah, I'm in."

"You mean it." Edwin's grin was incredulous.

"You see? I still listen to what you say. You think it'd be good for me to get religion, and I believe you. I'm tired of running around Mu, trying to keep the kingdom above water. Let's build it right. What do I have to do to sign up? Do you take me to your church?"

"Well, we could do that, but it might be simpler to—"

Downstairs, the front door slammed so hard the windows rattled. Four heavy feet came tramping up the stair. "Dad, you're awake!" Davey yelled. "Are you okay now?" He leaped onto the foot of the bed and bounced, boots and all. The opportunity for serious discussion popped like a birthday balloon.

Annie followed, shedding backpack and lunchbox right and left. "And Uncle Eddie, too! Boy, are you going to stay here forever?" She climbed onto the arm of the armchair and perched on the back.

Edwin grinned broadly. "Rob, what's underneath those uncomfortable-looking bandages, huh?"

"Yeah, I wanna see!" Davey said, jouncing with excitement.

"Can I help peel, Daddy?"

"Ouch! Watch it, sweetie—those are Daddy's tummy hairs you're uprooting."

Rob winced as the tape pulled slowly free. Davey said, "Oh, bummer, they took the staples out!"

"I wanted you to look like Frankenstein forever," Annie mourned. "Now you won't be any fun at show-and-tell."

Rob wadded the sticky tape up around the old gauze pads to form a roll the size of a soccer ball. The red ropy scars that crisscrossed his bare torso looked gruesome, but didn't hurt.

Edwin nodded. "Good enough, but not too good. What do you say?"

"Nobody will notice, as long as I reschedule my next doctor's appointment for much later," Rob agreed.

"Time for the acid test." Edwin stood and hoisted Annie up by an arm and a leg. She giggled and shrieked like a steam whistle. "Davey, Annie—I want you to tickle your daddy like mad, right now!"

"No, Ed!" Rob protested, but too late. Edwin dropped Annie onto his back, where she clung tightly. Davey attacked from the front. Rob collapsed laughing onto the bed, rolling and writhing. After a considerable noisy struggle, he pinned Annie squealing between his ankles and imprisoned Davey under his arm in a thrashing parcel. He was laughing so hard he could hardly hold on to them.

"Very good," Edwin approved. "You don't know how depressing it is, to converse with a mumbler who can't laugh out loud. Here it is almost four in the afternoon, and I haven't had any lunch. What about you, bud?"

"I could eat a bear raw without salt," Rob said, with feeling. "Pry these two leeches away, and I'll take a shower and dress."

"What shall we cook for your dad, kids? Let's go scope out the fridge." He lured the giggling twins downstairs, while

Rob stripped off his sweat-soaked clothing and dove into the shower. It was wonderful to bend and walk without pain, to feel energy and strength coursing through his veins. Never again, he resolved, would he take the precious gift of good health for granted. How could he not be grateful? And to have someone to be thankful to, actually increased the pleasure. Edwin had, as usual, been right—it was a relief.

Rob leaned his forearms against the tile wall, letting the hot water scour away the smells of illness and fear. He closed his eyes and stared, inarticulate, at the new silent presence in his life. He had plumbed so many different and painful holes in his life recently, and here, so close at hand, was the rock. Later on he could find out what bases to touch, how to actually access the help Edwin had mentioned. He could rebuild on solid footing. But for now, this wordless mutual regard was entirely satisfactory.

Clean and dressed, Rob came downstairs into complete chaos. A strong smell of scorching food filled the kitchen, and something fried in a fusillade of sputtering fat on the stove. The sink and counters were heaped with used dishes. Dog chow crunched underfoot. No one was watching the TV, even though it was turned all the way up. Crossing the living room was almost impossible, because the sofabed was open and unmade. The sheets on it were muddy with dog paw prints. An icy wind came howling in through the sliding patio door, which stood wide open. The kids were coatless, hanging by their heels from the swing set in the February cold and picking up leaves and twigs in their trailing hair. The dog ran barking joyously around and around the ice-rimed yard, one long fluffy ear flipped inside out over its head. Edwin, also in his shirtsleeves, sat on the swing talking with animation into the cordless phone.

When he saw Rob at the patio door, Edwin cut off his call and came running in. "We're pregnant!" He thrust the phone into Rob's hands and snatched up his coat. "Carina's been leaving messages all over for me. She's arriving at BWI in a couple hours—I have to dash, to beat the rush-hour traffic.

I'll call you tomorrow, Rob!" He vaulted neatly over the foot of the open sofabed and galloped down the hall.

"Thanks for everything, Ed," Rob called after him. The front door banged and the Porsche's six powerful cylinders came to life with a roar.

The twins and the dog came inside, too. "We turned off the stove burner for Uncle Eddie," Annie explained. "But we knew you wouldn't want us to try moving the pan."

"You did the right thing, sweetie." Rob used a potholder to pick up the still-hot frying pan. A thick, blackened cake of scrambled eggs clung to the inside. "I don't think even Sparky will eat this, do you?" He held the pan down for the dog to inspect. Sparky wagged politely, but looked away.

Davey made a face as Rob scraped the carbonized mess into the sink. His taffy-fair hair was so full of leaves it looked like a squirrel's nest. "Uncle Eddie says he's going to have a baby. Is that poor kid gonna have to eat like this?"

"Uncle Eddie can learn to cook," Rob said. "After all, I did." He inspected the sputtering pan remaining on the stove. An entire pound of bacon lay there in a solid slab, cooking unevenly and too fast.

"It was supposed to be bacon and eggs," Annie said dolefully. "We told him that bacon and eggs is for breakfast, but Uncle Eddie said that was all he could cook."

"I'm hungry, Dad," Davey said. "So is Sparky."

"I think the egg part is out," Rob said. How happy he was, so calmly joyful that these household problems became a pleasure to cope with! "There must be something we can do with all this bacon once it's cooked. Suppose you look if there's tomatoes or lettuce in the fridge, Annie. And bread. We could eat BLT sandwiches." He took the last clean fork out of the drawer and began teasing the bacon slices apart.

※ AUTHOR'S
NOTE

*I*n Chapter 5, Carina quotes from the Epic of Gilgamesh as translated by Stephanie Dalley. It is published in her book, *Myths from Mesopotamia* (Oxford University Press, 1989). That the ancient hero might have been childless, as Rob suggests, is a speculation that A. Leo Oppenheim advances in *Ancient Mesopotamia* (University of Chicago Press, 1977).

The German poem "Ode to Joy" was written by Friedrich Schiller in 1786. Ludwig van Beethoven's Ninth Symphony (opus 125) was first performed in 1824. The English hymn's words, which are quite different from Schiller's, were written by Henry Van Dyke (1852–1933). Biblical quotations are from the Revised Standard Version.

Edwin's Moonbase cake is based on one that the Artemis Society served up at the 1998 Worldcon in Baltimore, Maryland.

I owe a debt of gratitude to Michael Capobianco, for vetting all the NASA sequences, and to Carol Kuniholm and

Larry Clough for reading the first draft. Stephanie Mercier scouted out a file of data about Kazakhstan from the Internet for me. Cecile T. Kohrs scoped out Red Sage, and pointed out that from the evidence, Carina must use Addi Turbo knitting needles. Peter Heck found Mark Twain's cat for me, in Twain's *Following the Equator* (1899). A number of generous Internet friends helped with answers to my myriad questions.

Knitters will want to know that Carina made a saddle-shoulder crew-necked pullover in a basketweave knit-purl pattern, using blue worsted yarn in an alpaca-and-wool blend purchased from a (fictional) spinning cooperative in Peru.

DATE DUE			

F
CLOUGH

Clough, B. W. 67825

Doors of death and life

DISCARDED